THE GIRL BACK
HOME

Books by R.E. Bradshaw

RAINEY DAYS
(A Rainey Bell Mystery)

SWEET CAROLINA GIRLS

OUT ON THE SOUND
(Adventures of Decky and Charlie, #1)

Coming soon...
OUT ON THE ISLAND
(Adventures of Decky and Charlie, #2)

RAINEY NIGHTS
(A Rainey Bell Mystery)

The Girl

Back Home

R. E. BRADSHAW

Blue Crab Publishing

U.S.A.

THE GIRL BACK HOME

R. E. Bradshaw Books/ October 2010

All rights reserved.
Copyright © 2010 by R. E. Bradshaw

THE GIRL BACK HOME

Sometimes what you spend your life looking for is waiting at home, right where you left it.

Chapter One

On the drive across the state of North Carolina, from Durham to Currituck County, the view was dominated by farmland and forests. The winding four lanes gave way to two and back to four, passing little towns, most of which were dying because the main road by-passed them years ago. As the hours passed, layers of the modern world began to slip away. Turning off US highway 64, onto US 17 North, time began to stand still. The roadway took the driver through counties with names like Bertie, Chowan and Pasquotank, that traced their roots to a time when the land still belonged to the English Crown. Hertford County had the oldest brick home in North Carolina, the Newbold-White house, within its borders. The town of Edenton stood as a living history monument, and boasted of having the most intact colonial courthouse in America and houses dating from the early 1700's.

Passing through Pasquotank County and into the homestretch of the three and a half hour journey, the drive turned onto US 158, for the last twenty-two miles of the trip. Snaking through swamps and forests, the road opened on a view of the Currituck Sound, separating the Outer Banks' barrier islands and the mainland. Bearing to the right, onto Caratoke Highway, the sound became lost behind green trees and houses, lining the banks of the water. The road turned away from the shore line, making a long lazy curve around the old high school, which was now the middle school, and the new high school built right beside the old one. The highway would sway through several more languid curves, dividing the stretched thin county in half, like a long, gray, striped ribbon, all the way to Point Harbor, where the land met the water.

The Carolina blue sky overhead with only wisps of clouds, offered no barrier to the June morning sun. A black BMW convertible, top down, with Gucci luggage and what looked like an antique, cast iron, floor lamp sticking out of the backseat, approached the elevated bridge crossing the Intracoastal Waterway, at mile marker fifty, in the heart of the little village of Coinjock, North Carolina. The driver, Jamie Basnight, a forty-two-year-old lawyer, who looked much younger, was coming home, again. Jamie's body was hard with an athletic build that took a lot of work to maintain. Jamie Basnight was an attractive, hot shot lawyer, with the looks to match. Her shoulder length blonde hair was flapping in the wind, under a Duke ball cap, her baby blue eyes hidden behind dark sunglasses. She glanced down, from the apex of the bridge, at the tall sailboats cruising down the waterway. She really didn't see them. Jamie hadn't noticed any of the scenery she passed earlier this morning. Her mind had been busy replaying her every mistake and continued to take her back to three months ago, when it had all come crashing down around her.

Each time the replay would begin, the panic of that night crushed her chest again and her breathing became shallow. Jamie had pulled up in front of the luxurious home, she shared with Mary Ann, her lover of sixteen years, barely able to breathe and thankful Mary Ann's car was in the garage. She ran into the house, calling Mary Ann's name, but got no answer. Jamie found her out back, by the pool. Mary Ann's dark hair hung in curls over her shoulders. Her striking beauty always took Jamie's breath, but tonight she couldn't breathe for different reasons.

Mary Ann was dressed in an elegant white suit, sipping the remains of what looked like straight bourbon. Her back was to Jamie, but when Mary Ann heard Jamie come through the French doors she had slowly turned around. Her tear streaked face was red and blotchy, her beauty somehow making her look more tragic, but she wasn't crying anymore. Mary Ann was livid and turned away quickly, taking another drink. The dark curls swung around so violently, the ringlets bounced before settling against the expensive fabric of her suit.

Mary Ann leaned forward, elbows on her knees gripping the tumbler with both hands, as if, she were trying to keep from throwing it, or dropping it, Jamie wasn't exactly sure what was going to happen next. Mary Ann sat on a bench, built into the deck, that over looked the pool and the perfectly landscaped lawn, with its perfectly placed flower beds. Jamie never went near any gardening tools. She was too busy, fucking up her life, as it were.

Jamie, frozen a few feet behind the woman she slept with for the past sixteen years, was afraid to move or say anything. What could she say? She'd been caught.

The uncertain silence that fell over them was broken by Mary Ann, who said, in her silky manicured drawl, "I hope it was worth it."

"Mary Ann, please. You have to listen to me." Jamie pleaded. Her drawl wasn't as perceptible as Mary Ann's was. Years of polish and practice, in front of juries and colleagues, had taught her only to let the drawl out, when some man, or woman for that matter, mistook her southern charm for ignorance.

Jamie's plea fell on deaf ears. Mary Ann didn't raise her voice, in fact quite the opposite. She became very still, her entire demeanor darkened. With her clenched jaw muscles the only sign of her real emotional state, she said, calmly and evenly, "I have no intention of sitting here listening to you try to reason or lie your way out of this one."

Jamie bowed her head. Her voice weak, when she said the only thing she could think of, "I'm sorry."

The Girl Back Home

The stillness had been the calm before the storm. Mary Ann sprang up and whirled on Jamie, in a flash of anger. "Sorry? What are you sorry for, Jamie? Sorry you did it, or sorry you got caught?"

Jamie was so ashamed. She continued looking at the wooden deck. "I never wanted this to happen," she offered, trying for any redemption.

Mary Ann spit back, "And yet it did. Now you're going to have to live with consequences."

Jamie at last looked up from the deck. She pleaded again, "Please, Mary Ann, let me explain."

Mary Ann was having none of it. Mary Ann was beyond livid. Her voice grew higher and thinner, as the emotion seized her throat. She said, "Not this time counselor, you can't explain this away."

Jamie reached out to Mary Ann. She wanted to hold her and explain that this was some anomalous behavior, so out of the realm of possibility that it could never happen again, but that had turned out not to be a smart move.

Mary Ann slapped Jamie's hand away. In a voice full of rage, she said, "Don't, you dare! Don't you dare, touch me."

Jamie, shocked by the venom in Mary Ann's voice, backed away from her. Jamie looked at the woman she loved and knew she had made a fatal mistake. "So that's it, we're done, just like that?"

Mary Ann did not hesitate, when she replied, "Oh yes, we're done."

Jamie's heart sank with those words. She couldn't believe this was happening. "After sixteen years, I fuck up once and we're done?"

"Fuck up, what an ironic choice of words, and I'm sure it was more than once," Mary Ann said, sarcastically and then she asked, "How long has this been going on?"

Jamie dropped her head again, the shame and guilt were eating her alive. She whispered, "Four months."

Mary Ann sat down, burying her face in her hands. "That long. Fuck! I am such an idiot."

Jamie knelt down in front of Mary Ann. Her own tears flowing down her cheeks, she said, "It's over. I swear."

Mary Ann took her hands away from her face and locked her big dark eyes on Jamie's. She had been betrayed and it was written on her expression and dripping from her words, when she said, "And I'm just supposed to forgive you, is that it?"

Jamie bargained for her life, "How can I fix this? Just tell me, please."

Mary Ann said, softly through quiet tears, "You can't fix this. You've ruined everything." She paused and then stood up. She looked down at the still kneeling Jamie with pure indignation and said the last thing Jamie wanted to hear, "I will never forgive you." The scene ended the same way each time, with Mary Ann walking away from Jamie and their lives together.

In the car, Jamie put on the turn signal, turning onto old 158. She eased around the big curve where the country lane turned into Waterlily Road. On the right, past a few corn fields, several miles of swamp expanded and gave way to the wetlands of Currituck Sound. On her left, little white houses, beaten down by weather and time, lined the waterway.

A half a mile down the old narrow road, Jamie pulled into a driveway, on the left, marked by a For Sale sign. Hung diagonally, over the sign, was the word SOLD, in big bold letters. The small red house with white trim faced the waterway. The end of the dock, owned by the marina next door, ran in front of the house. Boats and yachts of all sizes were tied up, along the long dock. On the left, the marina restaurant filled the air with the aroma of frying seafood. Trees and thick undergrowth blocked the view of the house on the right. There were no houses across the road, because that was the edge of the swamp. The gravel driveway ended in front of a little barn, set off from the house. The barn

5

was painted red to match the house and joined the white picket fence that lined the walkway, to the backdoor. Jamie stopped the BMW and exited, stretching her five foot seven frame to its limits.

She looked around the property and smiled weakly. This was her new home. Jamie walked to the end of the driveway and pulled the For Sale sign out of the ground. She heard the truck coming toward her, and looked up to see the giant blue moving van slowing, as it approached. Jamie waved at the driver and the big truck miraculously was backed down her driveway. Let the unpacking begin, Jamie thought. She made her way to the backdoor of the house, to begin the process of restarting a life that she had single handedly dismantled. As she turned the key in the lock, she heard a little voice in her head say, "I might survive this, if the guilt and loneliness don't kill me first."

Chapter Two

After two a.m., Jamie fell asleep, wedged between boxes and the clutter of their contents, spread across her bed. She found a small blanket sometime in the night, covering her still clothed body, because she was too tired to look for her suitcases. Jamie was jarred awake by her ringing cell phone, located somewhere in the middle of the objects on the bed. Jamie began pushing boxes around until she uncovered the phone, on the fourth ring.

Answering, groggily, "Yeah... Hello."

"Get your ass out of bed. It's Saturday morning. Time to go to town."

The loud, fast talking, husky voice, on the other end of the phone, was unmistakable. It was her lifelong friend, Beth Etheridge. They were the same age and had graduated from high school together. The two women had remained friends through the years. Beth had been one of the few friends Jamie had not lost, when she became a lesbian, sixteen years ago. She could always depend on Beth to lighten the mood, but this morning Jamie was tired and overwhelmed with the move.

"Damn, Beth. What time is it?"

Beth had evidently finished a pot of coffee and was bursting with energy, which came through the phone in her raspy voice, "It's eight o'clock.

Daylight's burnin'. I'll be there in thirty minutes to pick you up, if I can get these damn teenagers out of bed and off to work."

Through the phone, Jamie heard a door open and a young teenage boy's voice cry out, "Mom!"

Beth said, to the protesting voice, "Rise and shine, Jake. Your daddy's waiting." The door closed and Jamie heard knocking, on another door, before Beth continued, "Jennifer, hurry up. You cannot stay in that shower forever. Get a move on."

Jamie laughed and said into the receiver, "I'm glad you weren't my momma."

"It's tough love. If they want to burn up and down these roads on Saturday night then they need to get up and earn the money to pay for the gas. The momma bank did not receive any stimulus funds."

Jamie laughed again, feeling better already. "I'll get dressed. See you in a bit."

She hung up the phone and looked around the room, at its current state of chaos. Jamie had so much to do that she didn't know where to start. Therefore, she wasn't going to do any of it. It would still be here when she got back. She would go to town with Beth and deal with the unpacking later. It wasn't as if she had a job to keep her busy. Jamie had time on her hands, if nothing else.

Jamie unpacked the bathroom things yesterday, so she had what she needed for a quick shower. She undressed and climbed under the spray of the hot water, letting her muscles relax from all the lifting. She washed the dirt and grime from her body and shampooed her hair. While rinsing the shampoo out, she closed her eyes and stepped under the steaming showerhead. Her mind flashed back to Mary Ann, her face streaked with tears, as she said, "I will never forgive you."

Jamie's eyes popped open, in an attempt to vanish the vision. The shower head rained down her face like heavy tears. She put her hands out on the wall, in front of her, steadying herself. She tried to fight it off, but the crush of emotion hit her in the chest like a fist, taking her breath. She barely had enough air to whisper, "I'm sorry... Oh God, I'm so sorry."

Slowly Jamie's knees gave way and she crumpled into a ball, in the bottom of the tub. The steaming water cascaded over her body, as she sobbed uncontrollably. The image of Mary Ann's face, looking at her with such disgust, seared her brain. If she could only forget that face, she could move on, but how could she? Until Jamie could forgive herself for what she had done, and that was something she thought she would never do, she would have to learn to stomach this burden, alone. Jamie had ruined both their lives. The pain was too much to bear.

Jamie cried it out and then pulled herself together. Beth would be coming soon. Jamie didn't want her to see her crying. She turned the hot water down and let the cool water bathe her face. When she was ready, Jamie turned off the water and stepped out of the shower. She checked her face in the mirror, while she toweled off. The crying hadn't done much damage, but she did look tired. That was understandable, since she had been up most of the night, unpacking. She hurried from the bathroom, quickly searching through a pile of clothes she had unpacked last night, finding a pair of shorts and a tee shirt to wear.

The move was a total readjustment for Jamie. Mary Ann was buying Jamie out of the home they built together, in Durham. Jamie was moving from a four bedroom, luxury home, in an upscale neighborhood, to a two bedroom, one bath, cottage, out in the country. The little house had a small kitchen on the back, just off the bedrooms. The rest of the house was a large dining/living room combination, accessed through an open archway, leading from the kitchen.

All of the interior walls, except for the painted crème colored kitchen, were made of thick hard pine paneling, stained a warm rosy red, with golden highlights. The waterfront wall of the house contained a row of six exterior windows that opened onto a sun porch. A step down and through a doorway, in the center of the wall, led out to the porch, which had eight wide windows. Starting about a foot and a half from the floor and nearly reaching the ceiling, the porch windows looked out over the waterway and the marina dock. The porch ran the length of the house and the view was fantastic. A single exterior door, in the center of the wall, was actually the front door of the house, although it wasn't used much.

The various rooms of the house were filled with boxes and unplaced furniture. Everywhere were signs of disarray. Stacks of books sat beside the floor to ceiling bookcases in the living room. Dishes had been unpacked on the dining room table. Jamie rid herself of many of the things she had accumulated over the years, before the move, but when she looked at all the stuff she still needed to put away, she wondered if she had gotten rid of enough.

Jamie was seated at the kitchen table making a list of things she needed to buy. She'd opened the backdoor that led into the kitchen leaving the storm door closed against the warming day. She heard Beth's voice, on the steps leading up to the backdoor. She could see that Beth had her cell phone pressed to her ear and was in an animated conversation, with one of her teenagers, Jamie assumed.

Beth barked, "I have said all I am going to say. Ask your daddy." Then she hung up the phone and spotted Jamie, who now was standing in the middle of the kitchen.

Beth broke into a big smile and throaty laughter, as she threw the storm door open and ran into the room. Beth was shorter and much smaller than Jamie was, with a wiry figure and brown wavy hair. She wrapped Jamie in a bear hug and squeezed her tight, while she said, "I am so glad you decided to come home." Beth relinquished her grip on Jamie and stepped back to look at her.

Jamie said, "I couldn't think of anywhere else to go, really."

Beth beamed. "There's no place like home. Everyone will be so happy to see you."

"I don't really know anybody anymore, Beth, except you and Robby. I haven't lived here since high school," Jamie said, turning to pick up her list.

Beth's throaty laughter filled the small room. "Damn, half the people who left have moved back. You know more people than you think."

Jamie wasn't as enthused as Beth. "I left here a much different person than I am now."

Undeterred, Beth continued, "You were popular girl in high school. Everybody loved you."

Beth couldn't comprehend what Jamie already knew. "You'll be surprised at how people react when they find out I'm gay."

"It's the 21st century. Fuck 'em."

"No, thank you," Jamie replied.

Laughing again, Beth said, "That's my girl. Keep up your standards." Beth then looked around the house, taking in all the chaos surrounding them. "Damn, you've still got a lot to do."

Jamie grabbed her keys and started toward the door, saying, "I've been here less than twenty-four hours and I've been doing this by myself, I might add."

Beth followed Jamie toward the door. "Okay, let's go shopping today, and then tomorrow I'll help you unpack."

Jamie smiled broadly, at the smaller woman. "That sounds like a terrific plan."

Beth hugged Jamie again, before they could get out the door. "Damn, it's good to see you."

#

The two old friends shopped all afternoon, only stopping to eat a piece of pizza, before continuing their hunt, for all the things a new homeowner would need. After cramming Beth's van with her own load of groceries and then adding Jamie's things, the only part of the van, not filled with plastic and paper bags, was the front passenger area. They left Elizabeth City, crossing the hump back bridge, which raised and lowered, allowing water traffic to pass, from the locks at Great Bridge through to the Albemarle Sound. The two women headed back across the causeway to Jamie's house. The road snaked through Camden County, the home of the hated rivals of Currituck County High School,

Jamie remembered once back in high school, in the dead of winter her sophomore year, someone brought a calf's head and put it on one of the medians, in the parking lot. The head was frozen and so was the ground. It was "colder than a witch's tit," as the old folks used to say. The northeast wind beat down on the outer banks with a fierceness, only someone who'd been through a "nor'easter," could understand. The needle sharp coldness of the wind seeped through multiple layers of clothing.

The head stayed in the parking lot all day. The temperature never rose above freezing, so it remained well preserved. Somebody stuck a cigarette in its mouth and a John Deere hat, with holes cut out for its ears, was pulled down low over its eyes. At the end of the day, the principal asked the boy who brought the head, a remnant of a recent slaughter on his daddy's farm, if he would please put it back in his truck. How the principal knew exactly who the culprit was remained a mystery. Principal Daniels had the uncanny ability to know exactly what was going on and who was doing it. It gave him a mystique among his students.

Later that frozen January evening, the hated rivals from the neighboring county came for their scheduled conference meeting against the "mighty, mighty Knights," perennial conference champions for the last decade, the boys Varsity, anyway. The girls, well, they competed in basketball, but ruled the region come softball season. Currituck wore red and white and were called the Knights. The Camden was called the Bobcats and wore blue and white. The historic rivalry packed the stands on both sides of the gym. The games that evening were thrilling. With the J.V. team losing their game, at the buzzer, and the girls team beaten by only five, it was up to the Varsity to stop the sweep. They did, winning a game that was close for awhile, until the Knights pulled away in the fourth quarter.

The next morning the principal came on the loud speaker and ordered all students and teachers to the gym, for an impromptu assembly. Rumors, of a pot bust or somebody important dying, abounded and passed unrestrained through the halls, compacted with students moving in mass, toward the gym. Principal Daniels cleared his throat in the microphone, once everyone was seated, and a hush fell over the room. Beside him on the floor was a blue and white, medium sized, Igloo cooler.

He began, "Now, students, I love a good practical joke, as much as the next person, but some among you crossed a line last night and caused a young woman extreme emotional stress."

A few snickers rippled through the student body followed by swift silence, as Principal Daniels mean-looked the crowd. He only had one good eye and

13

wore a black patch over the other one. When outside, Daniels always wore his black Stetson cowboy hat, which caused him to resemble Rooster Cogburn, in "True Grit," flying across that open field, reigns in his mouth, pistols firing from both hands. He looked more like Wayne, as the famous gunfighter from "The Shootist," without the hat, giving both resemblances an extra element of terror, when he stared the group, of nearly six hundred students, into submission.

He began again, "This is not a laughing matter. A serious accident was barely avoided and was caused by one of our students committing a very foolish act. I called you here to tell you what happened, so that we can learn to think through our actions to the consequences, before we do something that may harm others."

Jamie hated it when he spoke in terms of "we" and "our," as if he was one of them. A lot of adults did that. He was a strict disciplinarian, but fair and most everyone liked him, even if he was kind of scary.

Daniels continued, "One of our students broke into the Bobcat activity bus and placed the cow's head, from Billy Jo's truck bed, under one of the seats behind the driver."

More ripples of laughter, only the people laughing were trying desperately not to.

The principal cleared his throat again, adding, "A half hour before he was scheduled to leave, the bus driver cranked the engine and turned the heat on high, to warm up the bus. When the teams got back on the bus last night, a cheerleader put her pompons under the same seat, where the cow head had been placed. It turns out, the bus passed the cheerleaders house, so she was going to be let off at home, instead of riding all the way to the school. She began to gather her things, in the dark, as they approached her house."

Some of the boys, near Jamie, became restless and fidgeted, coughing, as their throats dried from fear. Billy Jo was one of them.

Daniels was winding up now, "Needless to say, the combination of the melting cow head, decomposing animal flesh, slime covered pompons and several hysterical cheerleaders set off a chain of events, resulting in the driver losing control of the bus. The bus careened through the ditch, until the offending pompon was removed from his face and he was able to steer the bus back on the road. He narrowly missed a culvert, which would have caused a serious accident."

The students were about to burst with laughter and maintained, as best they could throughout the incredibly funny story, that was being told to them in all seriousness. They could not, however, contain themselves any longer, when Principal Daniels reached into the cooler. He pulled out a clear plastic bag with the cow head inside. Through the plastic, the students could see the cow was still wearing the John Deere hat. It had melted enough that the jaw opened a little, allowing the tongue to flop out one side of cow's mouth. The tongue and face melded into the plastic, creating a comic, yet macabre expression. Daniels lost control of his charges. Even the teachers began to laugh. Daniels turned the bag around and seeing the bizarre look on the cow's face, began to laugh, as well. They all had a good laugh and were then sent back to class. Jamie was never sure what they were supposed to have learned from the assembly, other than frozen cow heads can be funny, especially when the story involves hysterical cheerleaders and John Deere hats.

Beth was just winding up the remembrance of another shared humorous event, from their past, when Jamie dropped back in from her own thoughts. Her ADHD, or as it was known in her school days, "self control issues that were usually taken care of by a few whacks with a wooden paddle," made it hard to focus when she wasn't concentrating. Her mind would ramble from subject to subject, until something or someone brought her out of it.

Through snorts of laughter, Beth was saying, "… and then you swam the length of the pool with your suit bottoms around your knees."

Jamie remembered what they were talking about, just in time to say, "I was going to lose the race, at that point, anyway. It just felt like the thing to do." Jamie laughed along with Beth.

Beth continued, "Those country club biddies didn't know how to react, so they just sat there with their mouths hanging open."

"I know. I could see them when I turned my head to breathe. I nearly drowned myself," Jamie said. "Laughing underwater is not easy."

When the laughter subsided, Beth sighed and looked over at Jamie. "So, are you going to tell me what happened? All you've said so far is you fucked up."

Jamie stared straight ahead. "Yeah, I did."

Beth prodded her, "Are you ready to tell me, yet?"

"I had an affair and I got caught," Jamie blurted out.

"That's it. That's all you're going to say. Shit, I figured that much out on my own," Beth said, unwilling to let it drop.

Jamie hadn't talked to anyone about the breakup, because she was so ashamed of what she had done. "I can't believe I did it. It's so out of character for me."

Beth waited, to see if there was more coming, then said, "You and Mary Ann always seemed so happy and in love, when you came to visit. Granted, it has been a few years since I've seen you together."

Jamie sighed, the air leaving her tightening chest. She hoped the crushing pain from this morning did not return. She looked away from Beth, focusing on the windshield. "We were happy, for the most part, but it wasn't perfect."

16

Beth let out a little laugh. She patted Jamie's hand. "Shit, nobody's perfect."

Jamie shook her head. "Believe me, I know that."

Beth looked away from the road, glancing at Jamie with a wicked grin on her face. "So what, some piece of ass came along that you couldn't resist?" Leave it to Beth to try and make Jamie laugh, while she poured her broken heart out.

Jamie didn't think it was funny. "No, it wasn't like that."

"What was it then?" Beth asked. Realizing humor may not have been a wise choice.

Jamie reluctantly began the story, "I hired a law clerk last fall that turned out to be trouble."

Beth's mouth dropped open. "Oh my god, how old is this person?"

"She wasn't a child, Jesus, I'm not a letch," Jamie said, defending herself. "Her name is Tara and she's a thirty-six-year-old divorcee. It just happened."

"Shit like that doesn't just happen, Jamie."

Jamie tried to explain, even though she still couldn't believe she had done it, "I wasn't happy, okay. Mary Ann has no sex drive at all. We were having sex maybe three or four times a year, six if I was lucky. I'm only forty-two. I'm not ready to give up sex, just yet."

Beth interjected, "Wow! If that happened to me, I would need a lot more batteries."

Jamie raised an eyebrow and grinned at Beth, then continued the story, "Now, to be honest, we could have probably had more sex, but it felt like she only did it for me. Like she could do without it. I got tired of asking."

Beth turned serious, asking, "Did you talk to Mary Ann about it?"

17

Jamie nodded yes. "About once every year or two, for the past ten years, we would have a huge fight, then we would talk and she would try to make things better, but it would always cycle back around, you know."

Beth raised a questioning eyebrow. "Ten years? I'm surprised your relationship lasted this long then."

Jamie didn't see it that way. "Yeah, well, I got caught up in how unsatisfied I was. Tara started flirting with me and it was exciting to be wanted by someone. I forgot to count my blessings."

"What about Tara? What happened to her?"

Jamie looked out the side window, before answering, "You know, the truth is I never cared about her at all. It was just sex. It only lasted four months. It was basically over when Mary Ann found out."

"How did she find out?"

Jamie sighed loudly, remembering the moment her world fell apart. "She walked into my office, totally out of the blue. She saw Tara come up behind me and put her arms around my waist, flirting as usual. Mary Ann confronted us, right there, and I couldn't deny it."

Beth said what Jamie was thinking, "Fuck!"

"Yeah, fuck is right. Mary Ann told me to get out of the house that night. That was three months ago."

Beth was still hopeful. She asked, "Would you go back, if she changed her mind?"

Jamie, who had run out of hope, answered, "She won't."

"How do you know?" Beth wanted it to work out, but she hadn't seen Mary Ann that night.

"The last time I saw her she made it quite clear." Jamie flashed back to the night she stood in the driveway, watching Mary Ann toss her clothes out the front door. She shook her head to make the image go away. She turned to

18

Beth, saying, "When the crystal vases shattered at my feet, I figured she was pretty much done with me."

Beth asked compassionately, "You're still in love with her, aren't you?"

Jamie had to turn away, because the tears were burning her eyes and she was losing control. She managed to whisper, "I always will be."

Chapter Three

The next morning, Jamie rose early and began unpacking more boxes. Last night, after putting away all the groceries and supplies she and Beth had gathered, Jamie sat on the sun porch, drinking bourbon, until she could no longer hold her eyes open. Her sleep was restless and filled with dreams of Mary Ann. Jamie woke herself, before the sunrise, screaming Mary Ann's name. She got up and made coffee, because she didn't want to dream anymore.

She managed to get all the dishes put away and then refilled the dining room table with the books she was unpacking. She was stacking the books by size, when she heard voices approaching the backdoor. Beth's recognizably throaty laughter and husky voice floated through the air. Jamie could almost imagine Kathleen Turner was approaching, and a few years back that would have been extraordinarily exciting. There went the ADHD brain again. A random thought could distract Jamie so easily, during the last three months. She guessed it was because she spent all her energy concentrating on not falling apart.

"Hell yes, I give my son condoms," Beth was saying. "He's a man. He's going to fuck."

An unfamiliar voice answered, "Well, you're probably right about that."

Beth entered through the backdoor, just as Jamie was coming into the kitchen. She was followed by an attractive blonde woman, with a tight athletic body, but very feminine. The woman was about an inch shorter than Jamie was. When she smiled at Jamie, her dimples lit up the room and her brown eyes sparkled. A spark of recognition hit Jamie like a lightning bolt.

Beth started speaking first, "Hey hon, we're here. I brought some help with me. Do you remember Sandy Canter? She was a Brown when you knew her."

"Yes, of course I do, Sandy Brown," Jamie said, extending her hand to shake Sandy's. "I baby-sat for your daughter, a hundred years ago."

Sandy shook Jamie's hand, smiling up at her. "She's no baby now. Dawn is thirty and married, with two daughters of her own. They live in Richmond."

"Wow, you're a grandma." Jamie blushed with embarrassment, as soon as the words left her lips.

Sandy got red in the face, in response. "Yes, I am."

Jamie looked at Beth, who had been watching the exchange between the other two women. Beth looked intrigued by their uneasiness. Jamie wasn't sure why she felt so awkward, but she had a sneaking suspicion that it was the mad crush she had on Sandy, when Jamie was just seventeen.

She was jolted out of her thoughts, by Beth saying, "Sandy is the librarian at the high school."

"So you two work together?"

Sandy looked at Beth for confirmation, when she answered, "For how long now, twenty years?"

"Oh god, don't tell me it's been that long," Beth anguished.

Still looking at Sandy, Jamie said, "I haven't seen you in what, twenty-five years, at least."

There was another awkward moment, as Jamie and Sandy smiled at each other, a look of remembrance passed between the two women.

Beth looked from Jamie to Sandy and back, and then said, "I didn't realize you two knew each other so well."

Not taking her eyes off Sandy, Jamie said, "We spent quite a lot of time together one summer."

Explaining to Beth, Sandy added, "Along with being my baby-sitter, Jamie was also on a traveling softball team I played on that summer."

Jamie laughed. "Sandy gave me my first beer."

"Oh my god," Sandy said. "What were you, sixteen?"

"I had just turned seventeen and I was a girl traveling with a bunch of women. You people corrupted me."

Jamie and Sandy laughed together. Beth lost interest in the two of them and began to evaluate the daunting task they faced. Boxes were stacked in every corner, some empty, but most were full. She put her purse down on the kitchen counter and said, "Let's take this walk down memory lane while we do some work."

"Okay, where do you want to start?" Jamie asked. She followed Beth through the archway, leading to the front of the house, stopping after only a step, to look back at Sandy once more. "It's really good to see you again, Sandy. Thanks for coming to help out."

Sandy tilted her head to one side and when she smiled, one corner of her mouth crept higher than the other, forming her darling dimple, again. She said, "I'm glad you came back home."

"Me, too," Jamie said, matching Sandy's smile.

#

The three women worked from eight thirty until they had to stop for lunch. They labored together, making sandwiches and pouring sweet tea,

22

laughing all the while. The house looked more like a home now. Jamie could see the top of her bed and many of the empty boxes had been neatly folded, tied up and placed in the attic. They may be needed later and Jamie hated to throw something away and then have to buy more, later. Although Jamie had money now, she had grown up the daughter of a high school math teacher and football coach, and a secretary mother. They were not poor, but Jamie learned the value of a dollar, early in life.

She taught tourists, at a local restaurant, how to open crabs, clams and oysters, for tips. That was her first job and she was only ten years old. She worked odd jobs to buy the first "big girl" ball glove she ever owned. Jamie paid for all her non-school related extracurricular activities, gloves, bats, balls, cleats and travel expenses to name a few. She had her own lawn mowing business when she was thirteen. She bought a John Deere riding mower at the end of that summer, increasing her speed and ability to take on more lawns. Before seven a.m. every weekday morning, during mowing season, Jamie set out on her mower, pulling her trimming mower chained behind her. Her other tools were strapped to the mower with bungee cords. She traveled like that to her job sites, until she turned sixteen and her dad built a trailer for her used VW bug, he had given her to drive. She did lawns for money until she left for college.

Some of her customers were more than two miles away. Before she got the trailer, she put-putted along Waterlily road happily, on her little green tractor. Once a week she had to traverse the main highway, just two lanes at the time, and cross the bridge into Coinjock, to mow for three clients. Her dad didn't want her on the highway, but he gave in, because two of the jobs were her biggest moneymakers. He bought a flashing red light and hooked it to the back of her mower and the battery. Jamie had to laugh at what she must have looked like. A lanky little girl, ball cap pulled low with a blonde ponytail

23

sticking out the back of the hat, slowing traffic to ten miles an hour, the fastest her ride could go, as she crossed the gateway to the outer banks during peak tourist season.

"Where did you go? Why are you laughing?" Beth inquired, bringing Jamie's brain back in focus.

"I was remembering being on that old John Deere mower, tooling across the bridge, like I belonged out there."

Beth said, "I remember that. You used to take me riding on it."

"I liked that job," Jamie said, before taking a bite of her sandwich.

Beth swallowed a bite. "You always had money."

"That's because I worked all summer, unlike you and your Florida vacations."

Jamie also worked for anyone who would pay her. She pulled a shift on the weekends in the off season, at a little country store in Barco, just up the road. She cleaned fish for boaters tied to the docks. During the school year, she babysat on the nights she didn't have a game of some kind. She met Sandy when she was still sixteen, at the first traveling team practice she attended, late in the summer and soon became her babysitter two nights a week, so Sandy could attend college classes. Jamie didn't play for the team full time, because she played on two teams already, one of which was the sixteen and under All Star team that represented the county, in tournaments all over Northeastern North Carolina. This limited her time with Sandy, but by the next year, she was playing fulltime for Sandy's team and spending the majority of her free time in Sandy's presence.

"I was not on vacation. I was visiting my grandparents," Beth shot back at Jamie.

Sandy joined in by asking, "What pray tell is the difference, when your grandparents live on the beach in Tampa?"

"People are not forced to go on vacation. I was forced to go by my parents," Beth said, sticking her tongue out playfully at Sandy.

Sandy feigned concern, "Oh, you poor thing, forced to spend six weeks on the white sands of the gulf coast. That kind of abuse explains a lot about you."

They all hooted loudly. Jamie let her head fall back and really laughed, for the first time in three months. She was taking pleasure in the comfort of women. A kind of peace bathed her in warmth. The warmth women give to each other when they gather in groups to laugh and share their lives. There is nothing sexual about it. Most women are different out of the presence of men. Women relax among their sisters and, given a common cause, can be a force to reckon with, not to mention how fiercely loyal they can be to each other. It was the kind of bonding Jamie needed, at the moment.

Mary Ann and Jamie had mutual friends, and both had friendly relationships with people they worked with, but never saw outside of work. They went to parties at friends they knew together or had dinner and drinks with a couple here and there. For the most part, Mary Ann and Jamie went to work and spent their free time with each other. So, when the break up happened, Jamie was left on an island by herself, with their former friends circling like sharks around her. If she made eye contact, they turned away, preferring to strike when her back was turned.

She paid Tara off, when she came back threatening to sue Jamie for sexual harassment. Jamie was the one who was harassed, but she gladly paid Tara's tuition, for her last year in law school at Duke. Jamie relived how dirty she felt, writing that check, for forty-six thousand, nine hundred and thirty dollars, the cost of attending the prestigious old law school for one academic year. She still remembered the exact amount. Tara was cunning enough to have Jamie pay the tuition directly to the university, so it didn't look as much like blackmail, more like a scholarship or grant Jamie had given her, for her exemplary service to the law firm.

Jamie, in turn, was clever enough to make Tara sign a confidentiality agreement and a legal document stating that if she ever disclosed the payoff or came back for more money, it would constitute a breach of contract. Jamie, then could have Tara arrested for blackmail and recoup her money. She didn't want the money. She wanted Tara gone forever and would have given her almost anything to get rid of her. As it turned out, Tara cost her more than money, and the things Jamie lost could not be replaced. Tara had been an extremely expensive piece of ass.

Mary Ann and Jamie's property on Chumsford Drive, in Cary, sat behind the gates of the privileged community, on almost five acres. It could rightly be called an estate. The home owner's association dues alone were twelve hundred dollars a year. Jamie scored a big win in a wrongful death suit. Collecting her contingency fee of one third, she received a check for almost five million dollars. The dead man's family ended up with over ten million, which the billion dollar corporation paid happily. The man had been killed by a piece of faulty equipment, scheduled for repair for two years and certified safe, by the manufacturer's OSHA compliance team. The jury actually awarded Jamie's client much more than they received, but she had encouraged them to take the settlement or the corporate giant would just tie the case up in court for years, in the appellate court.

Every year wasn't as good as that one, but Jamie averaged in the high six figures most years. Mary Ann made more than the salary she received from the university, of over two hundred thousand a year. She spoke to groups all over the county, as an expert on the sociology of crime, deviance and punishment. A day with Dr. Best cost a pretty penny and if you wanted her for a weekend seminar, your bank book had better be thick. She also received royalties from her published works. Therefore, when they decided to build the house five years ago, they spent freely; making sure the house had everything either of them had ever wanted. After all, Jamie had planned to grow old with Mary Ann in the dream home.

The luxury and sheer glamour of the home, they designed together, took visitor's breaths away. It had soaring ceilings, a fantastic spiraling stairway and a master suite encompassing the entire third floor. Besides the three other bedrooms and seven bathrooms, the kitchen was huge, equipped with top of the line stainless steel appliances, and Italian marble countertops. There was a spa, a sauna and exercise room, indoor lap pool, a theatre, and an elevator that terminated outside the third floor master suite, for when they got old and couldn't take the stairs. They built a guest house, which really served as the outdoor pool house and party central, when they entertained. In short, it was everything Jamie had ever wanted and it came with a beautiful woman she could watch out by the pool. Jamie had it made, and she blew it over unrequited sexual desires.

With the furniture and improvements made to the five acres, since they moved in, it appraised for over five million. They paid just under four million to have it built. In today's market, it would never sell and Jamie was lucky Mary Ann wanted to keep it. Jamie didn't ask for half of the current market appraisal. She took fifty thousand less than two million, for her buyout, letting Mary Ann keep the change, so to speak, for pain and suffering. She paid cash for her new house in Coinjock. Jamie had generated almost twenty million dollars in her fifteen years with her firm. With overhead, employees and the IRS taking their cuts, she still had enough money not to ever work again. For that she was thankful. Now, she wanted to practice law for the love of it and help out the wronged less fortunate, who could have never hope to afford a lawyer of Jamie's caliber. For that she was also thankful. However, Jamie was

27

most thankful for her friend Beth and reconnecting with Sandy, after all these years and the camaraderie the three shared over lunch.

When it was time to get back to work, Beth went to the guest bedroom, leaving Jamie and Sandy alone in the living room, placing books on the tall, built-in bookshelves. They both were drinking beer, now, and had been talking non-stop since lunch.

Sandy was saying, "...after the divorce I finished school. I've been married to Doug now, for fifteen years."

"I never saw you again, after your divorce from Gary was final. You just disappeared," Jamie said, sounding a little more hurt than she had intended to.

Sandy reached up to put a book on the top shelf, looking at Jamie from underneath her arm. "I moved to Greenville. I got lost in single motherhood and college. I'm sorry I didn't say goodbye."

Jamie didn't say anything. She was back in high school, experiencing those awful feelings of pain and loss, when Sandy moved away. She was only seventeen when it happened. The enormity of the crush, she developed on Sandy that summer, had hurt in ways she hadn't remembered, until she brought it up a minute ago. Sometimes, over the years, she thought about Sandy. She wondered where Sandy was and what she was doing. She even had some wild dreams about her. Looking back on that summer, Jamie recognized her young lesbian self, which at that time was not even a consideration. At that age, Jamie only thought of Sandy as a friend, with whom she desperately wanted to spend time. Now, Jamie knew the part of her that was a lesbian had been in love with Sandy. She smiled at the memory.

Jamie's thoughts were broken, by Sandy saying, "Is this your girlfriend?"

Jamie turned to see Sandy unwrap a framed picture of Mary Ann. It was one of Jamie's favorite photos of her ex. She was laughing, trying to hold her big floppy hat against the wind. Mary Ann was so happy in the picture. Jamie had taken it on the ferry, crossing to Ocracoke, on one of their vacations. It was just before they moved into the new house. Mary Ann's mouth was open in a smile, as she laughed at the gulls swooping down to peck the fake white flowers attached to her hat. The trip was one of Jamie's fondest memories of the two of them.

Jamie stared at the picture a few seconds, before she answered Sandy, "Yes, I mean, she was... that's Mary Ann."

Sandy, still looking at the picture, said, "She's absolutely stunning."

Jamie took the picture from Sandy. "Yes, she is."

Beth's voice came as a relief to Jamie. It snapped her out of that tumbling into darkness feeling she had, whenever she thought about Mary Ann not being in her life anymore.

Beth called, from the kitchen, "Jamie, where did you say you put the furniture polish?"

Jamie placed the picture on the end table, near the couch, and said to Sandy, "I better go help her."

#

Jamie left the room through the archway into the kitchen. Sandy picked up Mary Ann's photo again. She studied the face of the alluring Dr. Best, looking lovingly into the lens of the camera. Jamie had to have been behind the camera. Mary Ann looked like a movie star, what the love child, if it was possible, of Jennifer Beals and Julia Roberts would look like. She had perfect white teeth and the dark skin of someone of Mediterranean descent. Under the floppy straw hat her dark hair hung, in the perfect curls, that other women paid hundreds of dollars to recreate, only Mary Ann's looked natural. This woman turned heads, both men and women, Sandy thought. No wonder Jamie was so devastated. Jamie had won the hand, of the prettiest girl at the ball, and then simply threw away the glass slipper.

29

The Girl Back Home

Sandy heard Jamie tell Beth, she'd be right back. She had to go to the bathroom. She said something about the beer running through her and then Sandy couldn't hear the other women anymore. She put Mary Ann's picture back, where Jamie had placed it, so that Mary Ann peered out from the frame with those big brown eyes, at whoever occupied the room. Sandy reached in the box again and saw a small photo album. Opening it, she found pictures arranged in chronological order, of the happy couple. There was one, fairly early in the book, of the two of them in sparkling evening gowns, arms around each other's waist, posing in front of a gala poster. Undoubtedly, these two women had each been accompanied by the most striking woman at the event.

Sandy never saw Jamie, at the age she was in the picture, possibly late twenties, and she was amazed at the transformation, from the cute tom boy to the gorgeous woman, in the sequined gown. Sandy leafed through the rest of the album. Most of the pictures were of Mary Ann and Jamie vacationing, all over the world. To anyone looking at the pictures, it would appear that Jamie led a charmed life, with a beautiful woman, surrounded by luxury. Sandy's life couldn't compare to the glamorous one Jamie had thrown away. Sandy wondered how the adjustment to the simple life would affect Jamie.

When Sandy heard Jamie laughing, in the kitchen, she quickly put the photo album back in the box and went to find out what Jamie was finding so funny.

#

When Jamie first passed through the kitchen, she really didn't look at Beth. She rushed through the room, toward the bathroom, saying something over her shoulder about the beer running through her like water. That wasn't the real reason she went into the bathroom. After looking at Mary Ann's picture, Jamie needed a moment to collect her thoughts. She felt the emotion welling up inside, and was afraid another panic attack like yesterday morning was brewing. She splashed some cold water on her face and then sat on the toilet, relieving her bladder and breathing deeply, pushing the emotions back into the little box she built for them in her mind.

Once she was sure she had everything under control, Jamie went back into the kitchen where she found Beth up to her hips in the cabinet, under the sink. Jamie started laughing and thought how desperately she wished she had her camera-phone with her. It felt good to laugh and a wave of tension lifted from Jamie's spirit.

"What the hell are you laughing at?" Beth's voice bounced around inside the cabinet, giving it a hollow sound.

"She's laughing at the view," Sandy's said, suddenly behind Jamie. She added, "Those yellow pants really make the picture, don't you think?" Sandy winked at Jamie and gave her a dimpled grin.

"You damn well better not be taking a picture of my ass," Beth said, her head popping out from the cabinet. "Where in the hell did you put the furniture polish?"

Jamie was still chuckling, when she said, "You don't have to dust."

Beth stood up and dusted her hands off on her pants, leaving long fingerprints on her thighs. "I know I don't have to dust, I want to. It gives me pleasure."

"Who am I to deprive you pleasure? It's in the cabinet, over the washer." Jamie felt lighter from the laughter and added, "I can't thank you both enough, for all the help. Let me cook dinner for you tonight, at least."

Beth, who had located the furniture polish and an old tee shirt, for use as a cloth, smiled broadly. She said, as she headed toward the living room, "Anytime someone wants to cook for me, I'll take them up on it."

Sandy agreed, but added, "I need to call Doug."

"Call him and tell him he's on his own. I'll call Robby and tell him to microwave something for the kids," Beth said. "He's gotten quite good at it."

Jamie was pleased. The least she could do was feed them, after they had worked so hard. "That's great," she said, "I picked up some steaks and potatoes yesterday and I even have stuff for salad."

Beth, who had begun to dust the coffee table, in front of the couch, said to Sandy, "She bought groceries like she was setting in for winter."

Jamie shrugged. "I'm not used to doing my own shopping, yet. I'm not sure how much is enough for one person."

Sandy raised an eyebrow, questioning Jamie, "Mary Ann did all the shopping?"

Jamie answered sheepishly, "Not all... Well, most of it. Groceries, picking up laundry, cooking, and things like that."

"Damn, that's a straight woman's dream," Beth quipped.

Sandy jumped in, "No kidding. So, if she did all that, what did you do?"

Waves of guilt washed over Jamie. Mary Ann had been the caretaker in their relationship. Jamie dropped her head and answered, "Work mostly. I was so busy all the time.... She took good care of me."

Sandy and Beth must have sensed the mood swing in Jamie. Sandy quickly changed the subject, "That's the last box, except that one over there. It's pictures and things you should go through."

Beth stopped dusting. She stood up, saying, "Well hell, let's fire up the grill and call the husbands."

#

Out on the canal, boats passed down the waterway going north and south. Jamie had grown up not far from her new house. The variety of boats that used the canal and the people on them had mesmerized her in her youth. Large barges, pushed by smaller tug boats, tall masts on sail boats with their tanned

32

riders sitting on the deck, yachts the size of small cruise ships with people like Malcolm Forbes, Walter Cronkite and Roy Clark stopping their vessels to refuel and talk with the locals. The waterway was Jamie's glimpse, into the unexplored world, beyond her little village and represented everything the future had to offer. The old swing bridge was replaced by a much taller four-lane bridge to let the traffic flow unimpeded, on both land and water, and did not require an operator.

When she was younger, she would ride her bike down to the old battleship gray bridge, with its peeling paint and huge rust spots, from years of exposure to the salt air. No matter how many times she saw it swing open and close, it remained a fascination. Pilings, at least a foot in diameter, stuck up from the water. Bundled together by heavy cables and located on both sides of the canal, they were there to prevent a runaway barge from destroying the bridge. Other smaller bundles lined the shore on either side, preventing damage to the canal walls. Jamie would buy a popsicle or a mountain dew, in the Mr. Austin's store. Then she would sit on top of a bundle of pilings that she could reach from shore, and watch the boats for as long as the ADHD would let her. She dreamed of hopping on a southern bound sailboat to the Caribbean or a northern bound yacht to New York City, anywhere, but this backwater village.

Coinjock, located on US Route 158 between Barco and Grandy, about twenty miles south of the Virginia state line, traversed through mostly flat, lush farmland and swamps. Waterlily Road, past where Jamie's house was located, heads east through marsh lands, until it reaches Church's Island and the tiny village of Waterlily. The island got its name from the decayed old church that once marked the location of the village. Coinjock is bordered on the east by Currituck Sound, the North River on the west.

Jamie read somewhere that the name Coinjock came from the Native American word for mulberries. Jamie wasn't convinced, because she was told, by an old man Austin, who never missed a day on the bench outside his little country store, that mulberry trees hadn't been in this area for a very long time, even before the native Americans left. Well, some of them left. Most of them assimilated into the English culture, many of their ancestors still residing in the county.

Coinjock, a tiny village of unpretentious, coastal people, lies within the boundaries of one of the oldest counties in the United States. Currituck County was officially established in 1668, but English people were living in Currituck well before then. Colonists from Jamestown spread across the new land and Currituck was one of the first places they settled. The county became one of the five original ports used by the English. In the early 1700s, Currituck's original Courthouse was built and then replaced in 1842 and remodeled in 1898. The courthouse, still standing, currently houses governmental administrative offices. In 1776, the Colonial Legislature granted permission to build a jail in Currituck. The Old Currituck Jail and Historic Courthouse are two of the oldest county buildings in North Carolina and they are still in use.

Currituck was known for its quaint fishing villages and its slow, peaceful way of life. The Albemarle Chesapeake Waterway, which opened in 1859, became a vital water passage from Maine to Florida. By the late 1800s, Currituck gained a reputation as a "sportsman's paradise." Wealthy industrialists were attracted to the county for its abundance of wildlife and numerous hunt clubs, including the Pine Island Club and Currituck Shooting Club. In the old days, the geese and ducks were so thick, hunters used nets to snare hundreds at a time. The snow geese covered the fields like blizzards. Canadian geese were constantly overhead honking out orders to the flock. Mallard, Blue-winged Teal and Wood ducks swam, among the giant trumpeter swans, with the single mates they had chosen for life.

Jamie had grown up surrounded by history and nature. She never fully appreciated all that was offered, by this small coastal community, until she had grown up and missed it so. She graduated, at the top of the class, with a little more than one hundred people, the largest graduating class at the time. They all knew each other and their parents knew each other. They were sheltered and didn't even know it. Now, here she was, back in the land she had so desperately wanted to leave, as a child.

#

Jamie stood at the grill, contemplating her childhood in "Sportsman's Paradise," when Sandy came out of the house. Jamie had the moving guys put the grill on the patio, so that she could cook and watch the boats and foot traffic on the marina. The sun was setting, bathing the dusk sky in bright colors of orange and red. Beth leaned back in a deck chair, sipping a beer. Sandy bounded down the steps with a look a consternation on her face.

Jamie looked back over her shoulder, at Sandy, and asked, "Is everything okay?"

Sandy plopped down on the empty chair next to Beth. She sighed loudly, and then said, "Men are so helpless. He's packing and called to ask what tie went with what suit."

Beth took the beer bottle down from her lips. "Where's he going?"

"He has a big meeting in Norfolk, tomorrow. He decided that since I wasn't coming home until late, he's going to go up and get a motel room, so he doesn't have to fight morning traffic," Sandy answered. Sandy was seized by the smells from the grill. She stood up and walked over to Jamie, sliding up close to her, saying, "That smells incredible."

Jamie asked her, "What does your husband do?"

"He's in the aeronautical space industry, the business end. He deals with vender contracts and things. He pretends he's an essential part of the space

35

program, but he's just a glorified accountant," Sandy said, grabbing a beer from the cooler, next to the grill.

Jamie turned around, watching Sandy go back to the chair. She said, "That's mean, Sandy," but she was laughing and checking out Sandy's ass. Jamie caught herself doing it and it made her laugh even harder. She might be in mourning for Mary Ann, but her instincts to check out pretty women were not, and Sandy was an exceptionally pretty woman.

Beth chimed in on Sandy's attitude concerning her husband, "Yes, it is awfully mean, since he adores you. He thinks the sun sets and rises in you."

Sandy defended herself against Beth, saying, "You rag on Robby and he's put up with your ass all these years. He deserves a medal."

"That's because he knows I'd cut his dick off, if he tried to leave," Beth said, letting out a hoarse laugh.

Sandy and Jamie laughed, too. Sandy said, "So that's the secret to your happy marriage."

Beth toasted with her beer and said, "Yep, that's the secret.

Jamie said, "I'm glad I wasn't married to you."

All three women broke into peals of laughter. When the laughter subsided, Sandy asked Jamie, "So, how long have you been practicing law?"

Jamie flipped the steaks, as she answered, "Fifteen years. I started out in criminal law, but I have taken on some civil suits, usually when I felt my client had been harmed unjustly, by people who care about nothing, but money. I like to liberate them from some of that cash, for the folks they walked all over to get it."

"And you have your own firm?" Sandy asked.

Jamie closed the lid on the grill, grabbed her beer and sat down on the steps, leading up to the backdoor. "A small one, just me, a secretary and a paralegal."

"Don't forget the law clerk," Beth said.

Jamie glared at Beth, not angrily. She just didn't want everyone to know how stupid she had been. "Yes and a law clerk. I started in a big firm. At age thirty, I finally woke up, coming to the realization that they already had the prerequisite female partner and were not looking for another one. So, I went out on my own."

Sandy cocked her head quizzically and asked, "So, you're going to start your practice over, here? That must be frightening."

Jamie smiled. It was a question she had asked herself many times before, but she answered, "I don't think I'm as frightened as I should be. I'm looking forward to the country lawyer life. I'll do alright."

"Besides, she richer than two feet up a mule's ass, don't let her fool you," Beth said to Sandy.

Jamie looked at Beth, shook her head and said, "With that mouth and they still let you teach children? Amazing."

Beth feigned offense, "I know how to act in public."

Sandy shook her head in agreement, poking fun at Beth, "I don't know how she does it. It is truly a transformation, from gutter mouth to English teacher. You wouldn't believe it."

"I don't," Jamie said.

"Fuck ya'll," Beth said, and the three women erupted in laughter.

#

After the steaks were eaten and the dishes were put in the dishwasher, the three friends sat on the sun porch, drinking coffee. Beth had fallen asleep, in the chair nearest the door, with her feet up on the ottoman. Sandy and Jamie sat next to each other in matching dark wicker chairs separated by a small wicker side table. The furniture had belonged to Jamie's grandmother. It sat on her parents' back porch as far back, as she could remember. Jamie selected a nautical theme for the porch. The cloth covering the seat cushions depicted varieties of sailboats, and nautical flags, in blue, red and yellow, on a white background. Matching valances hung over the windows. Wooden shutters opened on the view of the marina's boardwalk and the waterway beyond.

All along the docks, on both sides of the canal, yachts and sailboats bobbed in the breeze, lit by the glowing amber lights from their cabins. Lines slapped against the masts, in a high pitched "ting," sounding out the rhythm of tiny waves, as they slowly rocked the hulls and their occupants to sleep. It was a cool night with a good breeze, so Jamie opened all the windows on the porch and shut off the area from the rest of the house. James Taylor sang quietly, in the background, merging with the sounds from the docks and the crickets singing loudly.

Sandy turned to Jamie, after a few moments of silence, from all the catching up they had done for the last hour. "I like this house. It's cozy and I like watching the boats."

Jamie watched as a couple boarded their cabin cruiser. Without looking at Sandy, she said, "It feels like home, already. Remember, I grew up just down the road from here."

"I remember that," Sandy said, then paused a few seconds before asking, "You don't think you'll ever go back... to Durham, I mean?"

"There's nothing for me in Durham," Jamie said, quietly.

Sandy reached over and patted Jamie's knee. She spoke softly, "I don't know what happened to you. Beth only hit the high spots, but I can tell you're hurt and I'm sorry for that."

Jamie grinned, to cover the pain, "It shows that much?"

"Not really, it's just that when I showed you her picture you went kind of pale."

Jamie was becoming increasingly uncomfortable with the conversation. "You're very observant," she said.

Sandy must have caught the tone in Jamie's voice, because she said, "I'm sorry. I shouldn't bring it up. It's none of my business, really... but if you need someone to talk to, I'm here for you."

"Thank you," Jamie replied.

Sandy prepared to stand, saying, "And now I think I should take sleeping beauty home."

Jamie was glad the subject was changing. She looked at Beth. "Man, she really crashed."

Sandy stopped, before she stood up, and looked back at Jamie. "Jamie, may I ask you a personal question?"

Jamie thought for a second and said, "I guess so. I might not answer."

"You don't have to, if you're uncomfortable," Sandy paused, as if to gather her courage, then asked, "When did you know you were gay?'

Jamie was just glad the question wasn't about Mary Ann or the Tara mess. She answered easily, "I understood I was gay when I met Mary Ann, I was twenty-six."

Sandy was confused by the answer. She raised one eyebrow, questioning Jamie, "What do you mean, you understood?"

Jamie elaborated, "I looked back over my life, and though I never acted on them, I had feelings... I mean I was attracted to women and just didn't put it together."

Sandy continued her questions, "Mary Ann is the only woman you've... uh, been with?"

Jamie wondered where this was going, she answered slowly, "Yes... Well, there was one other."

"Ah... I'm guessing she was the source of your trouble," Sandy said.

Here it comes Jamie thought, but she was honest when she said, "You could say that."

Beth rescued her by coming to life at that moment, saying, "That's a fucking understatement."

Jamie drew the attention from the conversation she and Sandy had been having, by leaping up and shouting, "It lives!"

Beth stood up and stretched, skewing the words with a yawn, as she said, "It needs to go home and get in its bed. Tomorrow's Monday isn't it?"

Sandy stood up, too. She answered Beth's question, "Yes, so thank God for summer vacation, right."

"There's no vacation this week. Mom and dad's big party is on Saturday," Beth said, as the three women walked back into the house and through to the kitchen. They continued to talk on their way to Beth's van in the driveway.

Sandy said, "That's right that is this weekend."

Jamie didn't know what they were talking about. She looked at Beth, who understood, and explained, "Mom and Dad have started having a big party every summer. They've been doing it for three years. I've invited you every year, but you were always too busy. Now, you have no excuse."

"I would love to come," Jamie said, excited about the prospects.

Beth continued, "Anyway, my dear mother has me doing something every day this week. It's the curse of being the child living closest to home."

Jamie joked with Beth, "Why do you think your siblings moved so far away?"

Sandy asked Jamie, "Where are your parents now?"

Jamie kicked at the gravel in the driveway. Sandy had a way of hitting her soft spots. "They moved to Belhaven after I graduated. They were killed in a car accident ten years ago."

Sandy was embarrassed that she hadn't known. She tried to cover it with, "I'm so sorry to hear that. They were such nice people."

Jamie gave her standard comeback, "Thank you," then added, "Hey thanks again. I owe you both."

Beth opened the van door and got in, saying, "You sure as hell do. You can help me with the party."

Jamie laughed. "Okay, just call me. It was great to see you again, Sandy."

Sandy got in the van, talking to Jamie through Beth's open door, "You too. I left my contact info on your counter. Call me if you need anything."

"I will. Thanks. I'll see you Saturday, at the party," Jamie said to Sandy.

Sandy waved and smiled, "Yeah, see you then."

Beth was looking back and forth between the other two women, with a look of puzzlement on her face. She smiled at Jamie and cranked the engine. "Okay, see you later," she said, before putting the van in reverse and pulling out of the driveway.

Jamie watched from outside until Beth's taillights vanished, then went in the house. She cut off all the lights and locked up. She went into the bedroom, shedding her clothes to take a shower and then she was off to bed. Jamie prayed before she closed her eyes. She beseeched the powers that be not to let Mary Ann haunt her dreams.

Chapter Four

The sun blushed pink, on the belly of the wispy clouds in the lavender sky, before peeking over the horizon and casting its first golden rays of the day. The wetlands stretched out on both sides of the narrow, two-lane Waterlily road. A small flock of white herons slowed in flight, circled slowly to the water and disappeared behind the reeds and cattails. Another beautiful June morning dawned over Currituck Sound.

Jamie had slept well. She figured she had been just too tired to dream. She had awakened just before sunrise and gone for a run, down to the sound and back. It was about a six mile run, which Jamie realized she needed, once she got warmed up. She had arrived at the water's edge just in time to see the sun clear the horizon, beginning its march across the sky. It brought back memories of long ago Easter sunrise services, on the water. Jamie smiled at the remembrance and turned back for the return home.

When she ran, Jamie usually used the time to think through a problem or a case. Over the last three months that problem was always Mary Ann. A Melissa Etheridge song began on her IPod and it caused Jamie to smile. At least, she was in good company. Melissa's marriage broke up, at about the same time as Jamie's and, rumor had it, for pretty much the same reasons.

Only, it appeared Melissa was doing a much better job of moving on, than Jamie was.

Jamie ran into the driveway of her home and checked her watch. Not a bad time, since she hadn't run in a week. Jamie picked up the towel she left hanging on a patio chair earlier and began to dry her face. She turned off the IPod and took the earphones out of her ears. Just then, Jamie heard her cell phone ringing, in the kitchen. Jamie bounded up the steps and finding the phone on the counter, answered it, without looking at the caller I.D.

"Hello," she said into the phone, breathing heavily.

There was no reply. She was too late and the call went to voice mail. Jamie saw Mary Ann's name on the missed calls list, when she checked to see who it had been.

"Damn," she said, and hit the recall button on the phone.

After four rings, Jamie heard, "You've reached the voice mail of Dr. Mary Ann Best. Please leave a message."

Jamie then listened to her own messages. The sound of a click was the only message Mary Ann had left.

"Fuck," she said and slammed the phone shut. The phone rang in her hand, startling her. She flipped it open and said into the receiver, "Mary Ann?"

"No, it's Sandy. Did I call at a bad time?"

Jamie was caught off guard. "I thought you were... no, no it's not a bad time."

"I can call back," she heard Sandy say, still rattled by the call from Mary Ann.

"No, really, it's okay." Jamie gathered herself and asked, "What's up?"

Jamie was glad Sandy let it drop, when she said, "Beth called. She wants me to pick up some lawn furniture in town. You up for a trip?"

Jamie began undressing, dropping her sweaty clothes in the washer, by the backdoor. She jumped at the chance to get out of the house today. She asked Sandy, "Do I have time for a shower? I just finished my run."

"I didn't know you were a runner. I could tell you were in great shape. Your body is incredible," Sandy said, drawing in a quick breath, as if she didn't mean to say the last part.

Jamie blushed, even though Sandy couldn't see her. Jamie wasn't very good at taking compliments. She said, shyly, "Thank you. It's a constant struggle."

Sandy laughed. "Some of us struggle more than others. I run every day and I don't look like you."

Jamie was naked now, ducking to avoid open windows, as she made her way to the bathroom. She held the phone against her shoulder with her cheek, while she grabbed a towel from the hall closet. Jamie thought Sandy looked fantastic and said so, "Sandy, you look great."

Sandy chuckled again. "Thanks. So how about forty five minutes, is that long enough?"

"Sure. See you soon," Jamie said, hanging up the phone.

Jamie stepped into the shower, a little twinge of the crush she used to have on Sandy, crept into her heart. She smiled at herself. Well, at least she had always had good taste.

#

Sandy stood at the big bay window, in her custom built kitchen, looking out over the landscaped yard and the water beyond. Her home, which sat on prime waterfront property, had an incredible view of the of Currituck Sound, and the Outer Banks' barrier islands beyond. Sandy still had the phone in her hand, after just hanging up with Jamie. When she had come home last night, Sandy sat on the deck outside of her bedroom upstairs, drinking tea and thinking about Jamie.

44

Sandy had not expected her heart to quicken, when Beth asked her to help move her friend, Jamie Basnight, into her new house. Sandy knew Beth and Jamie had been friends for life, but Beth rarely mentioned her and it was not a problem listening to Beth talking about Jamie. Jamie was a successful lawyer, in Durham. Sandy was proud of what Jamie had done with her life. At the sound of her name, Sandy had immediately flashed back twenty five years, to the lanky blonde and freckled teenager that Jamie had been, the last time she saw her. The rush of blood to her heart was so disconcerting it rattled her. Sandy had never told Beth that Jamie had been a friend of hers. She thought Beth knew about Jamie being her babysitter, but Sandy never elaborated on just what Jamie had been to her.

Sandy wasn't sure what to expect or what would happen, when she saw Jamie for the first time in twenty-five years. She certainly didn't anticipate her physical and emotional response to seeing the woman Jamie had grown up to be. Sandy had buried her attraction to women a very long time ago. It wasn't hard. She genuinely enjoyed the company of men, and found it easy to settle for a life, that may not have been in her true nature.

She buried it, because she fell in love with a teenage girl. Granted, there were only three and a half years difference in their ages, but Sandy was married, getting a divorce and the mother of a five year old. Jamie was about to be a senior in high school. They spent a portion of every single day that summer, in each other's company. There was never any discussion of how Sandy felt, or sexual interaction between them, but the crush had been exhilarating and oh, so painful, at the same time. Sandy had not been attracted to women before Jamie and found it easier to erase those feelings, after she moved away.

Sandy did not tell Jamie she was leaving, she just did. Jamie knew Sandy was going to Greenville for school, but she expected Sandy to go out to eat with her and a movie, before she left the next week, a sort of celebratory send off for Sandy that Jamie had wanted to give her. Sandy could not bring herself to say goodbye, so she got up early the morning of the scheduled dinner. She had been packing all week and was practically finished, so she packed the rest of her things into the little u-haul trailer, put Dawn in her car seat, and left without saying a word. Sandy was afraid of what she might say or do, if she saw Jamie that night. Sandy was afraid she might tell Jamie how she felt about her. She was afraid she might actually kiss Jamie, something she had dreamed about all summer, but never dared do. Her heart broke and she was crying, when she crossed the county line, but Sandy knew she was doing the right thing.

When Sandy walked into Jamie's kitchen and saw the gorgeous woman she had become, the long buried feelings she had for Jamie rushed up from her gut and crashed against the inside of her chest. Her heart literally palpitated and she felt the heat creep up her neck and bathe her face in a red glow. When Jamie had locked eyes with her, without saying a word, she knew that Jamie remembered, too.

Now, Sandy felt exhilarated. Young and alive again. The energy and excitement she was experiencing, just from the knowledge that she would see Jamie today, made her giggle like a school girl. The reasonable part of her brain sat back, arms crossed, tapping her foot, saying, "What in the hell is wrong with you?" while the part of her brain that had gone to mush, sang "Can't Fight This Feeling" by REO Speedwagon. It was a big hit in 1985. When it would come on the radio, Jamie and Sandy would crank it up and sing, at the top of their lungs, finishing in fits of laughter.

Sandy returned the phone to its base. She went up to her bedroom, took off the clothes she had on and searched for something to wear. She settled on khaki shorts, white tank and light-yellow linen over-shirt. Her tanned skin needed little makeup, but she took extra time on her eyes, trying for the natural beauty look with a little accent, here and there. Satisfied with her makeup, she restyled her hair with the blow dryer. She felt like a teenager, dressing up to go on a first date. The tapping of the foot of Reason grew louder in protest. Miss Mushy just turned the radio up.

#

Sandy picked Jamie up forty-five minutes later, as promised. Jamie was waiting in the driveway when Sandy pulled the big Ford truck to a stop. Jamie hopped in the passenger seat and they were off to town. They talked like old friends on the way. Sandy told Jamie all about her beautiful granddaughters and Dawn's life in Richmond.

Jamie listened intently and watched Sandy's animated joy, when she spoke of the children. Jamie found that she was once again mesmerized by Sandy, as if the twenty-five years they were apart had vanished. Jamie couldn't help but notice, how pretty Sandy was. This morning, Sandy wore a yellow linen over-shirt. The color set off her tan and gave her skin a glow. She was wearing just enough make-up to accent her natural beauty. Her blonde hair was pulled back away from her face and clipped up on the back of her head. Her dimpled smile lit her face and caused Jamie to smile back uncontrollably.

They made it through the shopping and were packing the plastic lawn chairs in the back of the truck, when Jamie said, "I really like this truck."

"It's Doug's," Sandy replied. "I borrowed it for the day or rather Beth told him I was going to use it."

Jamie tied the chairs down with a long bungee cord she found in the truck bed. "She is quite persuasive," she said.

Sandy laughed. "Threatening is more like it."

The Girl Back Home

Jamie finished the tie down and jumped down from the truck, closing the tailgate. As they made their way into the cab, Jamie asked, "So how did you and Doug get together?"

"Doug's son was in my daughter's class. He was divorced, too, and one thing led to another," Sandy said, while cranking the truck and pulling out of the parking space.

"Wow, not much for a romantic story, are you?" Jamie noted, teasing Sandy.

"It wasn't all bells and whistles. We just sort of started dating and after a couple of years we got married," Sandy answered and then directed the conversation back to Jamie, "How did you and Mary Ann get together? Do you mind talking about her?"

"No, I don't mind," Jamie said, and she didn't mind at all, because that was the nice part of their story. "It was my second year in law school at Duke. I went to a lecture in the Sociology department, given by Dr. Mary Ann Best, about the effects of sexual abuse on women and how it relates to their criminal behavior."

"Heavy topic," Sandy said.

Jamie went on, "She was very serious and incredibly brilliant, not to mention drop dead gorgeous."

"Was it love, at first sight?"

Jamie smiled at the memory and answered, "I didn't know that's what it was. Remember I was straight up to then. I even had a boyfriend at the time."

Sandy giggled, "I assume that didn't last much longer."

Jamie answered, "No, it didn't," and laughed along with Sandy.

"Go on, finish the story," Sandy said.

"I introduced myself after the lecture, which I couldn't believe I was doing, at the time."

Sandy interrupted, "I don't think anyone would accuse you of being shy."

"You don't understand. I was in awe of this woman. She was already a legend on campus, but she was gracious and took the time to talk to me for a few minutes."

Jamie paused, prompting Sandy to ask, "So what happened?"

"Nothing then, but a week later I still couldn't get her off my mind. I was working on a case for class and it involved an abused woman. I used it as an excuse to call her and ask if she would consult on the case and she accepted."

"Smooth move," Sandy commented.

Jamie continued, "I thought so. Anyway, she met with me several times. Finally, I asked her to have a drink after one of our meetings and as you said, one thing led to another."

Sandy asked, "Did she seduce you?"

Jamie laughed, answering, "That's the funny part. Mary Ann was gay before she met me, but I put the move on her. In fact, she resisted, because she was six years older than me, I was a student, and she thought I was drunk, but I persevered."

Sandy said, "She doesn't look that much older than you."

"No, she doesn't."

"And you were together for sixteen years after that?"

Jamie sighed. "Yep, until I fucked it up."

Sandy could tell the conversation was taking a turn for the worse, so she patted Jamie's hand and said, "Hey, we don't have to talk about that part. It's a romantic story, let's leave it at that, okay." Jamie nodded in agreement, but stayed silent until Sandy changed the subject. "So, are you excited about seeing everyone on Saturday?"

Jamie was snapped out of her misery. She asked, "What do you mean everyone? Who's coming to this shindig?"

Sandy grew animated again, saying, "Oh my god, everybody. I bet you will know most of them. People Beth's parents know, then people their kids know, and so on. It is usually a huge deal. You'll have so much fun, I promise."

Jamie was a little apprehensive about the party. She said, "Stay close to me. My memory for names is terrible. I'll need coaching."

Sandy said, "I promise to be by your side all day and don't forget to bring your swim suit."

Jamie grew more excited and asked, "Will there be ski boats?"

Sandy threw her head back and laughed. She smiled at Jamie and said, "Will there be boats? Ha!"

#

Tuesday through Thursday, Sandy worked at the school. She had to run the technology for a seminar. It was a boring assignment, but they were paying her and she could use the time to catch up on library paperwork. Sandy didn't see Jamie, after Monday, but they talked on the phone and exchanged emails. Their conversations were spent catching up on each other's lives.

Sandy noticed that Jamie's life revolved around work and Mary Ann. She had seen pictures of the two of them together and they were stunning. Sandy couldn't compete with that, she thought. For now she was just enjoying Jamie's company and the thrill she felt each time she heard her voice. Sandy waited with great anticipation for Saturday. She would spend the whole day with Jamie and that would be enough, she hoped.

#

Jamie spent the Tuesday through Thursday alternating between starting a new life and missing the old one. Sandy made her laugh and the memories they shared were healing, somehow. Still, the nights were cold and lonely with images of Mary Ann interrupting her attempts to sleep. Jamie tried to call, one more time, but the automated voice asked her to leave a message, yet again. No more messages. Nothing left to say.

Chapter Five

When Jamie's car emerged from the pines that lined the sandy lane and into the open air, she was overwhelmed with emotions from both ends of the spectrum. On one hand, she was washed with the smells and sights of her youth. The sound spread out in front of her, with the Currituck Banks on the horizon. The sun was in its mid-morning glow, shooting rays of amber into the clear blue sky. Jamie had the top down and let the warmth of the sun bathe over her.

On the other hand, her senses were on alert, because the yard and driveway of Beth's parents' home were covered in vehicles. Big four wheel drive trucks, with gun racks in the windows, were scattered among luxury cars, sedans, jeeps, sports cars, motor cycles, almost every make and model of vehicle one could imagine. Lots of people were at this party. People Jamie had not seen in years. It made her nervous. There always seemed to be some jack ass, at a party like this, who got just enough beer courage to ask her, "Don't ya' miss dick. I bet I could fuck the lesbian out of ya'," or some variant of that.

Jamie did not wear a flashing sign around her neck saying, "Lesbian! Protect your wives!" She was attractive, wore power suits and turned heads when she entered a room. Jamie and Mary Ann had made such an attractive couple, that rude men had not been a problem. They were too gorgeous and were unattainable to most men. The majority of men stood back, but a few would approach cautiously, only because they fantasized about being in bed with both of the women. A smile and a gentle rebuff were all that was generally necessary.

The most important thing, Jamie thought, was that those men lived in the city, not Hickville, USA. Not too many people knew Jamie's sexuality, but enough did that it had surely become public knowledge, by now. After all, she was the golden girl when she left. Jamie couldn't understand why she felt so uncomfortable, she was going to be with people she had loved and laughed with for the first eighteen years of her life. In her heart, she knew it was that one asshole in the crowd that made her cringe.

Jamie found a spot on the grass under a tree. She parked the car and grabbed a small canvas bag and a long black bag containing her skis, out of the back seat. She had her dark blue, one- piece, swimsuit on, under her gray cotton shorts and an old, light blue, oxford shirt, with the sleeves rolled up to the elbow and the front unbuttoned. She kicked off the sandals she was wearing and dropped them into the backseat. There was no need for shoes. She put the keys in a zippered pocket, inside the canvas bag, and with her skis over her shoulder began walking toward the house.

Beth's parents' home was a large, brick, ranch house situated on top of a low rolling hill, bookended on both sides, by tall pines and thick undergrowth. The front of the house faced the water. On one end of the house a three-car garage stood open, with large black cookers, smoking up the air with the aroma of roasting pork. Large trash cans containing iced down kegs, sat beside coolers crammed with water and other drinks.

On the other side of the driveway, the lush green lawn sloped down from the front of the house, to the bulkhead and the dock that extended into the Currituck Sound. Out on the water, pontoon party boats, bass boats and ski boats were all tied together end to end and side to side, so passengers could walk from one boat to the other, right up to the dock. It was a floating party in full swing, with people of all ages, colors, shapes and sizes. Ski boats and jet skis whizzed by. Boats dropped off and picked up a steady supply of skiers and wake-boarders. Some of the skiers were just learning how. Some of the skiers were showing off. Jamie longed to join them. She missed being able to ski nearly every day.

Jamie looked around for Beth or Sandy and had decided to head down to the dock, when a hand grabbed her shoulder and a man's voice said, "Turn around here, good-lookin'."

Jamie smiled and spun around. She hugged Robby's neck and said, "How the hell are you, Rob?"

"I'm better, now that you're here," he said, smiling down at her.

The old friends hugged again, then Jamie asked, "Where's that wife of yours?"

"Her mom's got her running around somewhere. I'll tell her you're here, if I see her," Robby answered.

"I guess I'll go down there and see if I can find someone who'll pull me on these skis," Jamie said, pointing the ski bag toward the dock.

"I'd do it, but I have to watch the cookers," Robby said and added, "Jake's down there with our boat. He'll pull you."

Jake was Robby and Beth's thirteen year-old son. The last time she saw him he was eleven, so when he stepped up on the dock to hug her, Jamie was shocked that he was now taller than her and his voice had changed.

"Damn Jake, you've grown into a young man," Jamie said, pulling back from their hug and sizing him up.

"Yes ma'am," he said, "I'm almost six feet now."

Jake was tanned all over, with just a thin band of white skin peeking out of the top of his swim trunks. His light brown hair had been highlighted with blonde streaks, by the sun. It was obvious he spent most of his time on the water. He was built like Robby, tall and lanky, not an ounce of fat on him.

"Well handsome," Jamie said, "your father said you could pull me on skis."

Jake grinned. "That's cool," he said, reminding Jamie that she was putting her safety in the hands of a thirteen year-old.

Jamie grinned back at him, saying, "Take it easy on me."

Jake and Jamie got into the boat, joining some of Jake's buddies, already aboard. As she was putting her ski bag in the hold, she heard one of Jake's friends, say to him, "Who's the hottie?"

Jamie blushed, but didn't turn around or indicate she had heard the kid. She heard Jake punch the kid in the arm and say, "Shut up, dude. That's my mom's friend. Jesus, she's like forty something."

The friend responded, "My mom's forty and she don't look like that."

Jamie shocked both of the young men, when she turned around and said, "I'll take that as a compliment. Thank you. Now, let's go ski."

The smell of boat engines burning fuel on the water brought back waves of happy memories. It smelled like home. Jamie put her shorts and shirt in the canvas bag and stored it in the bow. The ride out to the deeper water took a few minutes, because the Currituck Sound has an average depth of only five feet and maximum depth of approximately thirteen feet. A person could walk out over a mile in some places. Because it was so shallow, the water was warm, too warm in fact, and supported vegetation in the sand bottom shallows. The boat had to be taken out beyond the sea weeds to get full power.

Jamie slipped over the side, when Jake brought the boat to a stop. The familiar feel of the warm brackish water, thrilled Jamie. She was in her element. She slipped on the skis, grabbed the rope, and gave Jake the signal that she was ready. Once Jamie had finished a few warm up rounds on the skis, she signaled Jake to speed up, dropped a ski and began to attack the wake with the vigor of the teenage, water skiing phenomenon that she used to be, only a bit more cautious. She actually thought about breaking her neck now, as she whipped back around the boat, a huge rooster tail following behind her.

Jamie pulled Jake for awhile, so she could rest and then took out her trick ski. She decided to give it a try, even though she hadn't used it in two years. She gave Jake a few instructions on how to drive the boat and leapt over the side. Jamie felt better than she had in months. For the last hour she had done nothing but have fun. She never thought about Mary Ann. She only reveled in the experience of coming home again.

Jamie did only some simple tricks, but generally she just tried to get comfortable with the ski again. She fell a few times and came up laughing. Finally, when her body became too tired to hold on to the rope anymore, she asked Jake to take her to shore. She was dropped off, at the dock, and replaced by several young ladies, who giggled at Jake and his friends, as they climbed into the boat. Jake handed Jamie her bag and told her she could just leave the ski's in the boat. Jamie winked at him and thanked him for pulling her. She had just turned around, when she saw Sandy smiling at her.

Sandy was holding a towel and a cold beer. She offered them to Jamie, saying, "You look like you could use these. That was quite a show you put on out there."

Jamie said, "Thank you," taking the beer and the towel from Sandy.

Sandy picked up the canvas bag Jamie was holding between her feet, while Jamie dried her hair with one hand and held the beer with the other. Sandy looked at Jamie grinning. She said, "I can't believe you can still ski like that."

Jamie felt young and alive. She replied, "It's been a while. That was so much fun. I can't wait to do it again."

A good looking man, fifty something, with dark hair, graying temples, wearing stylish wire rimmed glasses, walked up behind Sandy and put his arm around her waist. He said to Sandy, "Hey babe, I'm going to go with Robby to get more ice."

Jamie saw Sandy flinch, just a little, before Sandy said, "Jamie Basnight, this is my husband, Doug.

He stuck out his hand, saying, "Hi, Jamie. I've heard a lot about you. It's nice to finally meet you."

Jamie shook his hand. "It's nice to finally meet you, too, Doug."

Doug kissed Sandy on the cheek and said, as he was walking away, "I've got to go. Keep my wife company for me, Jamie. Be back in a few minutes."

Jamie sat her beer on the dock railing and finished drying off.

"Well, that was Doug," Sandy said.

Jamie took the bag from Sandy, found her shorts and shirt and put them on over her almost dry swimsuit. The wet bathing suit bottom through the pants look was very prevalent among the guests. She talked while she did this, "He seems nice."

Sandy answered vacantly, "Yes, he is." Then the tone of her voice lightened and she said, "Hey, you want to go find Beth?"

Jamie hung the towel over the railing and retrieved her beer and bag, saying, "Sure, lead the way."

On the way off the dock and up the hill, Jamie ran into several people she knew and stopped to exchange handshakes or hugs. So far so good, everyone was glad to see her and she surprised herself, being happy to see them, as well. Young children darted about, chasing each other or playing a game of baseball with a stick and a pine cone. A Frisbee landed at Jamie's feet. Her hands were full, so Sandy flung it back in the direction from which it came. Over the speakers, set up by the small stage at one end of the yard, Jimmie Buffet songs played in the background.

They found Beth holding court, in a circle of seated women, on lawn chairs and blankets. Some held small babies or sat near strollers and sleeping toddlers. Others were more Jamie and Beth's age and older. Jamie sat down near Beth, in an empty chair. Sandy sat next to her. Beth was in the middle of one of her stories.

She was saying, "I kid you not, that child plopped a zip lock bag full of dog shit on my desk and said the dog ate my paper." She burst into laughter and had a hard time saying the rest. "You... you could actually see the little bits of paper in the shit."

The entire group of women burst into laughter. A small brown haired woman, holding a sleeping baby in her arms, asked, "What did you do?"

Beth gained her composure long enough to say, "Well, I figured he was either telling the truth or he had gone way above and beyond to create this excuse. Either way he deserved an extension."

This was followed by more loud laughter. Sandy made eye contact with Jamie and winked, as she laughed at Beth, her dimples showing in her smile. This did not go unnoticed by Beth, who was looking at Jamie, when she turned back around. Jamie thought Sandy was just being Sandy. She had always been quick with a wink and a smile. She wasn't quite sure what Beth was thinking, but she was sure giving Jamie a funny look.

Jamie was relieved when Beth said, "I saw you skiing. You're getting too old for that crap. You're going to kill yourself."

Sandy jumped in, "I thought she looked great out there. I had forgotten how well she could ski."

"God, I used to live in the water," Jamie said, "I really missed it. I only got to ski a couple of times a year in Durham and not once in the last two years. I think I need to buy a boat."

Beth poked Sandy knee, "See, I told you she was rich."

"Shut up, you," Jamie said, teasingly.

Beth turned back to Sandy, asking, "Did Doug find you?"

Sandy sighed. "Yeah, he tracked me down."

Beth explained to Jamie, "Doug always has to drive for supplies. He's our resident designated driver, because he doesn't partake." She held up her plastic cup and took a sip of beer.

"I see," said Jamie. "It's always good to have one of those. I've made a living off people who didn't."

Beth looked around the yard, saying, "You might make some money off of some of these fools leaving tonight. You should have brought business cards."

"I don't need the work that badly," Jamie said, laughing.

Sandy added, "Most people stay anyway."

Jamie was confused, "What? Here? They stay here?"

Sandy looked at Beth and then back to Jamie. She said, "Beth, you didn't tell her? People bring out tents and sleeping bags and sleep around the big fire pit. They'll start the fire later after the fireworks."

Jamie was taken aback. "Fireworks? Jesus, this is a big deal."

"What can I say," Beth answered, "my folks know how to throw a party."

"I don't have a sleeping bag or a tent," Jamie complained.

Sandy patted Jamie's knee. "I brought an extra bag. You can use it."

Jamie stood up, because when Sandy touched her, she felt electricity run up her leg. "Well, in that case, I need another beer. Anybody else?"

Sandy handed Jamie her empty cup. "Sure, I'll take another."

Beth said, "No, I'm good. Thanks."

"Okay, I'll be back in a minute," Jamie said and left for the kegs. She was lost in thoughts about how her skin had tingled under Sandy's touch. Jamie couldn't deny she was attracted to Sandy. Hell, Jamie still had a bit of a crush on Sandy, and it had been a long time since Jamie felt the touch of someone to whom she was attracted. That had to be what was making her heart race, when Sandy winked at her or showed her dimpled grin. Jamie was still very much in love with Mary Ann, and even though she felt so comfortable and thrilled in Sandy's presence, Mary Ann was never far from her thoughts.

Jamie filled the red plastic cups with ice cold beer and checked out all the food laid out on the tables, lining the driveway. Pulled pork, at a "pig pickin," is a dish a person never forgets. Carolina vinegar based sauces are famous worldwide. Some of the pork had been pulled and chopped, for sandwiches. The feast included multiple recipes for potato salad and coleslaw. Baked beans, pasta salads, cakes and pies, were among a few of the items Jamie knew she had to have a taste. Fresh vegetables, corn on the cob and sliced watermelon were calling her name. The skiing had made her ravenous. She decided to go get Beth and Sandy, so she could have some food.

Upon approaching her two friends, Jamie noticed that Beth was staring Sandy down over something. She slowed down and stopped, but she was already close enough to hear what they were saying. They didn't notice her. Jamie waited, because she didn't want to intrude on what appeared to be a very personal conversation.

Beth was hammering Sandy, "What's going on with you and Doug?

"What are you talking about? Nothing's going on" a shocked Sandy replied.

Beth was having none of it, "Bullshit! I saw the way you reacted when he kissed you earlier."

Sandy looked, at the other women in the circle, to see if they were listening. Luckily, they were engrossed in some magazine and hadn't noticed Beth's inquisition. Sandy turned back to Beth, "I just didn't feel like being pawed over. You know how it is sometimes."

"Are you sure?" Beth sounded doubtful.

Sandy looked away, flipped her hand in the air, and dismissed Beth with, "I'm fine. We're fine. Stop nagging."

Beth sat back, but she wasn't finished, "Okay... You and Jamie sure have become fast friends."

Sandy's head snapped back to focus on Beth. She said, "We were friends before. I like her and she's alone, except for you."

Beth was suspicious. She was like a dog with a bone, when she said, "I was never friends with any of my former baby sitters."

Jamie thought about stepping in and ending the conversation, but she was halted by Sandy's voice, saying, "I was just twenty-one. She was seventeen. We weren't so far apart in age and you know Jamie always acted older than she was. We spent a lot of time together. We played on the same traveling team."

For some reason, Jamie felt the need to rescue Sandy. Beth must have sensed Jamie coming, because when Jamie walked up Beth said, "Well, I'm glad she moved back. I think we'll have... speak of the devil."

Jamie handed a beer to Sandy, and returned to the seat, beside her. She said, "That's me," referring to Beth's remark.

Sandy tried to cover the previous conversation, as if she wasn't sure how much Jamie had heard, by saying, "We were just talking about how glad we are that you moved back here."

Jamie grinned and winked at Sandy. She held up her plastic cup for a toast. "Me too," she said, and the three women toasted to their friendship.

61

#

Jamie, Sandy and Beth all ate pulled pork sandwiches covered with coleslaw for lunch. Jamie had helpings of baked beans, potato salad and a piece of chocolate pie, before she finally had to quit eating or burst. To take care of the too full feeling, she and Sandy played kick ball with the kids and then danced and sang along, at the top of their lungs with Beth, to "Carolina Girls," blaring from the speakers someone had turned up, as the party moved into the late afternoon. Jamie skied again, pulled by Robby, with Beth and Sandy riding in the boat. The women spent the afternoon laughing and playing like old friends. Sandy never left Jamie's side, until they sat down at supper where Sandy resumed her place again, beside Doug.

After supper, Jamie helped Beth and the others clean up around the yard. The walking helped her stomach settle. Jamie hadn't eaten this much food in very long time, but the skiing, swimming, and the sun made her hungry, not to mention she had to soak up the beer she'd been consuming all day. Jamie had quite the little buzz going before supper and would probably drink more, after her food settled. She was among friends. Jamie wanted to cut loose and have some fun. This feeling of rejuvenation had been a long time coming.

By the time the red sunset disappeared behind the trees, giving way to an indigo sky filled with stars, Jamie was well on her way to a good drunk. The yard was now spattered with large and small tents. A bonfire roared in the center of the yard, behind a brick walled pit. Stacks of wood surrounded the pit. People in lawn chairs and on blankets covered the ground near the bulkhead. Lanterns were lit here and there. Fireflies blinked on and off, while being chased by jar bearing, giggling children. The flotilla's lights sparkled on the surface of the calm flat water.

Jamie sat on a blanket with Beth and Robby. Sandy sat with Doug on the blanket next to them. Sandy leaned back on Doug's chest. He had his arms around her. All eyes were on the fireworks bursting over the water. The crowd ooo'ed and ahh'ed. Jamie looked over at Sandy and Doug. Sandy caught her looking and they smiled at each other. Sandy's gaze stayed locked on Jamie for a few seconds, too long. They both felt it, which was obvious from the expression on Sandy's face. Doug kissed the top of Sandy's head, absentmindedly. Sandy quickly looked back up at the fireworks, just as a huge explosion of light expanded and then fell, into the water. Jamie knew she was drunk, when she didn't look up at the fireworks, but instead watched the reflection in Sandy's eyes, before excusing herself to take a shower.

#

Later, after the shower and some more food, a much more sober Jamie and a few others were seated, in lounge chairs around the now small and crackling fire. After midnight, the party had settled down, most of the drunks and children had long since passed out. A hush had fallen over the water and the yard. Random voices occasionally echoed across the silent surface of the water. Somewhere in the distance, Jamie could hear a guitar playing, accompanied by a single voice, in the middle of a lonesome country song. Jamie listening to the woman sitting beside her, but kept her eyes on the fire in front of her.

Jamie answered the question for the hundredth time today, "Yes, it feels good to be home."

The woman stood up and patted Jamie's shoulder. "It was good to see you again, Jamie. Welcome home."

Jamie had already forgotten the woman's name, before she left. She was exhausted from the day's activities and of course the alcohol didn't help her ability to focus either. Jamie closed her eyes and pulled Sandy's borrowed sleeping bag up to her chest. A moment later, she heard someone sit down in the chair beside her. She opened one eye to see that Sandy was next to her, covering herself with a sleeping bag.

Jamie sat up. "Hey you," she said, poking Sandy's leg. "What, now you want to sleep with me?"

Jamie had only been kidding, but Sandy looked stricken, before she realized it was a joke and recovered with a little chuckle. She said, "Doug was snoring like a freight train. I thought I would get more sleep out here."

"I'm glad for the company," Jamie said and settled back into the lounge chair, staring up at the stars.

After a moment of silence, Sandy asked, "So did you have a good time today?"

Jamie sat up on her elbow, turning to look at Sandy, and grinning broadly, she said, "I had a great time. I haven't laughed like this in forever and you were right, I did know a lot of people."

Sandy turned, smiling at Jamie and scolded her, "See, I told you so."

"It's nice to feel welcome. I hope it lasts," Jamie said, reflectively.

Sandy raised her eyebrow, a familiar expression when she had a question. It reminded Jamie of Vivian Lee's famous questioning eyebrow, curious and at the same time, so seductive. Jamie was lost in this thought when Sandy snapped her out of with, "What do you mean, you hope it lasts?"

Jamie was nothing, if not a realist, when it came to people's reactions to her choice to live with and love a woman. "When they find out I'm one of those dreaded Lezzies, some of them will change."

Sandy was an optimist. She said, "I think you underestimate people."

"I'm speaking from experience. People just up and disappear on you," Jamie paused, and then her mouth said what she was thinking, only she hadn't meant to say it out loud, "You disappeared on me. One day you were there and then you weren't."

Sandy looked shocked. She gasped out, "Not because I thought you were gay."

Jamie grinned at Sandy and in her most sincere voice said, "I was devastated when I showed up at your house that night and you were gone. I didn't know it at the time, but that aching in my chest was due to the huge crush I had on you. You kinda broke my heart."

Sandy looked sad, saying, "I missed you too, but I had to go."

Jamie winked at Sandy and grinned even bigger. Like an eager child, she said, "You did? You really missed me."

"Yes, of course I missed you. We were inseparable that summer," Sandy said, sitting up and swinging her legs over the side, placing her feet between the two lawn chairs. She leaned in closer to Jamie, as if she was going to say something else, but then she stopped herself.

Jamie waited, as Sandy looked out over the water. Jamie thought Sandy had tears in her eyes, but she didn't say anything. She was patient, as Sandy gathered her strength to say whatever it was she needed to get off her chest.

Finally Sandy took a deep breath and said, "Jamie," without looking away from the water, "I'm sorry I didn't talk to you. I was just overwhelmed at the time with the divorce and a five year old. It was complicated."

Jamie tried to lighten the mood, "It's okay," she laughed, "I got over you."

Sandy laughed, too, while she wiped away the one tear that had escaped, before she gained control. She winked at Jamie. "You really know how to hurt a girl."

Jamie suddenly realized how badly she needed to go to the bathroom. She stood up and her bladder screamed for relief. "Man, I have to go to the bathroom," she said, shifting her wait from foot to foot. "I don't want to go in the house. I might wake someone, and I will go back in the water, before I go in that port-a-potty."

Sandy stood up beside Jamie. She said, "Come with me. They just put a new bathroom in the garage."

Jamie followed Sandy, encouraging her to hurry. They arrived at the bathroom door, where Jamie pushed past Sandy. She tore open the jeans she had put on, after the sun went down, and plopped down on the toilet seat. She was concentrating so hard on evacuating her painful bladder, that she was surprised to see Sandy had followed her in, and locked the door behind them. As soon as she finished, Jamie stood, pulling her pants back up and stepped to the sink to wash her hands. Sandy took her turn on the toilet seat.

Sandy sighed with relief, adding, "I didn't know I had to go so bad, until we got here."

Jamie finished washing her hands and looked in the mirror. Her face was sunburned, except for the raccoon circles around her eyes, where her sunglasses had been. Sandy, who had finished on the toilet, stepped up to the sink. Jamie took a step back to give Sandy more room. Sandy looked at Jamie in the mirror, while she washed her hands.

"You got some sun, today," Sandy said.

Jamie looked at Sandy's reflection and pointed out, "You did, too."

The two women caught each other's eyes in the mirror and stared back at one another just a little too long. Sandy finally broke the stare-off, by turning around. She leaned on the sink, placing her hands on both sides of her, gripping the countertop tightly. Sandy looked up at Jamie, freezing Jamie to the spot on the floor.

When Sandy finally spoke, it was in a dry whisper. "You know, I didn't tell you the whole truth about why I disappeared on you back then."

Jamie cocked her head to one side, saying, "You didn't?"

66

Sandy looked down at the floor, still whispering, "No, I didn't say goodbye, because I couldn't. I was scared."

Jamie was intrigued. "Why?"

Sandy lifted her eyes back to Jamie's and with great difficulty said, "Because I was almost twenty two, with a child and I found myself with a crush on a seventeen year-old, girl, no less."

Jamie was completely surprised. She had no idea Sandy had a crush on her, too. She grinned at Sandy. "Really?" she asked, then after a pause she added, "Well, you know, you would have been run out of the county and my parents would have put me in a Psych ward."

Jamie laughed and Sandy joined her, saying, "Yeah, no kidding."

Jamie was still trying to laugh her way through this tense little scene, when she said, "It was probably for the best that neither of us really knew what was happening."

Sandy stopped laughing and held Jamie with her eyes, a gaze so intense that Jamie thought Sandy was trying to read her mind. Sandy only whispered, "Like now."

They stood like that for only seconds, but it felt like an eternity to Jamie. Sandy's eyes were boring holes in her soul and desire had somehow reared its ugly head. Jamie was lost in those eyes, when suddenly Sandy crooked a finger through one of the belt loops on Jamie's jeans and pulled her closer. When Jamie was standing over her, Sandy seemed unable to control herself any longer. She stood up, wrapped her arms around Jamie's neck and kissed her, as passionately as Jamie had ever been kissed. Sandy moved Jamie up against the bathroom door, pressing her body into Jamie's. Soft sounds of desire emerged from both of their throats, as the kiss grew more heated and frantic.

The only thoughts going through Jamie's head were about taking this woman to bed. She was overwhelmed with unfulfilled desires of years gone by. Sandy, it seemed, felt the same way. The only thing that stopped them from going any further was the sudden knock on the other side of the door. Sandy went into full blown panic mode. Jamie had to handle the situation, before Sandy imploded.

Jamie reached for the toilet handle and flushed it. She called out, "Just a minute," and then reached around Sandy and turned the water on in the sink. She mouthed the words, "Calm down," to Sandy. Jamie shut off the water and checked Sandy visually. She said to her in a whisper, "Smile."

Jamie opened the door to find two teenage girls waiting outside. They immediately recognized Sandy and said, "Hello, Mrs. Canter."

Jamie smiled at them and heard Sandy say, behind her, "Hello, girls."

Sandy passed Jamie on the way out of the garage. Jamie followed her silently, until they were far enough away from the garage and then caught up to Sandy.

"Hey Sandy, wait up," she said, grabbing Sandy's arm to stop her. Sandy pulled away, moving with a purpose, head down and walking fast. Finally Jamie stepped in front of Sandy and faced her, while walking backwards. She pleaded with Sandy, "Just stop for a minute."

Sandy finally conceded and stopped. She put her hands on her hips and looked at Jamie, saying, "Oh my god, those girls saw us."

Trying to diffuse the situation, Jamie said, "They saw two women coming out of a bathroom together. That's a pretty common occurrence."

"Yeah, I guess it is," Sandy paused, breathing deeply several times to calm herself, before adding, "What did I just do?"

Jamie grinned. "You kissed me."

Sandy was not so happy. "I'm sorry. That should not have happened."

Seeing that Sandy was upset, Jamie tried a new tactic, "I'm sorry, too. Look, it's okay. We just got caught up in a memory, that's all."

Sandy looked so confused. She said, "I feel like I'm going crazy."

Fear flashed across Jamie's mind. She begged Sandy, "Please don't let this ruin our friendship."

Sandy wasn't listening. She was too caught up in the moment. She looked at the sky and questioned herself, "What the hell was I thinking? I'm married."

Jamie spoke without thinking, "So am I."

This statement visually rocked Sandy. She hadn't been expecting Jamie to say that. She asked Jamie, "You're still in love with her, aren't you?"

Jamie was honest, when she said, "Yes, very much."

Jamie didn't mean she wasn't interested in Sandy, but Sandy took it that way. She said, "Let's just forget the whole thing ever happened."

Jamie said the only thing she could, "Okay, I think that's the best thing for both of us."

"Yes, it is." Sandy responded quickly, with a much different tone to her voice and not letting Jamie say anything to stop her, adding, "I'm going back to my tent now. Maybe Doug stopped snoring. I'll see you in the morning."

Sandy walked away, stopping by the fire to grab her sleeping bag, leaving Jamie standing there, staring after her. After a moment, Jamie said, "Shit," and went back to the fire, to sleep alone.

#

"Shit! Shit! Shit!" Sandy berated herself. She left Jamie standing by the fire pit and disappeared into the darkness surrounding the tents. Winding her way to the far side of the yard, using the darkness as cover, Sandy slipped through the trees and found the little cleared out area Jake had used as a fort not long ago. Jake had shown it to her when he was about eleven. He had outgrown it, but it offered Sandy the solitude she needed now.

The Girl Back Home

Sandy couldn't believe she finally kissed Jamie and it was everything she had ever thought that kiss would be. She would have stayed in that little bathroom forever, kissing Jamie, but the knock on the door hit her with such panic, she lost control. Sandy fled, like the teenagers she caught kissing in the stacks, at the school library. The fear of getting caught overwhelmed her. The same way it had twenty-five years ago. Having been told her whole life, that women who love other women are condemned to hell, an abomination, and then having to push those feelings down and lock them away. Fearing the consequences, she had driven out of Currituck County and away from Jamie Basnight.

Being afraid didn't stop her from melting into Jamie, as if it was the most natural thing she'd ever done. There was no awkwardness, no hesitation, they simply fit together like a glove and for one moment Sandy's soul soared. She felt, not a pain, but a longing deep inside her body. Desire burned between her legs so quickly, it startled her. No one had ever made her feel that way, not even Gary and he had been her first love, the mad love that made her crazy enough to get pregnant. Now, that she knew what it felt like to kiss Jamie, and knowing she couldn't have her, made the longing for her more intense. Before the kiss, she had not been sure of what she was missing.

Why did she have to deny herself this one thing? This one thing that she had prayed would never happen, because she was afraid of what people would say. There was, of course, the husband she wanted to be rid of. She never really loved Doug, and though he would do anything to please her, it wasn't enough to fill the void she felt. Sandy had convinced herself that everybody lived that way. That the myth of true love was just that, a myth. Beth and Robby the only exception she knew. Sandy believed, up until a few minutes ago, that the kind of love that rocked peoples' worlds only happened to teenagers and young adults, when their hormones were raging and their frontal

70

lobes were not fully developed, and of course, in the movies. After a certain age, people just settled. Settled for less than what they really wanted, and made do with what they had, in front of them. That's what Sandy had done.

On top of all that, Jamie said, she was still in love with her ex. The incredibly beautiful, accomplished, not to mention rich, Dr. Mary Ann Best. Sandy couldn't compete with that. It was ridiculous for her to think one magic kiss, and Jamie would forget about the woman with whom she had spent the last sixteen years. Jamie did not react badly to the kiss. In fact, the soft sounds in Jamie's chest, when Sandy kissed her, said she wanted to kiss Sandy, too, and she did. Jamie had kissed Sandy back with passion she had never known. Yet, there was the ex-wife standing in the way. Sandy had felt the pain of jealousy when Jamie told her she still loved Mary Ann. How could she kiss Sandy like that and still be in love with another woman?

Sandy sat on the log couch, Jake had made from toppled pine logs. He'd gone as far as hand carving notches into the logs, so they would stay together. Sandy brushed aside the leaves and fallen twigs, taking a seat with a heavy sigh. She could see the lights from the tents, through the branches and bushes, in front of her. Occasionally, a chord or note from the guitar and singer would drift on the wind and brush across her ear. Sandy sat there, alone, unmoving for quite some time. She tried to put her mushy mind back together. Reason was still tapping her toe and waiting for Sandy to get the rest of her mind in order. She needed to be rational and reasonable, because what she was about to do, would change her entire life, as she knew it.

She was leaving Doug. Whatever happened with Jamie, Sandy was ending her marriage. It had been over a long time and Sandy had just been dragging it out, waiting, but what for? Was she waiting for the happiness fairy to come down and swat her with her wand? No, she wasn't going to wait anymore. Sandy was going to start doing things that made her happy, not what other people expected her to do, of that she was sure. The first thing on the list was leaving her husband. She would soon turn forty-six, time to "piss or get off the pot," as her grandma used to say.

Sandy grew sleepy and cleaned off the wooden couch. She laid out her sleeping bag on the primitive furniture and climbed into it. She suddenly thought about all the bugs and things out here in the woods. She would probably be covered in ticks and chiggers, but she had sprayed herself well, before trying to sleep the first time, and she sure as hell wasn't going back to her tent or the fire pit. She needed to sleep, but every time she closed her eyes, she was kissing Jamie again. One question repeated itself over and over, in her head, "Did I miss my chance to be happy, twenty-five years ago, or do I have a chance of redemption, now?"

Chapter Six

The next morning, Jamie awoke to the aroma of bacon frying. She rolled up the sleeping bag and walked over to Sandy and Doug's tent to return it. She found the tent had been taken down and put inside its carrying bag. Two sleeping bags were rolled up and placed beside the tent. Sandy must have gotten up early and started packing. Jamie didn't see either Doug or Sandy anywhere, so she placed her sleeping bag beside the others and went to find the source of the bacon aroma.

When she reached the driveway, she saw that the big black cookers were open. The cookers were now being used to heat up the griddles, covered in frying bacon, and cast iron skillets, filled with scrambled eggs. Mounds of homemade biscuits waited on the tables nearby. A line of people stood at the open garage doors, filling plates and chatting. The sun was already bright and warm. Morning had come to Currituck Sound in all its glory.

Jamie found Beth already in line and joined her. "Oh my god, that smells amazing. I'm starving," she said, when she got close.

Beth was not as cheerful as Jamie was, replying, "I'm hung-over, so quell your enthusiasm."

"How much longer does this shindig last?" Jamie asked, wanting to ski again today.

"Usually, the breakfast wakes and disperses the crowd. A few of the boat people will hang around and ski today though, if you're wanting to risk your neck some more."

Jamie saw Robby approaching. He slipped up behind Beth and kissed her on top of her head. Beth looked up and smiled at her husband. It was obvious to anyone watching that these two were still very much in love. Jamie envied Beth's happy marriage.

Robby spoke to Jamie, "Hey how was your night under the stars?"

"It was beautiful. Thanks for the bug spray, by the way."

"No problem," he said, smiling and then turned to Beth, "Honey, I came to tell you Sandy took your van to her house."

"Why?" Beth asked.

Robby shrugged, "She didn't feel well and she asked if she could just drive your car home. She said she couldn't find you."

"Where's Doug?" Beth wanted to know.

"He went out early this morning with Billy, bass fishing. Sandy didn't want to take his truck. He wouldn't have a way home."

Beth nodded. "Okay, well, I'll call her later. Maybe Jamie can take me by there to get the car."

Jamie said, "Sure, no problem," but she was thinking, "I have a big problem."

Robby kissed his bride on the cheek and hurried away, calling back, "Okay, see ya' babe."

"I'm not surprised Sandy doesn't feel well," Beth said to Jamie. "She drank more than usual yesterday."

Jamie commented, "That can do it to you," but she was distracted with thoughts of Sandy and the kiss.

Beth prattled on, "I've decided that recovery from a hangover is directly proportional to age. Remember when we used to hoot all night and then go to class in the morning."

Jamie tried to stay in the conversation, "It is amazing the things we did and lived to tell it."

Beth laughed hoarsely, saying, "No shit."

When they reached the front of the line, the two women filled their plates and took them to a nearby picnic table. They sat near others recovering from the previous day and night's events, in various stages of misery. The sights and sounds of a camp breaking up went on around them. Tent poles clanged, babies cried and boat engines roared to life.

Beth finished her first bite and chased it down with fresh orange juice. After a big, "Ahhh!" she asked Jamie, "So how has your first week back home been?"

"I'm glad I moved back. I haven't been this relaxed in years."

Beth grinned and patted Jamie on the back. "That's good. You needed to relax."

Jamie grinned back. "It feels so good to laugh. Sandy almost made me wet my pants, telling stories about things we did back in the day."

Beth tried to sound innocent when she said, "It looks like you two just picked up where you left off," but she didn't do a good job of covering her curiosity.

Jamie replied, a little guarded, "Yes, we have. I had forgotten how much fun we used to have together."

Beth circled around what she really wanted to ask, "I think I was in Florida with the grandparents that summer."

"Yeah, you were always in Florida or somewhere." Jamie hoped to steer the conversation away from Sandy.

75

It worked. Beth became nostalgic, "I did get around back then. Ah... those were the days, before husbands, children and jobs."

Jamie encouraged Beth to think of anything, but Sandy, saying, "Yeah, but you're lucky. You love your life."

Beth smiled broadly and said, "Yes, yes I do."

Jamie held up her orange juice saying, "A toast to the luckiest woman in the world."

They bumped their plastic cups and laughed together. Another beautiful, sunny, summer day on the Outer Banks of North Carolina had begun.

#

Sandy awoke just before sunrise. She heard a boat motor crank, just as she emerged from the trees. She saw Doug and one of his friends leaving, in the boat. She vaguely remembered him saying he was going bass fishing this morning. Sandy quietly packed their tent and sleeping bags away, so as not to wake the still sleeping campers. She got the little duffel shaped bag with their extra clothes and things and went to the truck to put them away.

When she got to the truck, it was locked and Doug had the only key in his pocket. She couldn't just strand him here, anyway. She threw the bag in the back truck. "Shit." She started to cry. She said to the trees, "I have got to get out of here." She walked away to a part of the yard, where no one could see her and she cried. It exploded out of her, uncontrollably. It began as a whimper, followed by the, "why me," tears, then the reality of her life kicked her in the gut and doubled her over, and the sobbing began.

Once again Reason screamed, the tapping, a loud African drum now, "Stand up! Get up! Stop falling apart. Sandy, get your shit together, girlfriend, or this is going to be a lot harder than it has to be."

Sandy paid no attention to Reason. In some way, it felt good to let it go, to purge... to purge... to purge what? Sandy fell to her knees, because she had no

76

idea what was driving this emotional roller coaster she found herself riding, alone. This was going to be one of those cleansing cries. Something wanted to have its day and be done with her.

She felt it, before she realized what it was. An image flashed in her mind. It was the look on her mother's face, the daggered eyes of shame piercing Sandy, saying without words, "You little, whore," and that's the way she was treated for years, even after Dawn was born. Shame and the fear of it had imprinted on Sandy, compelling her always to do what was expected of her, never to step out of line, from then until now.

Sandy had borne the humiliation of being pregnant, her senior year in high school. Thirty years ago, it wasn't as accepted, like today. While still frowned upon, pregnant teenage girls today, are coddled, given classes and supported from inception to birth and beyond. Sandy bore it alone, with whispers and stares, from not only her classmates, but also her own family. Sandy rid herself of the shame they had heaped on her, the tears washing it out forever, and then she forgave herself for being too afraid of shame to be who she really was.

Sandy leaned back against the pine tree, but the tears flowed still. Quietly now, but somehow more distressing than before …and then it hit her. She heard a line from the Eagles "Wasted Time," in her mind first, and then she knew what, or maybe for whom she was keening. Sandy knew, after that kiss last night, her life had been filled with so much wasted time. Searching for that one thing that would make her happy and it had been inside her all the time, locked away and Jamie had the key.

It hit her so hard she fell forward onto her hands and threw up, and then she sat up sobbing silently against the base of a tree. Sandy was crying for the life she could have had, had she been brave enough. Sandy was purging all the tied up bundles of moments when, if she had done something or said something different, her life would have been altered.

77

The Girl Back Home

It wouldn't have been fair to Jamie, to involve her in a relationship, at that young age, and Sandy was positive she had done the right thing, by not acting on her feelings. Look what Jamie had become, a high powered lawyer and a polished woman, traveling in polished circles, way above Sandy's pay grade. Yes, she was proud of Jamie, of what she had achieved, of what a beautiful person she had become. Leaving Jamie had not been a mistake.

Now, she was facing that same moment again. Would she be brave enough to live the life, she now believed she had wanted all along? She was in love with Jamie, she always had been, but Mary Ann stood in the way of that. Sandy also had to consider that Jamie might not want to have a relationship with her, even if Mary Ann was out of the picture. What she needed to do was stop having this pity party and listen to Reason. Stand up! Get up, and get your shit together.

Sandy abruptly stopped crying. She wiped the tears from her face. She stood up and gathered her senses. She did feel better, but she was exhausted from the experience. She just wanted to go home. Sandy had a lot on her mind, when she found Robby, by the cooker. He had asked if she was all right and she told him she wasn't feeling well. He gave her Beth's keys and she went home. Home, where she would try to put her life back together or tear it apart, at that moment, Sandy had no idea how this was going to play out.

#

After another day of skiing, Jamie was exhausted and ready to call it a night. She was driving, top down, warm southern winds blowing through her hair. Beth was in the passenger seat. Jamie was taking her to Sandy's to get her van, before she could go home, take a hot shower, and crash into her bed. It was a beautiful warm evening, the bugs and frogs were in full voice. Jamie drove down the back road, a narrow two lane with huge cedar trees arching over the road, giving it a closed in feeling. Jamie rolled her neck, trying to relieve the pain of her stiff muscles.

"I'm going to feel that last spill tomorrow. I hit the water hard," she said to Beth.

Beth scolded her, "I told you, you're going to break your neck. We don't heal as fast as we used to."

Jamie stretched her shoulder and grimaced. "Believe me; I am very aware of that fact."

Beth continued, "Doug said Sandy was still in bed. The keys are in the van, so we can just take it and go."

Jamie yawned out, "That sounds like a plan. I'm getting sleepy, too."

Beth pointed down the road saying, "Turn up there, at that reflector on the left. They live on the water, down that lane. It's a really nice place."

"Sandy told me she worked with the architect to get it just right, her dream home."

Beth snorted a laugh. "Well, Doug would give her the moon, if she asked for it."

"That's really nice," Jamie said and meant it. She explained, "I'm glad she found someone who loves her. She deserved a good life after Gary."

Beth replied, "I never knew Gary. He was so much older than we were. He moved to Texas, I think."

Jamie turned the car down the path, while she elaborated, "I saw enough of him to know he was a jack ass. He knocked her up senior year and then blamed her for ruining his chances at a scholarship to play ball. He was really mean to Sandy. He hit her."

"Well, Doug treats her like a princess," Beth said.

Jamie felt a twinge of something, jealousy maybe, but she said, "That's good to hear."

Then Beth segued into the conversation Jamie had been trying to avoid all day, "That's why I can't figure out what's wrong with her lately. She doesn't seem to want him around that much."

Jamie offered an excuse for Sandy's behavior, "Maybe she's just in a mood, it happens."

Beth wasn't convinced. She said, "Maybe," and then pointed out the windshield saying, "That's it on the right."

A beautiful log cabin appeared among the tall pines, back-dropped by the moon shining on the surface of the sound. The house and yard were something out of a magazine. Perfectly manicured flower gardens were spaced around the property. Elegant outdoor lighting accented the yard leading up to the cathedral high ceilinged, mostly glass, foyer.

Jamie let go of a long and drawn out, "Wow!"

Beth chuckled. "I told you. Doug thinks the sun and moon rise in that girl."

"He must also make a crap load of money," Jamie observed.

Jamie stopped the car. She was still staring at the incredible house. Jamie's eyes traveled up to the second floor, where she could now see Sandy looking out of an upstairs window. Jamie couldn't take her eyes off Sandy. It took her a moment to realize Beth was talking to her.

She focused, just in time to hear Beth ask, "Do you want to go look for office space tomorrow?"

Jamie watched as Sandy left the window and then looked at Beth. She answered, "Yeah, sure. How about lunch? My treat, then we'll go look around."

Beth opened the car door and got out. "Okay, I'll be at your house at 11:30."

Beth turned to go to her van, when Jamie called after her, "I had a great time. Thank your parents again for me."

Beth said, "I will. See you tomorrow," waving and giving Jamie a big grin.

Beth continued on to her van, got in and started the engine. Her lights flashed on. Jamie looked back at the window and not seeing Sandy, she pulled away. Jamic's brake light cast a red glow on the trees that lined the sandy path. Jamie glanced, one more time, in the rearview mirror at the house behind her. She focused on the window where Sandy had been standing. Just before she rounded the next curve and lost sight of the house, she saw Sandy slide the curtain back and watch, as Jamie's brake lights disappeared from her view.

Chapter Seven

Two weeks after the party, Jamie walked down the back steps and followed the rock path to the little red barn, carrying a tray containing three glasses of iced tea. The river rock path was uneven and Jamie was glad for her experience as a waitress, during her undergrad years. She navigated the path without spilling too much liquid. It was a sweltering hot July afternoon. The humidity made the air feel thick and heavy. It felt like the yard had been engulfed in a cloud of steam. Jamie had begun to sweat as soon as she closed the backdoor behind her.

A pick-up truck, the paint scraped off in places and dents that were evidence of previous collisions, sat at the end of the driveway, close to the barn. There were ladders and saw horses in the back of the truck, which had been splashed with multiple colors of paint. The tailgate was down, making a temporary table for a miter saw. A hand painted sign, down the side of the truck, read, "Meachem Boys, Damn good Carpenters for Cheap."

A white post, with an old fashioned sign suspended by small silver chains, now stood by the driveway entrance. The sign announced, in large black letters, that this was the residence and office of J. L. Basnight, Attorney at Law. For the past two weeks, Jamie had worked on the yard, adding flowers in pots and beds around the property. She had even hung a hammock between the ancient twin oak trees by the patio and slept in it one entire evening.

Where once there had been white, wooden double doors, on the front of the barn, now stood the framework for a single doorway and a window. The interior of the barn had been gutted down to the studs and was, at this moment, being worked on by two men, in ragged tee shirts with the sleeves cut out and well worn painters' shorts, complete with paint stains and holes. The floor of the barn had been replaced by hard wood planking, creating a large, open, well lit, office space of about six hundred square feet. That was a real step down from the Durham office, which was located in an old Victorian mansion. Still, Jamie smiled at her new office space and at the two guys inside, as she neared them.

She offered the glasses to the men. "I thought you two could use some iced tea."

Billy Meachem and his brother Donny stopped working and came out of the barn, to take the tea from Jamie. They thanked her and the three of them stood together, admiring the progress, on the office.

Jamie was the first to speak, "It's coming along."

Donny, the smaller of the two brothers, with his year round deeply tanned tight body and sandy blonde hair, looked much younger than his age. That was until you got close enough to see the wrinkles on his face, put there by years of hard drinking and manual labor. Donny brushed his surfer bangs out of his eyes and said, "For a week and a half's work, it's not half bad."

"I think we're right on schedule. You should be in within a week. The plumber's coming tomorrow to do the little bathroom and set up the heat and air." It was Billy, the oldest brother speaking. In contrast to his brother, Billy had dark hair and fair skin. He was larger, with a thicker build, but shared the haunting eyes of a drinker with his brother.

The Girl Back Home

Jamie didn't care if they drank, as long as they were not working for her when they did it. She had grown up and graduated from high school with Billy. Jamie knew exactly what she was getting into, when she ran into them at the grocery store, the day after she and Beth had tramped all over Elizabeth City, looking for a good office space. Jamie and Billy had struck up a conversation and when she mentioned she had decided to turn her barn into a home office, Billy asked for the job. They worked out the price and the rules the next day, at Jamie's kitchen table. The price was reasonable and the rules were simply, on time, on budget, and off the booze. The Meachem boys were really good carpenters, as it turned out, and showed up every day, making fast work of the job.

Jamie tipped her tea glass in a toasting gesture. "You guys have done a great job. I'm glad I ran into you at the store that day."

Donny chuckled. "We're glad you hired us."

Jamie grinned at Billy, saying, "Well, if you can't trust your seventh grade boyfriend, who can you trust?"

All three laughed, when Billy responded, "I still haven't gotten over my broken heart."

Jamie poked Billy's shoulder. "It hasn't stopped you from being married and divorced three times, and fathering god knows how many children."

Billy feigned offense and blamed Jamie for his troubles, "You see. It's a pattern and it's all your fault. I could never love again, after the age of thirteen. You ruined my life."

Jamie laughed. "You'll live."

Unexpectedly, a car pulled down the gravel driveway. The rocks popping and crunching under the tires, alerted Jamie to its presence. Jamie peaked around the barn. She saw Sandy's car rolling slowly toward her. Jamie wasn't sure how she felt about Sandy's arrival. In the past two weeks, Jamie tried to get in touch with Sandy, multiple times. She had received no response. Beth was in Florida, visiting relatives, leaving Jamie alone, with no one to talk to. Her heart had begun to beat faster, not sure if it was anger or excitement, Jamie decided to stay put and try to be civilized.

Sandy pulled the car to a stop and got out. She was tanned and glowing, as usual, in a simple blue sundress, with tiny yellow sunflowers printed on the material. She wore sandals and Jamie noticed that even Sandy's toes were tanned. Sandy made casual look very, very appealing. Jamie's anger was losing out to lust, at the moment. Jamie tried to refocus, away from Sandy's amazing body and on the fact that Sandy had refused to communicate with her for two whole weeks.

Sandy spoke to the men first, "Well, hey boys. I haven't seen you in months. How's the family?"

Billy answered, "Good, good. Jimmy's playing in the twelve and thirteen year old league this summer. He's doing real good."

Sports was the language of the masses in this area and Sandy played the game well, saying, "Good to hear. I hope he makes the All-Stars."

"Thanks," Billy said.

Donny finished his tea and handed the empty glass to Jamie. "Thanks for the tea. Nice to see you Sandy," he said and went back to work.

Billy handed his glass to Jamie and she placed hers along with the other two on the tray. Billy followed his brother back into the barn saying, as he went, "Well, we need to get back to work. Thanks for the tea Jamie, and it was good to see you, Sandy."

Sandy smiled at the men, who were obviously charmed by her. "It was good to see you both." After an awkward moment of silence, Sandy spoke to Jamie for the first time, "So, you're turning your barn into an office?"

Jamie remembered to be civil, replying, "I looked around and decided I'd rather work from home than have to go to an office."

The awkward silence returned. Jamie finally broke it, by asking, "You want to come in, get out of the heat?"

Sandy nodded, yes, and followed Jamie into the house. Jamie went to the counter by the sink and sat the tray down. Her mind was racing with all the things she wanted to say. Namely how thoughtless Sandy had been, to not at least email Jamie and tell her she didn't want to talk to her, yet. Sandy stood in the middle of the kitchen, unsure of what to do.

Jamie turned and walked to the refrigerator, opening the door. She said, as she went by Sandy, "Have a seat. Do you want some tea or water?"

"Tea is fine," Sandy said, smiling weakly and taking a seat, at the small table in the corner of the kitchen.

"I hope you like it sweet. It's all I have," Jamie said with her back turned to Sandy. She poured the tea and brought the glasses over to the table. She sat down across from Sandy. Jamie had fought the urge to be tacky as long as she could. She opened her mouth and the words tumbled out, "So, you finally remembered where I lived."

Sandy lowered her eyes to the table, softly saying, "I'm sorry."

It wasn't enough for Jamie. "I called and left a message. I texted you. I even emailed you. Nothing. No response for two weeks."

"I said, I am sorry," Sandy responded, looking up from the table and into Jamie's eyes for the first time since she arrived.

Sandy, it seemed, need only look at Jamie with those big brown eyes and Jamie lost all ability to be angry with her. Jamie thought a moment, before she said, "Look I know that night at the party freaked you out. Hell, it freaked me out and I'm the one who's gay."

Sandy offered an excuse for not contacting Jamie, "I needed time to think. Time away from you and all these feelings."

"Then what made you show up here, today?"

Sandy tried a weak smile, when she answered, "You're the only one I can talk to about... what happened... what's happening to me."

Jamie smiled back at Sandy. She wanted Sandy to relax, so she said, "What happened is, you had too much to drink and kissed a girl. Believe me a lot of straight women have done that."

Sandy locked her eyes on Jamie's. "That wasn't just a drunken grope and you know it," she said, then quietly, timidly she added, "I've never felt anything like that before, never."

Jamie let the words slip out of her mouth, without thinking, "I felt it, too."

There was a moment between them, where they simply stared into each other's eyes.

Sandy broke the silence, "What are we going to do?"

Practical Jamie answered, "Nothing, you're married and straight." Jamie's evil twin whispered in her head, but not out loud, "Take her to bed and find out how straight she really is."

Sandy jarred Jamie with, "And you're still in love with Mary Ann."

"Touché," Jamie said and sat back against the chair. "Sandy, I cheated on Mary Ann. I know how it feels. People always talk about how getting cheated on is so terrible, but the one who cheats, well... at least in my case, the guilt was killing me... is killing me."

Sandy started to say something, but Jamie cut her off.

"Technically I wouldn't be cheating on her anymore, since we are obviously not getting back together, but you, you would be cheating on Doug. Don't make the same mistakes I did."

Sandy started to cry. She buried her head in her hands, saying, "I'm so confused."

"I know you are," Jamie told her. "I remember that feeling. One thing you should know is that I am attracted to you. I have been since I was seventeen. I can't tell you how many times I've thought about you, dreamed about you, over the years... and when you kissed me, I felt everything that you were feeling. Don't ever doubt that."

Sandy took her hands away from her face. She took a napkin from the holder on the table and dabbed the tears from her cheeks. She asked, "What about Mary Ann?"

Jamie grinned at her. "I have to admit, I'm a little confused myself."

Sandy slapped at Jamie's hand, on the table, playfully. "You're not helping."

Jamie grew more thoughtful. She took Sandy's hand and said, "I just don't want you to think you're crazy, like I did when it happened to me. If it is something you want to explore, I think that's great, but Sandy, don't cheat. Either work it out or get out, but don't do what I did. You'll be sorry and so will I."

Sandy gathered her composure. She waved a hand at Jamie, saying, "I know, I know. So, you'll understand if I don't see you alone, until I work some stuff out."

Jamie nodded in agreement. "I have some things of my own to work out."

Sandy stood and Jamie followed her to the door. Sandy turned and the two women hugged. Just before they released the embrace, Jamie whispered into Sandy's ear, "Sandy... don't kiss me again, I'm not that strong."

#

Later that same evening, after Jamie had gone to sleep, her eyes suddenly popped open. She had been having a dream. She tried to remember it, as she lay there catching her breath. In the dream, she was making love to Sandy. It had been incredibly hot and hungry sex. Just as Sandy orgasmed in Jamie's arms, Mary Ann had walked in. That's what woke Jamie up.

After a few useless attempts to return to sleep, Jamie got up. She was wearing only underwear and a tank top. When she went to the bathroom, she discovered that she was wet from the dream. She laughed at herself. It had been quite a hot little sex scene she dreamed up. Too bad, it ended the way it did.

Jamie took a water bottle from the refrigerator and stood drinking it, at the door on the sun porch. What was she to think about her attraction to Sandy? Jamie had lost all sense of what was the right thing to do. She knew she was still in love with Mary Ann, or was she? Was she holding on to Mary Ann, because that was all she had to hold onto? Was she really attracted to Sandy? Physically, absolutely, but emotionally, Jamie wasn't quite sure.

It would be ludicrous to think that she could have a physical relationship with Sandy and not become emotionally entangled. Jamie and Sandy were already emotionally tied to each other. This wouldn't be sport fucking or stranger sex, none of which Jamie had ever done with a woman. She had with men, but that had been easy. Jamie hadn't been a slut, but she had a few rolls in the hay, just for the hell of it. Even though she never cared about Tara, their relationship had left its emotional scars.

No, any relationship with Sandy was going to involve feelings. If Sandy left her husband to be with Jamie, what would happen? Jamie wasn't sure she was ready for that burden. How could she be involved in another relationship, when she hadn't put the last one to rest, yet? What if Mary Ann came back? It was a long shot, but it could happen.

Jamie felt something shift in her thinking. For the first time, she had wondered what she would do, if Mary Ann wanted her back. Up until now, there had never been any hesitation on Jamie's part. She had never thought about not going back to Mary Ann, but now Jamie wasn't sure about that either. She was beginning to think she wasn't sure of anything anymore.

Sandy awakened desires and needs, Jamie had long thought buried. Jamie wanted Sandy, but this was all getting way too complicated. Moving way out here to the coast was supposed to give Jamie time to get grounded again. Instead, she found herself confused and unsettled.

Jamie followed the reflection of the moonbeams on the water to their source. Somewhere under this same moon, the two women on Jamie's mind were probably fast asleep. Totally unaware that now they both haunted her dreams.

#

The moon reflected off the water behind Sandy's house. On the upper deck, Sandy sat alone, drinking tea, looking at the moon. She couldn't sleep. She sat wondering if she had come to the right conclusion. Doug slept in their bed on the other side of the deck doors, unaware that his wife was going to leave him on Sunday. She would spend the day with him Saturday, because he had asked her to, and then on Sunday morning she would tell him she wanted a divorce.

Sandy wanted to settle things with Doug first, before she did anything else. One thing at a time, that's how she decided to tackle her mountain of problems. Maybe it would give Jamie time to make up her mind about Mary Ann. She followed the reflection of the moon up to the sky and thought, Jamie was just down the road, under that same moon, fast asleep, and Sandy very much wanted to be there sleeping with her.

Chapter Eight

Since Sandy left her house five days ago, Jamie had tried to keep busy. She worked side by side with the Meachem boys for two days, painting and sanding, until the office was ready to move in. Beth came back from Florida on Wednesday and spent Thursday afternoon helping Jamie set up the office. Beth enjoyed being away from her family, after being cooped up with them at her brother's house for two weeks.

Beth brought up Sandy only once and must have realized it wasn't something Jamie wanted to talk about. Jamie hadn't meant to sound defensive, when she said, "I talked to her once. She's busy, I'm busy, what else can I tell you?"

Beth switched the subject to a no less controversial one, "Have you spoken with Mary Ann?"

"No," Jamie snapped.

Beth put her hands up in surrender, saying, "Okay... too tender... I get it." She paused and looked around the room and then cleared the pall from the air, "I love this office space. It looks old fashioned, but modern, very well done, counselor."

Jamie had smiled at Beth. She loved her. They would always be friends, because they didn't poke the tender spots. Oh there would be hell to pay one day, over this whole "Big Ol' Cheater," thing as Beth had once called it, but not until Jamie could take it. Until then, she could depend on Beth to be there when she needed her and back off when she didn't.

That had been on Thursday. Friday, Jamie settled into the office. She answered messages from the service she hired to field all her office calls. The service directed clients needing immediate advice to another firm, depending on their need. Other messages were transcribed and emailed to Jamie, sending a reply to the sender that J. L. Fisher was out of the office on an extended vacation. All clients would receive notice, when Ms. Fisher reopened her new offices in Currituck County. Jamie had contacted all her current clients personally and directed them to trusted firms, but a few people still called needing help or were just checking in.

Jamie contacted the service and changed her message to "open for business," but still, if it was an emergency, the service was to give out the appropriate firm's information. Jamie had enough clients on retainer to keep her invested in the work, until she could get some local clients. She only took on what she could handle, since she had to let her staff go, with healthy severance packages. Jamie would have to travel to Durham occasionally, to do business, but the age of technology made making a living from home a possibility. Jamie went to court, because she liked it. A competitor, all her life, winning was in her veins and winning was what she did. It was time to get back in the game.

Beth invited Jamie to ski with her family, minus the moody teenage girl, on Saturday. Jamie was happy for the distraction. Sandy had not called in five days. Five long days. Jamie found that she was thinking less and less of Mary Ann and oh, so much more about Sandy. Maybe it was just forbidden fruit syndrome or crush on a straight girl drama. Whatever it was, it was driving

Jamie nuts, not knowing what it would feel like to take Sandy to bed, and to Jamie that just didn't sound like a woman who was still in love with her ex.

That's why she was so thankful, when Beth called this morning. She could put away all her anxieties for the time being, out on the water. Jamie had ordered Jake a trick ski for his birthday, because he wanted Jamie to teach him some tricks. It arrived on Friday and she decided to give it to him a week early. They spent the morning, side by side, Jamie teaching and Jake mostly falling.

Robby drove the boat, while Beth looked on from the seat beside the driver. Beth looked tense as Jake prepared to give it another try. First, Jamie had to teach Jake to deep water start on a short, fat, rounded edge ski, which was much different from anything Jake had done before. That took a while. Then they worked on jumping the wake and getting some air. Jake caught onto that fairly quickly. Then she started teaching him the simple 'roast beef' trick of grabbing the ski between your legs while in the air.

Jamie did a simple twist over the wake, then Jake followed suit. So far so good. Jamie rolled off the wake and into the air with ease, flinging her ski up in the air, completing the trick and landing safely. Jake took off easily as well, but fumbled the hand work, coming down hard on his back. Jamie let go of the rope and curved back to Jake, before she swam up beside him.

Jamie praised him, "You almost had it that time."

Jake slapped the water in front of him. She was glad to see he was mad and not injured. Jake was angry with himself. "I knew I had it, but I got excited and I lost it."

Jamie patted him on the back. "You'll get it next time."

Robby pulled the boat up beside the two swimmers. Beth leaned over the side, taking the skis into the boat. Beth was grinning, ear to ear, when she said, "Damn, Jake, you almost had it that time."

93

Jake was excited. As he climbed the ladder into the boat, he said, "I know. Did you see it?"

Beth hugged him, "Yes, and if you don't land it soon, I'm going to have a heart attack."

Jamie's feet hit the bottom of the boat, as she said to Beth, "Relax Mom, this is just the first step. Wait till we add the flip."

Beth slapped at Jamie playfully, "You! Stop encouraging him."

They all heard the other boat approaching and turned to see who it was.

Robby pointed, "Hey, look. It's Doug and Sandy."

Beth waved happily at the other boat, while Jake slapped high fives with his dad, took his vest off, and grabbing a water out of the cooler, sat down in the bow. Robby pulled the ski ropes in and Jamie tried to get small. She got rid of her vest, dried off, threw a tee shirt on over her suit and grabbed her sunglasses. She got busy looking for a water in the cooler, while Robby and Doug pulled their crafts close together and tied off. Then while Beth and Sandy hugged over the railing, Jamie took a seat by Jake, in the bow. She forced a smile and concentrated on opening the water bottle and taking long sips.

Jake wanted to talk about the trick, so Jamie had a way out of the other conversation, but that didn't mean she wasn't listening to every word. The hair stood up on her neck when she just glanced at Sandy and saw that she was wearing a black two-piece bathing suit and a white sundress, unbuttoned all the way, hanging loosely over her shoulders. Sandy was built exactly as Jamie had imagined her. Soft feminine curves and a flat stomach, exposed hip bones and a soft peach fuzz blonde hair line leading down...

Jamie was jarred out of her fantasy by her name. She looked up to see Doug waving at her. He said, "I was saying, it's good to see you Jamie."

Jamie smiled and waved at the visitors. She covered her loss of consciousness a moment ago by saying, "Sorry, got water in my ears." She turned back to Jake, who had stopped talking and was just staring at her, "What were you saying, Jake?"

Jamie paid closer attention to him this time, but she still listened to Beth and Sandy, as they chatted, at the other end of the boat.

Beth was speaking, "What have you been doing? I haven't heard from you since the party."

"I've been doing some landscaping, at the house. You were in Florida, anyway."

Doug butted in, "Some landscaping? She put in a whole stone walkway from the shed to the backdoor."

Sandy took up for herself, "We needed the walkway."

Beth poked at Sandy. "Didn't they tell you summer vacation was for relaxing?"

"Hey, we're about to go in. Beth's dad cooked up a mess of fish. You should come eat," Robby said.

Sandy begged off, "No, we don't want to impose."

Beth was as persuasive as ever, "Since when is eating when you've been invited, imposing? Get your ass to the house."

Doug asked Sandy, "Honey, is that okay with you?"

"Sure, if you want to," Sandy answered, knowing she had been defeated.

Robby said, "Okay see you in a minute," and then untied the two boats.

He started the engine and the boat roared to shore, until reaching the shallows, where they slowed and crept toward the dock. Jamie sipped her water and begged her heart to slow down. She had actually stared at Sandy's body. Sandy had only worn shorts and a bathing suit top at the party. She never looked like that before, Jamie was sure she would have remembered. Thank god, Jamie wore dark sunglasses.

Lunch went better than expected. Sandy sat with Doug, at one end of the picnic table, and Jamie sat at the other end. She was careful to sit on the same side as Sandy, so she wouldn't have to look at her. Everyone had finished eating and Jamie was standing at the end of the table. She was helping Beth put lids on food containers, when she heard a car pull up in the driveway behind her. Beth suddenly shrieked with joy and ran from the table toward the new arrival.

All eyes followed Beth to the driveway, including Jamie's. Jamie was stunned and had to blink several times to make it real. Beth was hugging Mary Ann and welcoming her to the table. Mary Ann was dressed in shorts and a tee shirt, with her hair pulled back in a pony tail. She may have been going for casual, but as usual Mary Ann looked like a model. Jamie couldn't move, but she managed to make eye contact with Sandy. Sandy looked at Jamie and then at Mary Ann and back to Jamie. Jamie lowered her eyes and looked away.

Beth was saying to Mary Ann, "You remember Jake, don't you?"

Mary Ann smiled at Jake and he stood to give her a hug. Still enough of a boy to give hugs and be excited about birthday presents, he said, "Hey, Mary Ann, Jamie's been teaching me some stuff on my new trick ski."

Mary Ann chuckled as she squeezed him in her arms, "Oh my, you're not a little boy anymore. I didn't realize it had been so long."

Beth continued with the introductions, pointing at Doug and Sandy, "These are our friends Doug and Sandy Canter. This is Mary Ann Best, another friend of ours."

Jamie watched as Sandy and Doug shook hands with Mary Ann and exchanged greetings. Doug stood with his mouth hanging open, obviously bowled over by Mary Ann, when she smiled and said, "Nice to meet you both."

Jamie saw Sandy visibly steel herself. Smiling widely, she took Mary Ann's hand and said, "It's nice to finally meet you Mary Ann. Beth and Jamie have both spoken very highly of you."

Mary Ann, ever the southern belle, replied, "That's so nice of you to say." She turned to Robby and gave him a big hug, saying, "And you, how are you?"

"I'm great. You look as lovely as ever," Robby replied.

Mary Ann pecked him on the cheek, teasing him, "You are such a smoozer."

Jamie was the only person left to whom Mary Ann had not spoken. Beth played the peacemaker, pulling Mary Ann over to stand in front of Jamie. She said to Mary Ann, "And of course, you know my friend Jamie."

Mary Ann spoke first, "Well, you look like you've been having fun in the sun."

Beth spoke, because Jamie didn't, "She's been flying around behind that boat like a teenager. She's going to break her neck. I keep telling her."

Jamie finally managed to say, "What are you doing here?" Those were the first words she had spoken personally to Mary Ann in three months. Everything else had been communicated through email or lawyers. Jamie wasn't glad to see Mary Ann, not here and certainly not in front of all these people. She had imagined what her first words would have been to Mary Ann, if given the chance, but what she said was not on the list.

This wasn't going well for Beth either. She tried to help, saying, "She stopped by our house and Jen told her where we were. Isn't this a nice surprise?"

The Girl Back Home

Jamie had not taken her eyes off Mary Ann's, not since they first made contact. She was trying to read this woman she had lived with for sixteen years. Mary Ann was up to something, she was pretending too hard that she wasn't. Jamie asked her, "I meant, what are you doing here, in Currituck?"

Mary Ann's eyes softened, as well as her voice, "I need to talk to you and I didn't want to do it on the phone."

Jamie wasn't buying it. She had waited three months for this woman to speak to her. The first month Jamie called every day and left at least one message, sometimes more, if she was drunk. She had groveled on her knees and not once did Mary Ann respond. Not to cards, letters, flowers, nothing could touch the ice queen. The second month she cut the calls and messages to once a week, but by then she had lost any hope of reconciling. All she ever got in return were the hang up calls Mary Ann would make, not saying anything or leaving a message. Jamie thought Mary Ann should have to be the one waiting, this time.

"Okay," Jamie said, "but I promised Jake I'd teach him this trick today."

Beth butted in again, "Oh, you can do that some other time."

Mary Ann stopped Beth, by saying, "No, she promised Jake." Then she turned to Jamie. "I'd like to see you ski. I haven't seen that in a long time."

Jamie just stood there, still looking at Mary Ann. There were so many contradictory emotions swimming in her head, Jamie couldn't hold on to one, before another took its place. She hadn't forgotten about Sandy either, but could not bring herself to look that way.

Beth, thank god, realized her dilemma and rescued her by saying, "Alright then, let's get this mess cleaned up and we'll get back on the water. Mary Ann, do you have a swimsuit with you?"

"As a matter of fact, I did pack one. May I change in the house?"

Beth laughed at her and said, "Oh, shit. Quit being so proper. You are among friends now. Go get your suit and get changed. Do you remember your way around in there?"

Mary Ann, who had been here numerous times with Jamie, answered, "I think so. Where are your mom and dad?"

"They left a little while ago to meet some friends at the beach. They'll be back later tonight. Jake, go show Mary Ann in the house."

Jake and Mary Ann walked away together. All Jamie could think about, as she watched them walk away, was that Mary Ann had brought a bag with her. Was she assuming she could stay with Jamie? Jamie was thrust out of her thoughts by Doug's voice. When she turned around she realized they were all looking at her.

Doug asked Sandy, "Is that her girlfriend?"

Sandy only said, "Yes."

Doug reacted with a, "Wow!"

Robby seconded Doug's reaction, "No kidding."

Beth put a stop to their nonsense. She said, "Reel 'em back in boys and close your mouths."

Sandy backed Beth with a heartfelt, "Really!"

Jamie turned back to Beth. "Beth, did you..."

Beth interrupted her, "No, I did not ask her to come here."

Jamie wanted to know more, "Have you been talking to her?"

"A couple of times, but I just listened, I swear," Beth said, defensively.

Jamie let up, "Okay, okay."

Beth stepped closer and whispered to Jamie, "Didn't see that coming did you?"

Jamie looked past Beth to the house, where Mary Ann had disappeared. She said, quietly to Beth, "No, I certainly did not."

#

Robby took Jake and Jamie out in his boat. Jamie was thankful she didn't have to ride out with either Mary Ann or Sandy, who were both in the other boat with Beth and Doug. Jamie had left the rest of the crowd at the table and gone down to the dock, where she waited for Robby and Jake. She didn't want to talk to Mary Ann right now and she couldn't even look at Sandy.

Once they were back in the water, Jamie and Jake returned to their morning routine. Jamie would demonstrate and Jake would attempt to copy her. Jamie skied close to him and talked him through the trick, before each attempt. Doug had stopped his boat off to the side of where they were skiing, all occupants watching the skiers.

Jamie jumped the wake, doing a perfect twist and landing. Then Jake followed with his attempt and pulled it off flawlessly. The onlookers cheered and waved. Jake pumped his fist in the air. Jamie laid her head back and laughed. Jake's joy was infectious and Jamie started to relax a little.

After Jake successfully completed the trick several more times, Jamie slalom skied behind the boat alone. She wasn't ready to face whatever Mary Ann was up to, yet. Out here on the water, she could be alone. She jumped the wake and flew across the now glassy surface of the water. Jamie put one hand down as she leaned out and let her fingertips glide across the water. When she had gone as far out beside the boat as she could, she cut back sharply, sending a huge rooster tail of water out behind her.

#

Sandy stood alongside Mary Ann watching as Jamie carved the water with the edge of her ski. She was mesmerizing to watch. Jamie seemed to be in a world of her own, out there on the water. She was so graceful and smooth, crossing back and forth behind the boat.

Mary Ann spoke, interrupting Sandy's thoughts, ""God, I had forgotten how good she was."

"You should have seen her when she was a teenager. She was fearless," Sandy said, without taking her eyes off Jamie.

"Look at her. She's beautiful," Mary Ann said, wistfully.

Sandy answered absentmindedly, "Yes, she is," and then felt Mary Ann look at her, watching Jamie. She turned to see a look of confusion on Mary Ann's face. Sandy smiled at her and then retreated to sit by Beth.

"Oh, my god," she thought to herself, "she's come to take Jamie back." Sandy's heart was breaking, but she couldn't let it show. She stared out at Jamie, flying around behind the boat and realized she had missed her chance again.

#

Jamie crossed behind the boat, back and forth, sling-shotting her body faster and faster, until her muscles burned and she had to stop. She signaled Robby to go by Doug's boat. When she was close enough, she let go of the rope and slid across the water, turning at the last minute, showering the occupants of the boat, just for fun. She climbed into Robby's boat and rode back to shore, spent and starving. They ate leftovers standing around the picnic table and shared a cooled watermelon for desert. Jamie did everything she could to stay away from both of her tormentors. Jamie excused herself to change and headed into the house. No one followed her, but she locked the bathroom door, just to be sure. She wasn't ready to be trapped in the bathroom with either Sandy or Mary Ann.

Jamie was in a three F situation. She couldn't decide whether to fight with Mary Ann, fuck Sandy, or get in her car and flee. Any way she looked at it, Jamie's ass was in a tight spot. The very thing she had wished for had happened. Unfortunately, it had come on the very first day Jamie thought she

101

might not want it anymore. When she had seen Sandy on that boat and felt the obvious sexual tension between them, a crack had formed in her devotion to getting Mary Ann back. Today had been surreal. Tonight was going to be hell.

With that in mind, Jamie walked toward the end of the dock, freshly clean and dry, for the first time since nine o'clock, in the morning. She could see Mary Ann sitting with Sandy, Doug, Robby and Beth, in deck chairs on the dock. Beth was in the middle of telling a story when Jamie approached. Jamie had no choice, but to sit in the chair beside Mary Ann and join in the conversation, which as it turned out was about her.

Beth was going on, "Then the dean says, 'Jamie, what is your daddy gonna say, when I tell him you were the leader of this gang of skinny dipping girls caught in the university pool?' Without missing a beat Jamie tells the guy, 'I doubt he'll be the least surprised."

Everyone burst into laughter.

Jamie joined the group, taking the empty seat by Mary Ann. She tried to sound relaxed, when she said to Beth, "I forbid you to tell anymore Jamie stories without me present."

"Did I misquote you?" Beth teased her.

"No, but still, you've been known to embellish. I reserve the right to edit at anytime."

Beth conceded, "Fair enough."

Mary Ann turned to Jamie. "You really put on a show out there."

"I had forgotten how much fun it was. Thanks again, Robby."

Robby smiled and said, "Anytime."

Jamie was beginning to think she could handle being here like this, with both Sandy and Mary Ann, when the latter spoke, crushing her hopes.

"So, Sandy, you were saying you also knew Jamie when she was a teenager. Do you have any stories to share?"

Sandy fended her off with, "Oh no, I'm sworn to secrecy."

Mary Ann was fishing, "Did you go to high school with Jamie, too?"

And damned if Sandy didn't take the bait, "No, I graduated four years before her, but we played on the same softball team and she was my baby-sitter."

Jamie thought, whoa, too much information. She saw the flash of recognition on Mary Ann's face.

"Oh my god, you're Sandy Brown," Mary Ann said, and then added, "Jamie's talked a lot about you."

Jamie wanted to crawl under a rock.

Jamie admired the way Sandy could keep her cool under this much stress, because there was no doubt in Jamie's mind that Sandy was as uncomfortable as she was. Sandy acted intrigued, as if the thought never crossed her mind, she asked, "Oh really?"

Mary Ann was laughing now. It was her turn to tell a Jamie story, "You were her first girl crush."

"Mary Ann…," Jamie said, trying to stop her.

Mary Ann turned to look at Jamie. "Oh look, she's blushing." She turned back to Sandy, laughing while she said, "Jamie used to joke that if you ever changed your mind and came looking for her she'd have to leave me."

Jamie did not think this was at all funny. She said, more firmly this time, "Stop it, Mary Ann."

Naïve Doug asked Sandy, "Did you know that she had a crush on you, honey?" He laughed and added, "I guess I better watch you two a little more closely."

"Shut up, Doug," Sandy said, angrily.

A single look passed between Sandy and Jamie, which did not go unnoticed by Mary Ann. She looked from Jamie to Sandy and back again.

Mary Ann suddenly said, "Oh my god..." She stood up, stared down at Jamie, and then turned on her heels and walked off the dock.

Beth looked at Sandy and then at Jamie. She asked Jamie, "Are you going after her?"

Jamie was feeling spiteful and said, "No."

"Shit," Beth said, then took off after Mary Ann.

Sandy waited a second then took off after Beth, saying "Damn," when she stood up.

Jamie waited a beat. Stood up, looked after the three women, stomping up the yard toward the garage and said, "Fuck." Then she followed them.

As she was leaving, she heard Doug say to Robby, "Do you have any idea what just happened?"

#

When Jamie reached the top of the hill, she could see Mary Ann standing inside the open driver's side door of her car. Beth was very animated while she talked to Mary Ann, but Jamie couldn't make out what she was saying. Jamie grew closer, but the other three women didn't notice her. Mary Ann turned on Sandy, who had arrived only seconds before Jamie.

With venom in her voice she asked Sandy, "Are you fucking my wife?"

That, Jamie heard clearly.

Sandy was shocked by Mary Ann's bluntness, she answered, "No, I am not," but she sounded so guilty.

Jamie surprised them all, when she added her voice to the fray, "I wasn't under the impression that I was your wife anymore. You threw me out, remember?" Jamie had picked the first F and decided to fight with Mary Ann.

Mary Ann unleashed on Jamie, "Yes, I threw you out, because you were fucking somebody else. I see you haven't wasted any time finding a new piece of ass." She turned back to Sandy, "Did she tell you that? That she cheated on me?"

Jamie glared at Mary Ann. Beth, who was caught in the middle tried to make peace, "Ladies, let's calm down." She turned around, so she was facing Jamie. "Jamie, I think you and Mary Ann need to go somewhere and talk." Beth then moved over to the stricken Sandy, saying, "This is none of our business, so let's leave them to it."

Sandy was beginning to cry. She said, "I just want to go home."

Beth said, "Then I'll take you." She turned back around, pointing at Jamie and Mary Ann, with fire in her eyes, said, "You two, go deal with your shit."

Beth and Sandy started away, but Sandy turned back. Through her tears, she said, "Mary Ann, if it makes any difference, Jamie told me she was still in love with you."

Jamie looked at Sandy, who was looking back at her. Jamie could see the pain in Sandy's eyes and it stabbed at her. Then Sandy turned and walked away with Beth. Beth put her arm around Sandy, who leaned heavily into her. Sandy laid her head on Beth's shoulder. Jamie could see that Sandy had begun to cry harder, because her shoulders were shaking, as she sobbed into Beth's embrace. Jamie was so angry with Mary Ann she wanted to scream at her right there, but instead she remained calm.

"Do you want to follow me to my house?"

Mary Ann seemed much calmer, too, when she answered, "Yes, I'll follow you."

Jamie turned towards her car and walked away, without another word.

Chapter Nine

A few minutes later, in Sandy's kitchen, Beth sat at the bar, while Sandy paced back and forth.

Beth asked, "So, are you going to tell me what's going on now?"

Sandy was on the verge of totally losing it, when she answered, "I don't know... I don't know... I think I'm losing my mind... I don't know."

"Let's start with what's going on between you and Jamie, and don't bullshit me. I'm not stupid. I've watched you two dance around each other all day. I see the looks that pass between you."

Sandy stopped pacing and thought for a second, before answering. She sounded almost relieved to say it aloud, even though tears were rolling down her face, when she said, "I think I'm in love with her."

"Are you two having an affair?"

Sandy was adamant, "Like I told Mary Ann, no we are not."

Beth continued asking questions, "How does Jamie feel about this?"

"She doesn't know, I mean, I haven't told her, if that's what you mean."

Beth was confused. "You haven't talked to Jamie?"

"No, not about this. She doesn't know I'm in love with her. We talked about the kiss."

"What kiss?" Beth was even more perplexed.

"At your folks party, that night, after everyone had gone to bed."

"Did she just grab you and kiss you?" Beth just assumed Jamie had been the aggressor.

Sandy hesitated, replying bashfully, "No, I grabbed her in the bathroom and kissed her, before she knew what was happening."

"That's why you've been hiding," Beth said, beginning to get the picture.

"I needed time to think about what was happening to me."

Beth laughed, not at Sandy, but the situation. She said, "And now that you've had time to think, you've come to the conclusion that you are in love with Jamie."

Sandy cried harder, "Yes, but she's still in love with Mary Ann."

Beth got up and walked around the bar. She took Sandy in her arms and let her cry on her shoulder. Beth said to Sandy, "This is so fucked up."

"I know."

Beth became practical for a moment, "What about Doug? What are you going to do?"

"I was going to ask him for a divorce tomorrow." Sandy righted herself and moved to the paper towel dispenser. She pulled off several sheets, blew her nose and wiped her face.

Beth, who had been looking out the windows toward the water, said, "Because of Jamie?"

"No, because of me. Beth, I want to be happy. I just don't know if being alone the rest of my life is better than staying here."

"It sounds like to me, you were counting on Jamie being there when you got out from under Doug, no pun intended," Beth said.

"She's either going to be there or not, but I have to get out of here. There has to be more to life than this. Doug loves me. I know that, but it isn't enough. I'm just not sure how to tell him."

"Well, you better think of something, because he'll be here in a minute, and you are going to have to explain what the fuck just happened back at the house."

"Beth, what is happening to me?"

"Hell if I know," Beth said, "Maybe it's menopause."

"I'm not in menopause, yet."

Beth was undeterred, "I'm just saying, hormones can make women crazy."

Sandy tried to explain, "It's not hormones either. I love Doug, but I haven't been in love with him for a long time, hell I don't think I was ever in love with him now. Not now, not after..."

Beth cut her off, "Shit, here comes Doug. I'm going to go."

Sandy looked scared when she asked Beth, "What am I going to say?"

Beth gave Sandy a quick hug. "Sorry darlin', but you're on your own."

#

Over at Jamie's house, she entered the backdoor with Mary Ann right behind her. Jamie dropped her keys on the counter and went straight for the refrigerator. She opened the door and took a beer off the shelf. She looked at Mary Ann.

"You want one?"

Mary Ann replied, "No, water for me, please." She had obviously had time to regain her composure and was back to the pleasant Mary Ann, the one everyone adored.

Jamie took a bottled water off the shelf, handing it to Mary Ann. She closed the door to the refrigerator, twisted the cap off of the beer and threw the lid into the trash can under the sink. She leaned back on the counter, crossed her legs at the ankles, and took a long pull on the beer. Mary Ann stood in the center of the kitchen, looking around.

Jamie spoke first, "You drove all this way to talk to me, so talk."

Mary Ann began, "You know, I actually thought I saw Tara today, when I first came through Coinjock. I almost followed the car to see where it would go, but I decided I should just go to Beth's."

"I told you, I would never see her again, and I didn't until she blackmailed me, for nearly fifty thousand dollars. I paid her in full and sent her packing. You've never believed me. I guess you still don't." After an awkward silence, she added, "I'm sure you didn't drive all this way to talk about Tara."

"I'm just shocked that you paid her. Why? What could she have done to you? Male lawyers fuck around on their wives all the time."

Now, here was the Mary Ann she lived with. The passive aggressive, who just sounded like she was taking up for Jamie, when in fact she was, once again, pointing out that Jamie cheated on her. Jamie felt the sting. It initiated a defensive strike of her own.

"I did it so she wouldn't embarrass you. I don't see how she could have made a scandal without your name popping up, do you?"

"How chivalrous of you," Mary Ann said, sarcastically. Falling on her sword for Mary Ann had won Jamie no points.

Jamie was defensive. She had her guard up against the pain, this night was inevitably going to cause, and Mary Ann's barbs had a sharp edge to them. Jamie wanted her to cut to the chase, saying, "Again, I ask you, why are you here?"

Mary Ann stood still, trying to think of what to say. Jamie could see her brow wrinkling, as she searched for the right words. Eventually she said, "I thought about this moment all the way down here, but now I'm at a loss for words."

Jamie said, with much cynicism, "I find that hard to believe," as she took her beer and walked around Mary Ann, heading to the sun porch.

Mary Ann followed Jamie, saying, "I'm just in shock. I never imagined you would already be involved with your teenage crush."

"Goddamnit, Mary Ann," Jamie said, as she plopped down on the chair in the corner, "I told you, I am not involved with Sandy."

Mary Ann, it seemed, wanted to fight, too. She raised her voice, "Jamie, come on. You two are obviously involved in something. You can see it all over your faces. Does her husband know?"

Jamie wasn't going to back down this time. "There's nothing for him to know. We're friends. You embarrassed us both, with your little story about my crush, when I was seventeen years old."

"Bullshit, Jamie. You look just as guilty as you did when I caught you with Tara, so don't lie to me."

"I wasn't fucking Tara then either, but you never let me explain."

"Explain what? That you felt so guilty that you had to stop, but you didn't feel guilty enough to get rid of her, did you?"

The fight escalated, when Jamie stood up, shouting, "What if I was having an affair with Sandy? I'm not, but what if I were? What right do you have to come here and judge me? Do I have to continue to remind you, that you told me you never wanted to see me again?"

Mary Ann tried to top her, "I had every right to throw you out. You were fucking your god damn law clerk and for all I know she wasn't the first."

Jamie grew angrier. "That's not true and you know it. I know what I did. You don't have to tell me. I live with the consequences every day."

"You look like you're doing just fine to me," Mary Ann spit out.

The two women stared at each other. They didn't speak for a moment. Jamie finally took her seat again and Mary Ann sat down, in the chair across from her.

110

Jamie was calmer and more reflective, when she said, "There hasn't been a day gone by, that I haven't asked myself why? Why did I fall for her come on, when you know I'd been hit on before and so have you? Why did I cross the line with her? It wasn't as if I was in love with her or anything. If I had been single, I probably wouldn't have dated her."

"Have you found your answer yet?"

Mary Ann had calmed down, miraculously, while Jamie had been talking. She almost looked sympathetic, but Jamie was sure she was just misreading her expression. Jamie shook her head, from side to side. "No, I still don't know why I did it."

Mary Ann spoke with a different tone now, softer, kinder, "Tara was younger and sexy and she gave you what you didn't get at home. She wanted you."

Jamie choked back unexpected tears, when she said, "I wanted so badly for you to want me."

"I know, Jamie," Mary Ann began, "I've repeatedly told you it wasn't that I didn't want you. I just don't think about sex until you initiate it. I've been to doctors. You know that. I've tried to find out why."

"And yet we've been talking about this for ten years. I don't want to talk about it anymore."

Jamie stood and headed back toward the kitchen, draining the beer bottle, as she went. Mary Ann stayed still for a moment and then followed Jamie, stopping at the kitchen doorway. Jamie could feel Mary Ann's eyes on her. She stood there watching, as Jamie threw away her empty bottle. Still with her back to Mary Ann, Jamie snatched open the door to the refrigerator, popped the top off of another beer, took a long drink, then turned around to face Mary Ann.

"Why did you come here? I did what you told me to do. I got the hell out of our house and your life. What else do you want from me?"

This time Mary Ann spoke softly, "I needed to see you."

Jamie didn't know where all the anger was coming from. She had wanted so desperately for Mary Ann to come back to her, and now, here was her chance to make it right, but all she felt was hurt and anger. She said, "Why? What is so important that you couldn't tell me on the phone?"

Mary Ann's eyes glistened with tears. "When you were still in Durham, I was so angry, I couldn't see past it. Nevertheless, when you left and came here, the anger was slowly replaced by an ache. It won't go away."

Jamie smirked, "I'm all too familiar with that feeling."

Before Jamie could react, Mary Ann closed the gap between them. She put her hand behind Jamie's neck and pulled their lips together. She kissed Jamie long and deeply. Jamie responded in kind. After what seemed like minutes, they separated their lips and stared into each other's eyes.

Mary Ann's voice dripped with lust, when she said, "What if I told you, I've never wanted you more than I do, right this minute?"

Jamie did not hesitate. She forgot she was angry and grabbed Mary Ann, walking her backwards toward her bedroom, kissing her the entire way. They tore at each other's clothes. Mary Ann spun them around and pushed Jamie backwards, onto the bed. Mary Ann then slid her naked body on top of Jamie. She kissed Jamie from her belly button, up to her chest and then took one of Jamie's nipples in her mouth. Jamie arched off the bed and moaned from deep down in her soul.

#

At Sandy's house, a much different scene was unfolding. Sandy stood by the kitchen breakfast bar, wondering what was going to happen next. She told Doug, as soon as he came in, that she wanted a divorce. She thought it would be easier just to go ahead and say it. Sandy had expected that Doug would not take the news well, at all, but she had not expected him to get blind drunk.

Doug never drank, as long as Sandy had known him. He told her when they first met, that he was an alcoholic and he had been dry for two years. Even though he did not drink, he stocked his bar with the finest liquors, for his friends that did. He always enjoyed playing bar tender and never let anyone drive away drunk.

Now, fifteen years later he was pouring liquor down his throat faster than Sandy had ever seen anybody drink. It hadn't taken much, to begin with, for his personality to change. Loving, sweet Doug was now a raving lunatic. She prayed he would pass out, so she could go upstairs, get the already packed suitcase out of her closet, and leave before he woke up again. No such luck.

She wasn't looking at him, so he reached out and spun Sandy around. He slurred out, "Why? That's all I want to know. After all these years, you suddenly don't love me anymore. Why?"

"It's not all of a sudden. I've been trying to figure out how to say this for a long time. There is no easy way," Sandy offered, as an explanation.

"Why now? What's changed?" Doug was pleading with her.

"Nothing's changed. That's the point I need you to understand. Something has always been missing, but I thought it was enough that you loved me, but it isn't and I just can't settle for that anymore."

Doug wasn't satisfied, "Why? Why can't that be enough?"

Sandy was losing her cool and her ability to censure her own words. She blurted out, "Because I know there is something better out there."

Doug finally got it. His personality snapped and the angry drunk reared its ugly head. Even his voice changed and the glare he was giving Sandy had an evil cast. "So, the dyke licked your pussy and you liked it."

"Jesus Doug! I haven't had sex with Jamie. You're drunk, go to bed."

The Girl Back Home

Doug grabbed Sandy by the wrists, hard. He pulled her closer to him and growled out, "I'll go to bed if you go with me. I'll fuck the dyke right out of you. Is that what you want?"

Sandy screamed at him, "Let go of me!"

Doug was out of control. He grabbed Sandy's shoulders and shook her, screaming, in her face, "Why are you doing this? Why can't you love me? Why? Why?"

Sandy straightened and tried to pull his hands away. When she couldn't, she looked him dead in the eyes. "Because, I'm in love with Jamie."

Doug let go of Sandy and then he slapped her, across the face, with his open hand. The noise of the loud smack, sounded like a gun going off, and echoed around the kitchen. It felt like a fist and Sandy's nose began to bleed. Blood trickled out of the corner of her mouth and her cheek was already swelling.

Sandy was in shock for a moment. Doug had never raised his voice at her, let alone, hit her. She'd been down this road with Gary. She wasn't going there again. When Doug turned and walked back toward the bar in the den, Sandy grabbed her purse and keys, and headed for the backdoor before Doug could turn around. On her way out, she took off her diamond engagement ring and wedding band and threw them on the counter, where they spun like tops and then fell over with a tenor ringing, as they wallowed to a stop.

#

In the meantime, Jamie and Mary Ann had finished having sex. Jamie knew they hadn't made love, they had hot, angry, break up sex with no love involved. There was a lot of desire and need, maybe even a little passion, but not love. It didn't feel right, at least not to Jamie. Their relationship was broken, not because Jamie slept with someone else, but because Jamie was not in love with Mary Ann, anymore.

114

Jamie lay back in the bed with Mary Ann's head resting on her chest. They were covered loosely with a sheet. Jamie stared up at the ceiling. The tears welled up in her eyes and trickled down the sides of her face. She stroked the back of Mary Ann's hair and mourned the loss, of what might have been. Sandy floated through Jamie's mind, time and again.

Mary Ann didn't lift her head, when she asked Jamie, "What are you thinking about?"

Jamie whispered back, "You and me," because if she tried to talk louder, she knew she would lose control.

"Me too," Mary Ann said, into Jamie's belly button. She sat up, leaning on her elbow, so she could look at Jamie. Mary Ann was smiling, until she saw that Jamie was crying. "Baby, why are you crying?"

Jamie wiped the tears away with her free hand. She looked up at Mary Ann and said, "We shouldn't have done that."

"Oh, I don't know. I enjoyed it immensely." Mary Ann was in the afterglow and giggled, like a school girl. Jamie smiled weakly at Mary Ann, but she didn't laugh. Seeing that Jamie wasn't as happy as she was, Mary Ann tenderly wiped away the still falling tears from Jamie's cheeks. "Talk to me, Jamie. Tell me what's wrong."

Jamie tried to explain, "Sex was never our problem. I never had any complaints about the quality. It was the quantity that bothered me."

Mary Ann pushed strands of Jamie's damp hair, away from her face. She smiled sweetly and in all sincerity said, "All you have to do is ask. Jamie, I adore making love to you. I'm just wired differently."

Jamie sat up and leaned back on the headboard. Mary Ann sat up in the middle of the bed, letting the sheet fall away from her chest. Jamie looked, but that familiar twinge wasn't there. Not the, 'Hey, look! Boobs!' twinge. That was still there. The wanting of Mary Ann was not.

Jamie needed Mary Ann to understand, "I don't want to ask or make an appointment with you for sex. I want to be wanted, who doesn't?"

Mary Ann finally caught on to where this conversation might be going. She said, in her defense, "I do want you. I realized how much when you were gone. I don't want to live without you. I'm going to do whatever it takes to keep you, doctors... therapy... whatever it takes."

"Do you remember when we first got together? How you would call me out of the blue and we'd rush to your house between classes, just to make love?" Jamie chuckled, and then added, "We couldn't keep our hands off each other."

"Yes, I do," Mary Ann said, laughing along with Jamie, "but we were younger and in heat, as I recall."

"What happened to the heat? I didn't stop wanting you. That's what hurt the most, knowing it was there and then it was gone."

"It isn't gone," Mary Ann, countered. "Every time you walk in a room, my heart skips a beat. I'm so proud to be with you. When you smile at me, I feel it all over, like sunshine," she grew quieter, "and when you were gone, I ached for you. Isn't that wanting you?"

Jamie cut to the chase, "I lived in the same house and ached for you for ten years. I don't think I can do that anymore."

"You shouldn't have to," Mary Ann responded, still unable to except what Jamie was trying to say. "I will have sex with you, everyday, if that's what you want."

"It's not all about sex, Mary Ann. It's a wink, an unexpected phone call, coming into the study when I'm working, just to give me a kiss and then scurrying away. Just feeling wanted is enough. The sex is the cherry on top."

Mary Ann interrupted, "You do all those things for me. I guess I just took it for granted that you would..."

Jamie held up her finger for Mary Ann to stop, so Jamie could continue her thought. She had to say everything now, there wasn't going to be a second chance. Jamie reached for Mary Ann's hand and said, very softly, "Baby, I need some romance in my life. I want to fall in love every day. I tried to tell myself to grow up, but you know what, I don't want to, if it means I will never feel the thrill of a woman coming up behind me and whispering in my ear, 'Take me to bed or let me make love to you, something totally corny, but oh, so hot."

Mary Ann was beginning to panic. She squeezed Jamie's hand tighter. "Jamie, we have to try to make this work. We have sixteen years invested in this relationship, in each other. I love you too much, not to at least try."

Jamie knew in that instant, absolutely, that she wasn't going back to Mary Ann. She didn't have the heart for it. She smiled weakly at Mary Ann, the tears coming freely now, for she did love Mary Ann, but she had fallen out of love with her and she hadn't even realized it. Until that kiss in the garage. The one that lit her soul, in its darkest places. The kiss that told her there was more, so much more than Jamie, up to now, had believed was enough.

Jamie wasn't going to say that to Mary Ann. There wasn't any need to hurt her any more than she already had. She simply said, "If we tried and failed, I don't know... I don't want to go through that again. I'm still trying to get over the first time."

Mary Ann was crying now, she whispered, "I said, whatever it takes. Jamie, I love you. I need you."

"It isn't enough." Jamie stung Mary Ann with those words. She hadn't meant to, it was just the truth. It hurt Mary Ann, making her flush with either anger or the recognition that Jamie was right. Jamie wasn't sure which, but she was saved by an urgent knocking on the backdoor, or so she thought.

They both stopped and listened. The knocking persisted.

The Girl Back Home

Mary Ann asked, "Are you expecting somebody?"

Jamie shook her head, "No."

A second later, louder knocks followed. Jamie jumped from the bed, found a pair of sweats and a tee shirt and threw them on. She didn't have time to find her underwear. She turned back, at the bedroom door. "Stay here," she told Mary Ann, "I'll be right back."

Jamie left the room, leaving Mary Ann naked, covered by only a sheet. When she reached the threshold of the kitchen, she could see Sandy's profile in the backdoor window. Sandy was looking toward the driveway, as if someone were following her. Jamie sped her steps to the backdoor and opened it quickly.

Sandy rushed in, pushing past Jamie. Jamie shut the door and locked it. She turned around, just as Sandy revealed the other side of her face, which was bruised and swollen. A large red handprint was clearly visible on her skin. Dried blood, from her nose, was crusted on her upper lip and in the corner of her mouth.

Jamie rushed to Sandy. She gently put her hands on Sandy's shoulders and straightened her up, so she could get a good look at her. "Oh my god, what happened? Who did this to you?"

Sandy was crying and barely able to make herself say the word, "Doug."

Jamie asked the obvious question, "Why?"

"I told him I wanted a divorce. He got really upset and then he started drinking."

"You said, 'Doug doesn't drink."

Sandy clarified for Jamie, "He's an alcoholic. He hasn't had a drink in seventeen years. Well, until tonight anyway."

118

Jamie tried not to treat Sandy as though she was questioning a witness, but she needed to know what happened. "He hit you when you asked for the divorce?"

Sandy started to pace, gesturing with her hands, as she talked. "He started screaming at me. I tried to talk rationally to him, but it just made it worse. Jamie, I have to get out of this marriage. I'm dying in there. He's smothering me."

"I don't know him that well, but I would never have imagined he'd hit you." Jamie thought there was more to the story.

Sandy continued pacing. "He cornered me in the kitchen. He was screaming at me, 'Why? Why?' over and over. Suddenly it just came out. I couldn't help it."

"What did you say?"

Sandy stopped pacing and looked down at the floor, stammering out, "I told him... I told him..." She looked up into Jamie's eyes, and finished, "I told him, I am in love with you."

Jamie took a step back, saying, "You did what?"

At that very instant, Mary Ann appeared in the bedroom doorway, draped only in a sheet. Sandy looked beyond shocked. Jamie was sure that was the look on her face, too. The only one smiling was Mary Ann. It was a self-satisfied smile, because now Mary Ann knew, she had been right about Sandy and Jamie, all along.

#

Enjoying a quiet evening on their screened in back porch, Robby and Beth were relaxing, after the excitement of the day. Robby watched a baseball game, with the volume down low and Beth read a book, but her thoughts were never far from her friends, who were both dealing with incredibly difficult endings to their respective marriages. Beth had no doubt that Sandy had fallen for Jamie and after today, she was sure Jamie had been smitten by Sandy, too.

The crickets and frogs sang their summer songs, at the top of their lungs. Over the cacophony of nature sounds, they heard a car pull up in front of the house. A car door opened and closed followed by Doug's drunken voice, shouting from the front yard, "Sandy! I'm sorry! Sandy!"

Beth sat up. "Is that Doug?"

"Sounds like him," Robby said, "Who else would be looking for Sandy?"

Doug shouted again, "Sandy! Please come home. I'm sorry! Sandy!"

Beth stood up, setting her book down. "It sounds like he's drunk off his ass."

Jake came onto the back porch. "Did you know that Mr. Canter is in our front yard, screaming for his wife? He sounds drunk."

"I better go get him," Robby said, standing and stretching. Robby was that kind of guy. As wired tight as Beth was, Robby was just as laid back. It worked for them.

Beth looked at Jake. "Go make coffee. I'm going to find Sandy."

#

Mary Ann stood in the doorway of the bedroom, with that stupid grin on her face. Sandy stood unmoving, still in shock, and Jamie was caught in the middle. Sandy suddenly regained her powers of movement and speech.

Sandy started toward the backdoor, trailing out words rapidly, "Oh my god. I am so sorry. I didn't notice her car. I need to leave."

Jamie stepped in front of her. "Wait, where are you going?"

Sandy looked at Jamie, as if Jamie didn't understand the magnitude of the situation. "I don't know, but I can't stay here."

Jamie took Sandy gently by the shoulders and said, "Yes, you can. You are not leaving, understand?"

120

Jamie led the emotionally drained Sandy out of the kitchen and into the living room. She glanced over her shoulder at Mary Ann, who turned and went back in the bedroom. Jamie sat Sandy down on the couch. She looked down at Sandy's swollen face. Jamie saw the purple fingerprints starting to show on Sandy's wrist. She had to take care of Sandy first, and then she would deal with Doug.

"I'm going to get an ice bag for your face, okay? Do you want something to drink?"

Sandy didn't raise her eyes to look at Jamie. She said, "Yes, I need a shot of bourbon, maybe two shots, if you have it." Sandy dropped her head back against the couch cushion.

Jamie started for the kitchen. She was almost out of the living room, when she stopped and turned around, because she thought Sandy said something. Sandy must have assumed she was alone. Jamie watched as Sandy slowly raised her head and then lowered it into her hands. Sandy ran her fingers through her hair and then in slow motion, she raised her head and sighed out loudly, "F...U....C...K!" She drug out each letter and raised her hands to the heavens in a "Why me?" gesture.

Jamie knew how confusing this must all be for Sandy. Here she was professing her love to Jamie and out walks a naked Mary Ann, from the bedroom, wearing "I just had great sex," all over her demeanor and a shit eating grin on her face. Damn it. Mary Ann had done that on purpose. Jamie figured she deserved that kind of attitude from Mary Ann, but she didn't want to hurt Sandy.

Jamie stuck her head in the bedroom, but Mary Ann was not there. She heard the water running in the shower. Okay, one woman locked away behind closed doors. Now she had to deal with the broken one on her couch. She couldn't let Sandy leave, without explaining what was really happening. She could try, "Yes, I slept with her, but now I know I don't love her." Yeah, right. That would go over so well. All Sandy would hear, was the part about sleeping with Mary Ann.

Jamie kept ice bags in the freezer, because she was always hurting, somewhere. Too many hard spills and slides had left their toll on her body. She took a bag out and found a soft tea towel to wrap it in. She took a wash cloth from the hall closet and ran cold water on it from the kitchen faucet. Then she grabbed two shot glasses and the bottle of Old Weller from the cabinet, over the sink. Maybe she should let Sandy get drunk and pass out. That would give Jamie more time to get rid of Mary Ann. How did the simple country life become so complicated?

The water continued to run, in the shower. Jamie still had a little time alone with Sandy, before Mary Ann would make a grand entrance. Mary Ann wasn't one to show her ass, but she was a bit pissed off, at the moment. Jamie went back to the couch and sat on the coffee table, in front of Sandy. She put the bottle of bourbon down with the shot glasses. Then she handed the ice bag to Sandy and poured them both a shot. Sandy gingerly tried to apply the ice bag to her swollen, already black and blue eye.

Jamie handed Sandy a shot glass and took one for herself. "First things, first," she said, and both women slammed the bourbon down with gusto.

Sandy let the liquor bathe her body with warmth and her face flushed. "Thank you so much, may I please have another." She held out her empty glass to Jamie.

Jamie filled the glass and watched as Sandy slammed the second shot, just like the first. She gave the empty glass back to Jamie and went back to trying to find a place to put the ice pack, that didn't hurt like hell. Jamie took the cold wet washcloth and gently dabbed the dried blood from under Sandy's nose and on her chin.

"Stay here." Jamie said, "I need to get you some ibuprofen to help with the swelling. I'll be right back."

Sandy grabbed her arm, as Jamie stood up. "I should go, Jamie. I shouldn't be here."

"I need to talk to you, please just wait a minute," Jamie pleaded.

Sandy didn't release Jamie's arm. She asked, "What about Mary Ann?"

"That's what I need to talk to you about. Just relax. I'll be right back."

Sandy let go of Jamie's arm and reached for the bourbon bottle. Jamie left the room, while Sandy was pouring herself another shot. The water wasn't running in the shower anymore and the bedroom door was closed. Jamie slipped into the bathroom, took a bottle of ibuprofen from the medicine cabinet and, on her way back to Sandy, grabbed a water bottle from the frig. Jamie sat back down in front of Sandy, got out two pills and opened the water bottle. She handed them to Sandy, watching as Sandy washed them down.

After a moment, Sandy tried to smile, but winced instead and said, "Now what am I going to do about falling in love with you?"

Jamie needed to know if Sandy was sure, "How do you know? Maybe it's just the first time you kissed a woman, it happens."

Sandy had relaxed a little. The effects of the alcohol evident when she replied, "You're not the first woman I've kissed."

Jamie grinned at Sandy. "Oh my. You are full of surprises."

"You have no idea," Sandy said, grimacing again, when she tried to smile.

Loud banging, on the backdoor, startled both of them. They relaxed when Beth shouted, "Hey, unlock the damn door."

Jamie called out, "I'm coming," and went to let Beth in. The bedroom door was still closed. Good, Mary Ann was still laying low. The anticipation, of what Mary Ann had planned for her exit, was like waiting for a jack-in-the-box to explode. Jamie hoped the music would keep playing a little while longer. She opened the door and Beth rushed in.

"Where is she? Is she alright?"

Jamie pointed, "She's in the living room."

There was evidence of Sandy taking another drink, while Jamie went to get Beth. A little bourbon had been spilt and both shot glasses were bottoms up on the coffee table. Sandy had gathered herself up in the far corner of the couch. She was leaning back with the ice pack on her face. Beth rushed into the room. She saw Sandy and ran to her. Beth reached out, gently lifting the ice pack from Sandy's face and examining her wrists.

"That son of a bitch."

"How did you know Sandy was here?" Jamie's house was becoming drama central.

Beth explained, still looking over Sandy for signs of injury, "Doug is at my house, drunk as hell, doing a Marlin Brando impression, screaming for Sandy. After what she told me today, I just thought she might come here."

Jamie looked in disbelief at Sandy. "What did you tell her?"

Beth answered for Sandy, "She told me she was in love with you."

Sandy shrugged her shoulders and cocked her head, showing a little crooked smile, as if to say, "Yep, I did it."

Jamie had gone from no women in her house, to now three women, in the span of a couple of hours, all with their own accompanying drama. Well, except for Beth, she just made the drama worse, by escalating everything to a high energy pitch. Jamie had always been counted on to be the cool head in a crisis. Today, not so much. Jamie was in need of a good scream. Instead, she took a deep breath and tried not to sound tense, when she spoke to Sandy.

"Sandy, honey, has this proclamation just been spontaneously erupting from your mouth all day?"

124

Sandy had a buzz on. She giggled and said, "Yep, pretty much, but so far only to you, Beth and Doug... well... and now, Mary Ann."

That set Beth off, "Doug? You told Doug that you were in love with Jamie?"

"Yep," was followed by more giggles.

Jamie had become a bystander. Beth and Sandy were having their own little conversation.

Beth asked, "And Mary Ann? When did you tell her?"

Sandy leaned up and whispered to Beth, "Well, she overheard me professing my love for Jamie, just now."

"Mary Ann is still here?" Beth gasped.

"She was naked," Sandy giggled and then pointed toward the bedroom. "Yeah, she's putting her clothes back on."

Beth reacted, "Holy shit. Holy fucking shit."

Jamie interjected, "I know, can you believe it?"

Sandy's giggles began to change into the nervous laughter of a desperate woman, "No, not really. I not only told my husband I wanted a divorce, I told him I was in love with a woman. A woman who, at the time I was ending my marriage, was just down the road, screwing her ex. It is more than fucked up. It's some kind of cosmic joke."

Beth was hung up on the details. She said, "So, you did tell him you wanted a divorce?

"Yes, that's all I intended to tell him, then he went nuts and the rest just slipped out."

Beth, who let things slip out all the time, said, "Sandy, shit like that does not just slip out."

"He kept screaming 'Why,' and my mind kept screaming back, 'Because I'm in love with a woman.' Finally I lost it and I said it out loud."

The Girl Back Home

Jamie wanted Beth to know all the facts, "Not only did she say it, but she used my name."

Sandy jabbed at Jamie, with, "Well, he'd have to be an idiot not to know it was you, after Mary Ann's little scene."

Beth played referee, "Well, she's gotcha there."

Sandy moaned and sighed out, "Oh my god. What have I done?"

Beth patted Sandy's hand, saying, "It's okay. The truth is out now, so you just need to breathe. The worst part is over…"

The three women looked up to see Mary Ann walk in.

Beth finished her thought aloud, "Well, maybe not."

#

Beth drove down the narrow winding road, back to her house, with a dazed and tipsy Sandy in the passenger seat. The hands free device was ringing in the car speakers, while she waited for Robby to pick up the phone at home.

Robby answered, "Hey babe, did you find her?"

"Yes, she was at Jamie's. I have her in the car. We're on the way home. Is Doug still there?"

Robby's disembodied voice said, "Yes, he's here."

Beth was very angry with Doug and it sounded out clearly in her voice. "Did you know he hit her?"

"He just told me."

Beth raised her voice to the little speaker in the roof of the car, "Did you tell him you'd kick his ass if he did it again?"

"Yes, dear," sounded nasally through the speakers.

"Take him home. Stay with him in case he passes out," Beth said, adding, "I don't want him to choke on his own vomit, until I get a chance to kill him."

126

There was laughter from the speakers, followed by, "Okay, I'll keep him alive. Love ya'. See you in the morning."

Beth said, "Love you too, and hey, pour out all the alcohol in the house."

Robby didn't sound like he agreed with pouring out perfectly good liquor. "All of it? He's got some real expensive scotch in there."

"All of it, Rob."

"Yes, ma'am. See you tomorrow."

Beth punched the button on the mirror, hanging up the call. She glanced at Sandy, asking, "Are you okay?"

Sandy was in a more contemplative portion of her buzz, winding down for the big blow out at the end. Whether it was sobbing or screaming, it was bound to happen, if she didn't pass out first.

Sandy watched the swamp pass her window, calmly saying, "I can't believe, I didn't think about Jamie still being in love with Mary Ann. She even told me she was, but after we kissed, I thought something changed. I'm so stupid."

Beth tried to stay out of Jamie's love life, and they respected each other enough not to get involved unless asked. Hence, the reason she had not known Jamie's life with Mary Ann was in such a mess. This time, however, she stuck her foot right in the middle of it. "You're not stupid. I've seen the way Jamie looks at you. She doesn't look at Mary Ann like that, I'm not sure that she ever did."

Sandy turned to Beth, her face a swollen purple mass in the shadows, inside the car.

"What am I going to do, Beth?"

"Be patient. Let Jamie finish this," Beth told her.

"Finish what?" Sandy didn't know.

127

"Sandy, Jamie was breaking up with Mary Ann for good. Didn't you see their body language?"

Sandy sniffed, "What I saw was a gorgeous naked woman, wrapped in nothing but a sheet, and not much of her was wrapped, either."

"Did Jamie have a chance to tell you what happened?" Beth asked.

"No, you burst in just when we started to talk," Sandy said, flipping her hands up in the air, as if to say, the fates would not have it.

Beth said, "If it's meant to be, it's worth waiting for." Realizing, only after she said it, how corny it sounded.

Sandy didn't seem to notice. She went on with her lament, "I've been waiting for her to come back for twenty-five years and I didn't even know it."

"You're really in love with Jamie, aren't you?"

Sandy was reflective, saying softly, "I fell in love with Jamie a very long time ago. Seeing her again just brought it all back, so fast. I feel my world spinning away from me, and I can't stop it."

Beth whistled. "Wow. You've got it bad sister."

Sandy slapped her thigh, shaking her head up and down, like now you get it and said, "Tell me about it."

#

After Beth and Sandy left, Mary Ann and Jamie sat down in the living room. The shot glasses remained on the table, in front of Jamie, and she was tempted to take another drink. Mary Ann sat across from her, in a wing backed chair that used to be in Jamie's study, in Durham. Jamie had sat across from Mary Ann, while she sat in that exact same chair, during many of their most private discussions. Mary Ann was an adult and tried to handle her affairs gracefully, the crystal vases, notwithstanding. She was also a very well educated student of human behavior. Both factors made winning an argument with her challenging.

Mary Ann spoke calmly, "I need to know. Is this some payback, for throwing you out?"

"No," Jamie answered. She had asked that same question of herself and could honestly say it wasn't. "Mary Ann I love you, but…"

"But what?" Mary Ann asked. When Jamie didn't answer right away, she asked, "Jamie, are you in love with Sandy?"

Jamie was staggered a little by the question and even more so by her reply, "I don't know, Mary Ann." Then Jamie decided to be honest. She owed Mary Ann that much. "Yes, I think I am."

Mary Ann was taken aback and the color drained from her face. She was quiet for a moment. Then she looked at Jamie, who quickly began staring at the floor.

"Jamie, have you fallen out of love with me?"

Jamie took a slow deep breath, trying to fight back the tears, but she couldn't. When she looked up, the tears fell down her cheeks, as she said, "Yes, Mary Ann, I think I have."

Chapter Ten

Jamie woke up on the couch, stiff and a little hung over. After Jamie told Mary Ann she wasn't in love with her any more, Mary Ann left the room and locked herself in Jamie's bedroom. Jamie sipped bourbon alone, into the wee hours of the morning. She had gone out to the sun porch, put on an old Joan Armatrading CD and bathed in her own misery.

Jamie had fallen in love with Sandy. It wasn't just the old crush. She had fallen in love with the woman Sandy had become. Could Jamie have chosen a more complicated situation, in which to become involved? If Mary Ann had not come to Beth's house, would Jamie have kept hanging on to the hope of getting back together, out of guilt?

Jamie knew she was smart. She was a fucking lawyer, for Christ sake, and a damn good one. Somehow, she missed the signs that pointed straight to falling out of love with Mary Ann. She would never have had the affair in the first place, if she was happy and in love. The secrecy had been exhilarating and her sexual life had been... Jamie groped for the word... enlightened.

During the four months that Jamie was sleeping with Tara, she wondered if Mary Ann felt the other woman's presence, the two times they made love in the same time period. The first time, Jamie had been so horny she had playfully teased Mary Ann into bed with her. They spent an entire rainy afternoon, laughing and playing and of course having sex. It had been so much fun that Jamie had been consumed by guilt afterwards. She promised herself that she would not sleep with Tara again, but a week later, when Tara locked her office door, pulled the blinds and did a strip tease, she hadn't resisted.

Jamie started staying at work later, finding excuses not to spend time at home. Every time she looked at Mary Ann, the guilt would stab at her heart, but she couldn't stop. Tara fulfilled a need that Mary Ann was obviously not interested in satisfying. Jamie's guilt started to turn to anger. She began to pick fights with Mary Ann about the dumbest things. After one of those fights, over which side of the garage Mary Ann parked on, Jamie shut herself up in her study, fuming over nothing. Mary Ann chose to get drunk.

About two hours, after Jamie had taken sanctuary in the study, Mary Ann opened the door with a drink in her hand. She was wearing a black sheer nightgown, over a black, very sexy bustier and matching black panties. Jamie had given her the Victoria's Secret ensemble several years earlier. Mary Ann had on black high heels and draped herself against the door jam. She was drunk.

"I came to apologize," Mary Ann had said, playing the seductress, which was so out of character for her.

Jamie had leapt to her feet, crossed the room in seconds and kissed Mary Ann with such passion that they had ended up on the study couch, naked and spent. Mary Ann had been the aggressor. Mary Ann wanted sex and she wanted it bad. She had practically lived out every fantasy Jamie had ever had about her. She tore Jamie's blouse off, sending the pearl buttons scattering across the floor. She pushed Jamie down into a sitting position on the couch and straddled her legs. She grabbed Jamie's hand and shoved it into her crotch. She kissed Jamie and rocked against her until she came in violent jolts, then she fucked Jamie's brains out. They continued their marathon sex up in their

131

bedroom and when Jamie woke in the morning, she knew she had to tell Tara it was over.

Jamie did tell Tara the sex had to stop, but it wasn't long after that, when Mary Ann had caught Tara trying to seduce Jamie and Jamie had not been putting up much of a fight. That's when the guilt took over and Jamie tried so hard to get Mary Ann to forgive her. Was that all Jamie had really wanted, forgiveness? Once Mary Ann told her, she knew part of it was her own fault, Jamie had let some of the guilt go. She would always feel guilty about betraying Mary Ann's trust, but at least Jamie knew now that she had not been alone in letting their relationship fall apart. It made it easier for Jamie to leave Mary Ann behind.

Jamie still had to face Mary Ann this morning and then she had to talk to Sandy. She never had time to explain to Sandy what was going on last night. Jamie couldn't imagine what Sandy must be thinking. Jamie stood and stretched. She needed a shower and fresh clothes. She hoped Mary Ann was up and would let her into the bedroom.

When she came through the kitchen, Jamie saw the bedroom door open. It was eerily quiet in the house. She went to the door and looked in. Mary Ann wasn't there. She wasn't in the bathroom either. Jamie was heading for the backdoor, when she saw the note on the kitchen table. She read it.

"Dear Jamie. You were sleeping so soundly, I didn't want to wake you. I'm going back to Durham. I have a seminar to conduct tomorrow. I'm sorry that I couldn't be what you wanted. I hope you know how much I love you, and if you ever remember how much you used to love me, I'll be waiting. Love, Mary Ann."

Jamie looked up from the note. She whispered, "Mary Ann."

#

Down at Beth's house, Sandy was lying in Beth's guest bedroom, staring at the ceiling. Her swollen cheek was now different hues of black, blue and yellow, with Doug's hand print easily distinguishable across her face. Her lip was a little swollen on one side, but there was no crack in the skin. The ice had helped. Sandy held up her arms in front of her and looked at the imprint of Doug's fingers on her wrists. She slowly rolled over and began to cry quietly, into the pillow. Soon Sandy's whole body was racked with sobs.

A light knock on the door startled her. The handle turned slowly and Beth entered the room. She was carrying a glass of orange juice, with two pills in one hand, and an ice bag in the other. Seeing Sandy's condition, Beth immediately went to comfort her, setting the juice and pills on the night stand, by the bed. She gently placed the ice bag on the swollen side of Sandy's face and let her cry.

Beth rubbed her hand in a circle on Sandy's back and patted her every few seconds. She said, "It's okay, baby... It's going to be okay... Get it out. It's okay."

Through her sobs, Sandy responded, "No, it's not. I have truly fucked up my life this time. I mean I thought Gary was the biggest mistake I ever made, but this takes the prize."

"You don't know that's the case, at this point. It's been less than twenty-four hours. Give it some time." Beth was the voice of reason this morning.

Sandy sat up. Beth went to the adjoining bathroom and brought back a box of tissue. She also gave Sandy the juice and ibuprofen and made her take it. Sandy gradually went from sobs to the occasional sniffle or gasping breath, as her diaphragm recovered from the emotional stress. When she was able to speak, her words were interspersed with hiccups as her torso went through one spasm, after another. The breakdown had drained much of her energy and she spoke in hushed tones.

"Jamie is probably...hiccup... packing to go back...gasp... to Durham...hiccup... as we speak."

"I'm sure she would have talked to me, if that was happening. Don't make up things to worry about. Concentrate on what's in front of you," the voice of reason, spoke again, but Beth had a battle getting Sandy to focus.

"There's nothing...hic... in front of me," Sandy said, defeated.

Beth was going to have to lay it all out for Sandy, who obviously couldn't think straight. "You asked your husband for a divorce. Do you still want to go through with that?"

"Yes, that's been coming...hiccup... long before Jamie came back."

"Okay, then tomorrow we set you up with a lawyer. The teachers' union provides a free one, as part of your benefits." Beth had helped other women at her school get through domestic issues. She had done her homework.

Sandy began to examine the practical aspects of her decision, "Where am I going to... hiccup...live?"

"You can stay right here, until you find a place," Beth offered.

Ever polite, Sandy said, "I don't want...hiccup... to put you out."

Beth reassured her, "You're my friend and I love you. You are not putting me out. Who knows, Doug might just move out and leave you the house."

"I don't know...gasp... if I could live there, now."

"Sandy, you put your heart and soul into that house. If Doug doesn't want it, do you really want someone else living there?"

Sandy didn't have the energy to care about the house. She said, "We'll see...hiccup... I just want this whole...gasp...thing to be as painless...hiccup... as possible."

Beth smiled at her friend. "Honey, there is no such thing as a painless divorce."

"Hiccup."

#

Jamie sat at her kitchen table, drinking coffee and staring at the note in front of her. Jamie had showered and dressed, in a tank top and shorts. She had just finished eating some yogurt and a piece of toast and had settled down at the table, to plan her next move. It was still early, so she was going to wait a few more minutes, before calling Beth's house.

She would have called Sandy's cell phone, but Jamie was afraid she wouldn't answer and that would be a bad sign. No, she had to go to Sandy and look her in the eyes, tell her how sorry she was and what a big mistake it had been to sleep with Mary Ann. Jamie only wanted Sandy, and had ultimately come to the conclusion, that she always had. Then again, Sandy might not ever want to see Jamie again, after Mary Ann's little show.

In the middle of evaluating her position and how best to get Sandy to listen to her, she heard a knock on her backdoor. She could see Doug standing on the other side of the unlocked screen door. They made eye contact. Jamie folded the note and slid it into her pocket. She rose slowly and crossed to the door. After taking a deep breath and a quick look around her surroundings for a weapon, she opened the door.

"Come in."

Doug stepped around her, entering the kitchen. "Thank you," he said, sheepishly.

Doug was bowed with shame, not the confident, happy guy Jamie knew before. He had slept in his clothes, he wasn't wearing his glasses and he reeked of alcohol. She was suddenly more at ease, because he seemed broken, without the inclination for a fight. Still, she was on guard. After seeing what he did to Sandy last night, Jamie wasn't sure what Doug was capable of.

"Can I get you a cup of coffee?" Jamie offered.

Doug stood in the middle of the room, unable to decide what to do next. He replied, "Yes, please. I take it black, no sugar."

Their was an awkward silence between them. Doug looked around anxiously. Jamie brought the coffee pot to the table, with a mug for Doug. She said to Doug, "Please, sit down."

Doug took a seat, saying, "Thank you." He took a sip of coffee and then cleared his throat. "I guess you know why I'm here," he said.

"I think I have a pretty good idea," Jamie answered.

Doug continued to look around anxiously. He was nervous and fidgety, and sounded afraid the answer would be yes, when he asked, "Sandy isn't here, is she?"

Jamie eased his mind, "No, she is at Beth's house, or at least that's where she was going when she left here last night."

Doug began rambling, "I vaguely remember being told that by Robby, but I wasn't sure and then I saw her car here..."

Jamie interrupted him. She was about to badger the witness. "So, you thought you'd stop for a visit. What makes you think she wants to see you, after what you did?"

Doug hung his head, "I know, I know. I'm so sorry. That's why I can't drink. I become violent."

The pain he had caused Sandy drove Jamie to say, "Then you shouldn't drink. How irresponsible of you."

Doug looked up. "In my defense, she just told me she was in love with you. That was quite a shock."

Jamie was suddenly seized with Momma Bear fierceness, "I don't care what she said, you don't hit her, ever, are you hearing me?"

Doug's eyes came to life. He straightened his back and said, "Are you threatening me?"

Jamie wasn't intimidated. She had confronted murderers and bigger men than Doug, but this was different. There wasn't a cop or bailiff around, but she meant what she said next and she wasn't afraid of the repercussions.

"No, I'm promising you. If you raise a hand to Sandy again, I will bring all hell down on you. You won't have a pot to piss in, when I get through with you. The time you will spend behind bars will sure as hell dry you out. You are extremely lucky I won't be her divorce lawyer, now," Jamie said, and added, with as much sarcasm as she could muster, "Conflict of interests and all that."

Doug thought for a moment, and then he asked, "Did you encourage her to divorce me? If you did, I can sue you for alienation of affection."

Jamie laughed at him. "How could I encourage her? She never told me she was even thinking about divorcing you and I happen to have an ex-wife who can testify that she was present last night, when I learned all this, after Sandy arrived at my house."

Doug hit home with his next shot, "Are you in love with my wife?"

Jamie went on the defensive. "I don't see how that's any of your business."

Doug was beside himself, "None of my business? We were doing just fine, before you came back here."

"Doug, you had problems before I came along, you just didn't notice how unhappy Sandy was."

Doug needed someone to blame. He accused Jamie, "No, it's you. You caused this."

Jamie ignored the accusation and said, "Look Doug, I have my own divorce from Mary Ann to deal with. I know what it feels like to all of a sudden, after sixteen years, be faced with starting over. It's frightening."

137

Doug took another shot at Jamie's character, "You cheated. You got what you deserved. I would never cheat on Sandy."

Jamie smiled, saying, "No, you probably wouldn't, but still, if she's ready to go, trust me, nothing you say or do is going to stop her."

Doug began to plead with Jamie, "If you don't love her, give her back to me."

Jamie was growing tired of his poor pitiful me act. She said, "That's your problem Doug. You want to possess her. She's not property. She has a mind of her own and can do what she wishes."

Doug bowed up again, "I won't let her leave me."

Jamie laughed at him again, which was making him angrier. Jamie grinned and said, "What are you going to do, force her to go home and lock her in her room? Let me know how that works out for you."

Doug turned bitter. He leaned across the table. Jamie could smell the alcohol, when he spoke, "You talk about divorce, like wallowing around in bed with another woman is a marriage. We are a real family, a marriage with kids and grandkids. How do you think they're going to feel about their grandmother being a dyke?"

Jamie didn't flinch. She wasn't afraid of pissing him off. Jamie decided she really didn't like this man and if he hit her, she'd have him locked up for a very long time. She answered, mockingly, "I would hope they would be more enlightened than you. If you were, you would know that, by definition, dyke is an offensive term for a lesbian who is noticeably masculine. Sandy is no dyke."

Doug slammed his hand on the table, "I'm going to fight for her."

Jamie smirked, "Knock yourself out."

Doug growled, "You sit there so smug. How can you ruin a family like this?"

Jamie raised her voice, just enough to let him know she wasn't frightened by his histrionics. "When and if, it ever dawns on you why she left, you're going to realize I had nothing to do with her leaving. She's doing this all on her own, and frankly, I'm proud of her for finally doing what she wants, instead of what is expected of her."

Doug stood up from the table. He shook a finger in Jamie's face, saying, "I'm warning you. Stay away from my wife."

Jamie remained seated and un-intimidated. She said, still with the smirk on her face, "Or what, Doug? Are you going to hit me, too?"

"You'll see. This isn't over, not by a long shot." Doug turned and left quickly, the screen door slamming behind him. Jamie waited a few seconds and then let out a huge sigh of relief.

She said to the air around her, "Sandy, what have you gotten me into?"

#

Down the road, Beth and Sandy were crossing back and forth, from the kitchen to the dining room, cleaning up the dishes, from Sunday breakfast. The ice and pills had helped with the swelling on Sandy's face. She had taken a shower and borrowed sweats and a tee shirt from Jake, because they were about the same size. Cleaned and refreshed, Sandy was actually looking pretty good, considering.

Beth was saying, "I told the kids not to mention that huge bruise on your face to anyone. That's your private business."

"I appreciate your efforts, but I don't care who knows," Sandy said, "I won't be ashamed. Too many women stay in abusive homes, because of shame. I won't participate in that behavior."

Beth let out a throaty laugh. "Listen to you, a martyr to the cause."

"Fuck you," Sandy replied, but she was smiling.

Beth added, "In this county, they'll make up their own stories anyway, and I really think the abuse is going to take a back seat to the Lesbian thing."

Sandy laughed then. "You have a point there."

Sandy crossed back to the dining room. Even though Beth could not see Sandy, she continued the conversation, "So, are you attracted to women in general or just Jamie?"

"Oh, I don't know" Sandy said, from the other side of the wall, "I know I had girl crushes, most people do, so I thought nothing of it, but this, this is different."

Beth looked up, and saw Jamie standing in the doorway of the kitchen. Jamie had just heard the last part of the conversation.

Jamie put her finger to her lips, silently asking Beth to be quiet. She whispered, "Jake let me in."

Sandy continued from the other room, "There's just something about Jamie. I feel like we belong together. It's like destiny or something." She laughed and said, "Listen to me. I sound like I'm in a Shakespearean play."

Beth looked at Jamie and called back to Sandy, "And the plot just thickened."

Sandy re-entered the kitchen. She didn't notice Jamie right away, because she was carrying a large platter, looking down, making sure not to spill the left over juice. She was concentrating hard when she asked Beth, "What did you say?" She looked up and followed Beth's gaze to Jamie. She stopped dead in her tracks. The juice went over the edge of the platter and onto the counter.

Beth answered Sandy, but kept her eyes on Jamie, "I said, 'the plot has thickened.' Destiny has arrived and I think that's my cue to exit, so you two can talk." Beth looked from one friend to the other, shook her head in wonder, and then left the room.

Sandy put the platter on the counter. She turned toward Jamie and leaned back on the counter, both hands gripping it for support. Jamie came into the kitchen and leaned against the opposite counter. The two women were face to face, about ten feet and a kitchen island separating them. They just looked at each other for a few minutes.

Sandy broke the tension with a question, "How much of that did you hear?"

"Enough," Jamie replied.

Sandy appealed to Jamie, to speak to her with no coded messages, they had tiptoed around this...whatever this was, for too long. "What does that mean? Talk to me, Jamie."

Jamie couldn't suppress the grin, when she said, "There's something about you too, Sandy."

Sandy brought up, what was to her, a major stumbling block, "Where's Mary Ann?"

Jamie knew that was what Sandy was going to ask her first, and she could not suppress the little grin, when she said, "She went back to Durham this morning. I didn't see her. She left a note."

"What did it say?" Sandy asked

Jamie told the truth, "She said she was sorry things didn't work out for us." Jamie skirted the real substance of the note, that Mary Ann was waiting to see how this all played out with Sandy. There was another awkward silence between them, as Sandy processed the information. Then Jamie said, "Doug came to see me, this morning. He told me to stay away from you."

Sandy was shocked, "What did you say?"

Jamie grinned again, "I'm here aren't I?"

Sandy looked at the floor. She said, "What are we going to do now?"

"I don't know...I seem to be saying that a lot lately." Now it was Jamie's turn to stare at the floor. Jamie didn't know what to do next. She wanted to cross the room and hold Sandy to her. She wanted to tell her she loved her and probably had her entire life. She wanted to keep Sandy safe and love her forever, but Jamie was afraid. Afraid to let her heart run wild. Afraid of falling for and then losing Sandy, because she didn't think she could stand the pain of another loss.

Sandy brought Jamie back from the place she kept her fears. She asked, "What else don't you know?"

"I don't know if I did the right thing, telling Mary Ann I wasn't in love with her, anymore."

Sandy brightened a bit, but continued her line of questioning, "What else?"

Jamie bit the bullet and laid out her true feelings for Sandy. Once she crossed this line, there was no going back. She captured Sandy's eyes with her own and said, "I don't know if I've fallen in love with you, or if this is some kind of residual crush, from the past."

Sandy smiled and said, "I thought about that, too."

Jamie relaxed a bit, but the sexual tension in the room was building. She winked at Sandy and grinned. "Oh yeah, and what did you decide?"

Sandy went on, "I've thought about a lot of things, but I keep coming back to the fact that when you walk in a room my heart nearly jumps out of my chest, when you smile at me I want to kiss you, and when you barely touch me I feel electricity shoot through my entire body."

Jamie grinned wider, "I know what you mean." Jamie felt the same way about Sandy. It was also, the second time a woman had told her something similar in less than twelve hours. It was different when Sandy said it. It didn't sound rehearsed, it sounded real.

Sandy continued, "But then I see Mary Ann naked, in your house, and I don't know what to think."

Jamie tried to explain, "I should not have had sex with her. I don't know what happened, one minute we were yelling at each other and the next..."

Sandy interrupted, "You don't owe me an explanation."

Jamie wanted Sandy to understand, "I'm just saying, it didn't help the situation, other than, I realized I wasn't in love with her. We're done, Sandy. Mary Ann and I are finished."

"So, now I need to finish my business with Doug. It isn't quite as simple as just saying it. I have to tell my daughter and I have to know if I'm doing the right thing," Sandy lamented.

"This isn't easy for me either, Sandy. I don't want to make a huge mistake here."

Sandy raised a questioning eyebrow, the look that made her resemble Vivian Leigh, and asked, "And you think being with me would be a huge mistake?"

Jamie took a couple of steps forward, and leaned on the island in the center of the room, because her legs were shaking. She locked Sandy's eyes with her own and said, "No, I think not letting myself fall madly in love with you, would be the biggest mistake I could ever make."

Sandy closed the space between them in a flash, but it felt like slow motion to Jamie. Jamie took Sandy in her arms and kissed her tenderly, careful not to hurt her injured face, but Sandy kissed her back deeply. Longing took over, and all the passion Jamie had craved, since they kissed in the garage, burst out of her chest, in a long groan of pleasure. Sandy kissed her harder, and pressed her body into Jamie's, trembling with emotion. Jamie held her tightly and whispered in Sandy's ear, "Come home with me, now."

Sandy's answer came in the form of a breathless kiss.

#

Jamie led Sandy, by the hand, into the bedroom. They stopped just inside the door and Jamie kissed Sandy, not wanting to move too fast, but Sandy kissed her back so hungrily that Jamie started moving her toward the bed, when Sandy balked.

Jamie held Sandy in her arms and let out a little laugh. She said, "I changed the sheets."

Sandy kissed Jamie lightly on the lips, and then looked at the bed again, "It's not that."

Jamie tenderly brushed her lips across Sandy's swollen cheek, "What is it then?" she whispered. Jamie was taking in all of Sandy. How she felt in her arms. How she smelled fresh and clean, with her own underlying scent beneath. It was intoxicating. Jamie stopped kissing Sandy's neck, when she realized Sandy was frozen in place. She pulled her head up, to look into Sandy's face.

Sandy stared into Jamie's eyes. Looking back and forth between each one, searching for something, trust maybe. She said softly, "I told you I kissed a woman before, really, it was a girl in high school and we were both very drunk. I've never even come close to having sex with a woman."

Jamie kissed Sandy sweetly, grinning she said, "You'll be fine."

Sandy whispered, against Jamie's lips, "I don't know what to do."

"You are a woman aren't you?" Jamie asked, kissing Sandy's neck again.

Sandy pressed her body against Jamie and let her head fall back, as Jamie kissed down her chest and between her breasts. "Yes," Sandy gushed out, breathlessly.

Jamie brought her lips back to Sandy's, whispering against them, "Then you'll know what to do." Jamie followed the statement with a deep kiss that brought sounds of desire from Sandy's throat.

Sandy became very involved in kissing Jamie and their need to be free of their clothes grew more frantic, as their breathing quickened. Jamie ran her hand up Sandy's shirt, feeling her soft skin for the first time. It made her weak in the knees. She was thankful when Sandy pushed her back on the bed and fell into her arms. Sandy's hands were tangled in Jamie's hair. She kissed Jamie so madly, so passionately, they had to come up for air.

Jamie easily flipped Sandy over and started removing Sandy's shirt, slowly, trying to catch her breath. Her hands were trembling. That hadn't happened to her in a very long time. She wanted this woman so badly, that her body could no longer control itself. The adrenaline had to go somewhere, so she was shaking uncontrollably and suffering from a lack of oxygen.

Sandy tried to pull Jamie back to her lips, but Jamie needed to calm down. She whispered, "Wait a minute, baby. Let me just look at you."

Sandy smiled up at Jamie, her own chest heaving up and down. She settled back on the bed and relaxed, her eyes locked on Jamie's, while Jaime peeled her clothes away, one piece at a time. Jamie slid the bottom of Sandy's shirt up, gradually revealing her perfect breasts. Sandy hadn't worn a bra today. She adjusted on the bed so Jamie could get her shirt off.

That's when Jamie saw Doug's fingerprints, where he had grabbed Sandy and shaken her. He had done all this to Sandy, because she loved Jamie. Something cracked inside of Jamie. A wall crumbled down, showering her heart with the want of this woman. The need to have her always in her life. To let Sandy into places Jamie dared not let others go, not even Mary Ann. Jamie would never let anyone lay a hand on Sandy again. She would protect her with her life.

Jamie thought of this while she kissed the bruises on Sandy's wrist and arms, and then gently brushed her lips against Sandy's swollen cheek. She looked in Sandy's eyes, which were burning with desire and the want of Jamie, and at that moment, Jamie knew she had made the right decision.

Jamie slid down Sandy's body, kissing down her neck and onto her chest, where she explored Sandy's perfectly round breasts and pink nipples, with her mouth. Sandy tangled her hands in Jamie's hair again, pulling her down against her chest and arching her back off the bed. A sound rose out of Sandy's chest, it said to Jamie take me, take me now and then Sandy began to tear at Jamie's clothes.

Jamie stood up, shedding her shirt, pants and underwear while Sandy watched, growing hotter and hotter. Sandy wriggled out of her sweat pants and underwear, with Jamie's assistance. Jamie then lowered her naked body onto Sandy's, and kissed her with all the feelings she had bottled up, for the 25 years she'd been gone. Guttural sounds of pleasure escaped from both of them.

When Jamie took Sandy, Sandy whispered, "Oh, my god. Oh, my god."

Jamie's cell phone rang on the dresser, but nobody heard it.

#

Outside the bedroom window, Doug peered inside. He was revolted by what he saw, but he couldn't pull himself away. He couldn't see all of them, through the crack in the blinds, but he could see enough. He recognized his wife's naked legs wrapped around Jamie's ass, grinding her pelvis into Jamie's. A couple walked by on the marina dock. They noticed Doug and looked on with suspicion, forcing him to leave.

#

Sandy slept soundly in Jamie's arms. Jamie lay there as long as she could, but she had to pee. Jamie slowly slid out from under her and got out of bed. She found her underwear on the other side of the bed and a pair of sweats on the back of a chair. She grabbed a tee shirt out of the dresser drawer. She looked back at Sandy lovingly and smiled. Jamie took her cell phone and left the bedroom.

After she went to the bathroom, Jamie went to the sun porch, making a call on her cell phone. Mary Ann answered.

"Hey," Jamie said, "I missed your call earlier."

"Yes, I called when I got home," Mary Ann explained. "Did you forget to plug your phone in again?"

Jamie lied, "No, I guess I didn't hear it ring."

Mary Ann grew quieter, she asked, "Jamie, what's wrong? I can hear it in your voice."

"Nothing. I'm just tired. It's been a crazy weekend." At least that part was the truth.

"Jamie, I'm glad we talked. I've missed talking to you."

Jamie did not notice the sheet wrapped Sandy approach and stop in the doorway.

"I'm glad we talked, too. Mary Ann, I want you to talk to me, whenever you need to. You are always going to be a big part of my life, you know that don't you?"

"Jamie, I hope she makes you happy, I really do, but I can't help wanting you back. I love you."

"I love you, too," Jamie said, "I don't want to hurt you anymore, I'm sorry for the way things ended, but…"

Mary Ann cut her off, "But you're in love with Sandy. I get it, Jamie. I'm a smart girl."

"I know you are," Jamie said.

Mary Ann continued, "So, I'm going to let you go, do what you need to do, but when it's over, I'm begging you, come back to me."

"Mary Ann, nobody can predict the future, but I'm pretty sure I'm not coming back. Don't wait around for me."

Mary Ann grew silent for a second or two. Jamie could hear her breathing. Then Mary Ann said, "I guess there is nothing left to say, is there?"

"No, there isn't. Good night, Mary Ann."

"Goodbye, Jamie."

Jamie hung up the phone. She sat gazing out at the docks. She sighed loudly and stood up. Jamie saw Sandy and realized she had been standing in the doorway. She didn't know how long.

Jamie said, "I didn't hear you come in."

Sandy grinned, "I'm stealthy like that."

Jamie explained what she had been doing, "Mary Ann called earlier, so I was returning the call. I just wanted to know she got home safely."

"Jamie, you need to do what you need to do. I want you to have no doubt you've done the right thing."

Jamie crossed to Sandy and tugged at the sheet, gently. "I have no doubt that you look really sexy in that sheet."

Jamie started kissing Sandy's neck, which drove Sandy crazy. Jamie pushed Sandy backwards and up against the wall in the living room. The sheet fell by the wayside. Jamie kissed her way down Sandy's body. Sandy threw her head back, clutching at the wall behind her and moaned in ecstasy.

#

Jamie awoke a couple of hours later, with Sandy draped over her. Jamie started kissing Sandy tenderly around her swollen face. She was surprised Sandy hadn't complained, at some point during their love making, of her face hurting. Sandy opened her eyes and Jamie kissed her on the lips.

Sandy smiled up at Jamie and said, "Not until you feed me, I'm starving."

"I am, too," Jamie said. "I make a mean omelet. Do you like breakfast for supper?"

Sandy rolled off of Jamie and got out of bed. "I love it. Do you have some clothes I can wear so I can help? I don't have anything with me, except what I had on earlier."

Jamie got up and grabbed the clothes she had on, at least the pants and underwear. She couldn't find her tee shirt and thought it might be still in the living room. She opened two drawers in the dresser. Sandy shuffled after Jamie, wrapped in the sheet.

Jamie said, "Here, help yourself. Tee's in the top drawer, sweats in the next one." Jamie grabbed a Tennessee Lady Vols tee shirt and put it on. She would locate the other one later.

Sandy dug through the drawer making her selection, saying, "I'm going to need to go get some things from my house. I left with nothing, but my purse."

Jamie grinned at her, "I don't mind sharing, but I'd really rather keep you naked." Sandy immediately dropped the sheet and did a sexy pose. Jamie laughed and said, "You are a very bad girl and if you want food, you better cover that up, before I become distracted."

Sandy said, "Well, we wouldn't want you getting distracted now would we," and with that she turned her back to Jamie and deliberately bent over in front of her, to retrieve the sheet.

#

Outside of the bedroom window, Doug was back for another peak. He saw Sandy's sexy pose in the doorway. He took another pull, one of many, on the liquor bottle he was holding and snuck back into the darkness, under a tree.

#

Jamie left the bedroom and entered the kitchen, looking over her shoulder at Sandy. She said, "I'm leaving the room or we'll never get fed." Jamie began

149

pulling ingredients out of the refrigerator, putting them on the counter. She called out to Sandy, who was still in the bedroom, "Onions, peppers, mushrooms and cheese sound good?"

Sandy answered from the bedroom, "Yes that sounds amazing. I'll help chop."

They continued their conversation through the open door of the bedroom, "Did you find anything to wear?"

Sandy emerged in one of Jamie's old faded Duke t-shirts and grey sweats. She let Jamie inspect her with her eyes, asking, "Do you approve?"

"I don't think that t-shirt ever looked that good on me."

Sandy went to Jamie and gave her a kiss on the cheek. They were just smiling at each other, as though neither of them could believe this was actually happening. Both women jumped, startled out of their romantic moment, by the sound of glass breaking and something heavy crashing to the floor, in the bedroom.

Jamie instinctively threw her body around Sandy and pulled her down to the floor, where they crouched and listened. Once Jamie was sure Sandy was okay and all was quiet, she started for the bedroom. Jamie peeked into the doorway and quickly pulled her head back. She didn't see anybody, only glass and a brick in the floor. Sandy crept close behind her. Jamie picked up the brick. It had "FUCKING DYKES" written on it, with a Sharpie. She flipped it over and read the message on the other side of the brick. She put it down on the bed and stepped over to the bedside table, removing a 9mm Beretta. Her jaw was set in anger.

Jamie held up her hand to Sandy and said, "Don't come in here. There's glass everywhere," as she slipped off her sweats and put on a pair of jeans. She picked up her purple Converse from the bottom of the closet and sat on the bed to put them on.

Sandy saw the pistol on the bed beside Jamie, where she sat tying her shoes. With a frightened look on her face, she said, "What are you going to do with that?"

Jamie stood up, picked up the pistol, peering out the window, into the darkness, and said, "I'm arming myself, in case that asshole out there decides to come in here."

Sandy pointed at her shoes, near the end of the bed. Without a word passing between them, Jamie picked up the shoes, dusted the glass off and handed them to Sandy. She had a connection with Sandy that Jamie had never experienced with another person. Maybe her dog, Beau, when she was growing up, but not a human who could read her like a book and who she in turn understood every little gesture. Sandy finished her sentences or said out loud exactly what Jamie was thinking.

Sandy asked, "Do you think it's Doug?" She leaned on the doorframe, putting on her sandals.

Jamie picked up the brick, handing it to Sandy, saying, "I can't think of anyone else that knows anything about us, besides, turn the brick over."

Sandy turned the brick over to see, "FUCK YOU SANDY" written on the other side.

Jamie tucked the pistol into the back of her jeans and began closing the bedroom blinds tightly. Then she checked the locks on the other windows and doors, in the house.

Sandy trailed behind her. "Do you know how to use that weapon?"

"Yes, I am licensed and trained," Jamie said. "I practiced criminal law in Durham. Some of my clients were really criminals."

Sandy was a little alarmed by the gun. She asked, "Well, can you not kill him? Maybe just scare him or wound him in the leg. He has children."

Jamie stopped, turning back to Sandy, "He has kids?"

Sandy continued, "From his previous marriage. They are grown, but I'm sure they would prefer he not be dead."

"I don't want to shoot anybody. I'm calling the police and swearing out a warrant for him."

Sandy was stricken, "You can't do that."

"Why not?" Jamie didn't need to ask the question, she had a good idea why Sandy didn't want the police involved.

"Because, I will have to explain why I'm here and why Doug is so pissed and of course the writing on the brick pretty much says it all. The news would be all over the county by tomorrow morning, hell by midnight tonight, probably. Jamie, I'm not ready to face that just yet. Does sleeping with one woman make you a lesbian?"

Jamie smiled at Sandy's naiveté. She stepped closer, opening her arms for Sandy to step into them. She enveloped Sandy in her arms and hugged her tight. Jamie whispered in Sandy's ear, "Honey, you just blew the doors off the closet. The hinges are still smoking, sending out little smoke signals to all the lesbians in the world. I should get a new toaster any day."

Sandy pulled back, so she could see Jamie's face. She asked, "What?"

Jamie laughed and grinned at the beautiful woman, in her arms, even with the bruising. "Lesbian joke. I'll explain it later."

Sandy began to think about who knew about them already. She said, "Beth and Robby won't say anything."

Jamie countered with, "Doug will. He's extremely angry and probably drinking again. He'll tell somebody, if he hasn't already."

The panic set in for Sandy. "Oh my god, suppose he called my daughter, or my mother?"

Jamie picked up her cell phone from the living room floor, where she had dropped it, when she and Sandy got busy, earlier.

152

Sandy put her hand over the phone, so Jamie couldn't open it, yet. She asked, "Are you calling the police?"

"No, I'm calling Beth and Robby, this time… but Sandy, if we are going to have a relationship, you will have to be ready to live as an out lesbian. I am not ashamed of who I am and I won't be anybody's dirty little secret."

Sandy removed her hand, but looked deeply into Jamie's eyes, "I don't want to keep you a secret. I want everyone to know how much I love you. Nothing anyone says or does will change that."

Jamie reminded Sandy, "What about your job? They don't look too kindly on lesbians teaching children, around here."

"I'll deal with that when the time comes," Sandy answered, adding, "besides, I have enough sick leave built up to retire anyway."

"Just be sure this is what you want," Jamie warned. "You can't take it back, once it's out there."

"Same back to you," Sandy said, tapping Jamie on the chest.

Jamie raised her brows, questioning, "What do you mean?"

Sandy smiled, as she said, "You need to be sure I'm what you want, before I go making any more life changing proclamations."

"And I need to be sure that I'm not just some temporary diversion, into the lesbian world, for you," Jamie said, "I don't want to wake up one day and hear you say, you're going back to men or you think you're bi-sexual."

Sandy slid her hand down to Jamie's crotch and gripped her solidly. It sent shivers down Jamie's spine. Sandy whispered against Jamie's lips, "Baby, you are no diversion. I've never wanted anything as desperately, as I want you. You have all the equipment I need. I have no intention of ever making love to anyone else, ever again. Are you ready to make that commitment to me, Jamie?"

The Girl Back Home

Jamie fixed her eyes on Sandy's. "Let me show you." Jamie pressed her lips to Sandy's and melted into a kiss that said, "I only want you." Jamie pulled away, but kept her lips brushing against Sandy's. She whispered, "I'll love you forever." This was followed by another long, deep kiss, initiated by Sandy.

When they came up for air, Jamie flipped the cell phone open, saying, "I need to call Robby. That idiot, Doug, is probably home by now, but I want him to stay there."

Sandy still had her arms around Jamie's waist. She had the smoky veil of desire on her face and in her voice, when she said, "Okay, but after you feed me, I want you to take me back to bed. If I'm going to be a proper Lesbian, I need more practice."

Jamie made the call and then led Sandy to the kitchen, where they worked side by side, chopping the ingredients for their omelets. They couldn't keep their hands or lips off of each other, which made the cooking slower than necessary. Once Jamie had the omelets started, she fetched the vacuum cleaner from the hall closet and went into the bedroom. She left Sandy in charge of not letting the food burn.

After she vacuumed, Jamie came back into the kitchen, took a tape measure out of a drawer and disappeared back into the bedroom, but not before she kissed Sandy again. Jamie re-emerged with the tape measure now clipped to her jeans pocket. She said, "I think I got all the glass out of the carpet, but I need to cover the window with something."

Sandy flipped one of the omelets onto a plate. She asked Jamie, "Did Beth say she'd call back when Robby finds Doug?"

"Yes, don't worry. I'm sure he's home, passed out by now."

"I hope so," Sandy said, bringing the plate to the table.

"I'm going to put something over the window, before I eat. The Meachem boys left some plywood, out by the office. I think there's a piece that will fit nicely."

Sandy was leery, "Are you sure you should go outside?"

Jamie reassured her, "Oh, he's gone by now, surely. I don't want to leave the window as it is. We would be fighting mosquitoes all night. Do you think you can handle that second omelet on your own?" She winked at Sandy.

Sandy stood over by the stove, pouring coffee from the fresh pot. She said, "Oh, I think I can manage," smiling and winking back at Jamie, "Be careful."

Jamie went to Sandy and pecked her on the cheek, saying, "I will."

Jamie went towards the door, stopping to grab her big black Mag light, out of a drawer. When she started cooking earlier, she had taken the Beretta out of the waistband of her pants and laid it on the counter by the sink. Her mind was on a thousand different things at once. Most of her thoughts were dedicated to Sandy. Jamie thought of how they fit together perfectly, how Sandy's skin was so soft, how Sandy melted into her and how she knew that Sandy was the one she had always been looking for. It wasn't just the sex, although that was incredible. Her heart had gone astray for twenty-five years and now, it had finally come home.

Her other thoughts were of wanting to wring Doug's neck. At least, Mary Ann had the grace to leave without causing a scene. Doug was his own worst nightmare. He needed to sober up and get on with his life. His wife was not in love with him and she wanted out of their life together. Sandy and Jamie were living very parallel lives, each dealing with relationships that were ending and a new one just beginning. Doug was in the way of that. He had to be stopped. Jamie could only hope Robby could talk some sense into Doug, before he really hurt someone or himself. She half hoped he wrapped his truck around a tree. She didn't want him dead, but injured enough to send him to the hospital, where they could deal with his current mania.

With all the things churning in Jamie's head, she never even thought about picking up the pistol, as she went out the door. It was a new moon night. Jamie hadn't installed the motion sensor light on the outside of the new office. It sat in a box, unopened, in the corner of the office. With no help from the moon and no artificial light out by the office, Jamie stepped out of the patio light, cautiously.

She aimed the flashlight at all the dark shadows. Ambient light, from the docks, cast just enough light to show that no one was in the front yard, on this side of the house, anyway. The hammock rocked slightly in the evening breeze. The sound of someone laughing, on the dock, echoed across the water giving it an evil, unnatural sound. All was quiet in the yard. Jamie bet Doug was passed out in his truck somewhere, so she headed for the garage.

Jamie found the pile of lumber on the side of the office and began to look through the plywood pieces leaning against the wall, measuring each one. She didn't want to have to get out a saw, so if she could find the perfect piece, life would be good. At least it would be a barrier to anymore flying bricks. Jamie said out loud, "What a jack ass," referring to Doug's childish behavior and lost herself in her search.

#

Inside the kitchen, Jamie's cell phone rang on the counter. Sandy, who had been standing by the backdoor, listening, picked up the phone and read Beth's name on the caller ID.

She answered it, "Hey, Beth. Did Robby find Doug?"

Beth sounded worried, "No, he didn't. Doug wasn't at home so he drove towards Jamie's. He found Doug's truck about 500 yards down the road from you. Stay in the house, Robby's on the way...." Beth reacted to the sound of Jamie's cell phone hitting the floor. She cried out, "Sandy? ... Sandy?"

Jamie's phone spun slowly on the floor, coming to the end of its violent landing. It was still open, with Beth's voice a tiny high pitched sound, unheard by anyone. Sandy and the Beretta were both gone.

#

Jamie was still hard at work, crouching beside a piece of plywood she thought would work, when the two-by-four connected with the back of her head. Then everything went black.

Doug stood over her with the two-by-four poised for another strike, when Sandy appeared, aiming Jamie's pistol at Doug.

She screamed in horror, "Doug! What have you done?"

Doug turned to see Sandy with the gun shaking in his direction. He said, in a drunken slur, "Well, if it isn't my wife." He was grotesque in this state of self pity and intoxication. He lowered the two-by-four and continued with a base insult, "So did you enjoy it, getting your pussy licked by this pervert?"

Sandy kept the weapon pointed at Doug. She sneered at him, hissing, "Go to hell, Doug."

Doug chuckled a mad laugh. He growled, "You first."

Sandy couldn't believe she had been married to this creature in front of her, "What is wrong with you? Have you completely lost your mind?"

"Me? Lost my mind?" Doug shouted, "I think it's you that's lost your mind."

"I'm finally doing what's right for me. Can't you see that? I'm in love with Jamie, I always have been. Now leave us alone."

"Sandy," Doug said, wallowing in self pity, "What will people think. My wife left me for a dyke. How will I show my face?"

"This isn't about you," Sandy retorted.

157

Doug screamed at her, "Yes, it is Sandy. If I'm not man enough to keep you, then I don't want to live and I'm going to take both of you with me."

Sandy tried to stop the gun from shaking, but her hands were trembling so much, it was almost impossible. She narrowed her eyes and said, "Over my dead body."

"That's the idea," he said, with an evil glare. Doug dropped the two-by-four and reached in his jacket pocket. He pulled out a revolver, saying, "Hey, look. I got one of those, too." He pointed it at Jamie, still unconscious at his feet.

Sandy was as frightened as she had ever been. Her hands were frozen to the Beretta, but she couldn't bring herself to pull the trigger, yet. She tried instead, talking to him, "Doug, it's me, you're mad at. Not Jamie. Don't make me shoot you."

Doug turned his weapon on Sandy. "You're right. I should probably shoot you first. You having a gun and all. I wouldn't want to die before I kill this fucking bitch on the ground."

Sandy tried to reason with him, "Nobody has to die. Just put the gun down and I'll put mine down."

Doug looked at Sandy with such malice it made her skin crawl. He spat out, "Oh, somebody has to die, Sandy."

Jamie stirred at Doug's feet. She opened her eyes and realized Doug was standing over her, pointing a pistol at something. She followed his line of fire and saw Sandy aiming a pistol at Doug. She tried to sit up. She was too weak and groggy. She couldn't get herself up and she desperately wanted to.

Jamie called out weakly, "Sandy."

Jamie blacked out again. Just as she lost total consciousness, she heard a gunshot and a body hitting the ground, heavily.

#

Moments later Sandy held Jamie's head in her lap, with a bloody towel pressed against the back of Jamie's head. Sandy had blood on her clothes and hands. Head wounds bleed profusely. Jamie had an L shaped gash, on the right side of the back of her head that looked deep. The blood looked much more serious than it was, and it had really frightened Sandy, until the bleeding slowed down. Doug writhed in pain on the ground nearby. Jamie became conscious of someone calling her name.

Sandy was saying, softly, "Jamie, open your eyes."

Jamie opened her eyes to see Sandy's concerned, still a bit blurry, face looking down at her. Behind Sandy, she could barely make out Robby, bent over, looking down at her. Jamie became aware that Doug was squirming on the ground near her.

Jamie asked, "What happened?"

"Doug shot at me, but he missed," Sandy said, as if he had thrown a snowball at her.

Jamie grinned, "Did you shoot him?"

"No, I forgot to take the safety off."

"Then why is he screaming?" Jamie looked at Doug, who was moaning, in between screams of pain and holding his leg.

Robby spoke up, "I broke his fucking leg."

Jamie looked up at Robby. "You what?"

Sandy answered for him, "Robby came out of nowhere and tackled Doug."

"You're lucky I played linebacker," Robby added, "If I had been a kicker, this would be a different story."

Doug cried out in pain, "Jesus, somebody help me." The others looked over at his writhing body, but nobody offered any comfort to him.

Robby went over to Doug and told him, "Shut up or I'll break the other leg."

Jamie's head was throbbing. She put her hand on the back of her head and felt the warm moist hair and knew she was bleeding. Sandy pulled Jamie's hand away, placing it back down on Jamie's chest. Doug must have hit her with something. Whatever it was, it hurt like hell. Jamie had no idea how much time had passed. She grimaced and then tried to sit up, but Sandy stopped her.

"Whoa. You stay where you are. You got whacked pretty hard."

Jamie could hear sirens off in the distance, wailing their way down the highway, coming closer.

Robby heard them too, he said, "The ambulance is on the way, along with the sheriff."

At that moment, Jamie heard car tires squeal, as the driver braked hard and then plowed down the gravel driveway. Jamie craned her neck to see Beth jump out of the car, almost before it came to a stop.

Beth ran to Robby, "Oh, my god. Are you all alright?"

Robby hugged her, saying, "Yes dear, we're all okay. Except, Doug here. I don't think he feels so well and Jamie needs some stitches."

Sandy spoke to Beth, "I think she'll have a concussion, but she'll live," and then smiled down at Jamie.

"Thank god," Beth gushed out.

Beth looked down at Jamie, "Did you shoot him?"

Sandy and Jamie spoke at the same time, "No, Robby broke his fucking leg."

Beth walked over to Doug and stood over him. He continued to groan in pain. Beth kicked his injured leg, which caused a blood curdling scream from

Doug. She said, "Don't fuck with my friends again, you son of a bitch, and stop screaming like a girl."

The others laughed quietly at Beth,

Sandy said, "She is a force to be reckoned with."

"You can say that again," Robby added.

The sirens grew louder and much closer, and then faded again. That meant they had just crossed the hump backed bridge, rising over the tree tops, where the sirens had no impediments to their lonesome call, which echoed down the canal. The sirens then dipped back behind the trees, until once again, in clear voice, the sirens made the turn off the highway. They were on Waterlily road now, a half a mile away. The sound became deafening, as they closed in on Jamie's house.

An ambulance followed by a sheriff's car pulled into the driveway. Another ambulance and more sheriff's patrol cars pulled off the road in front of Jamie's house. There was even a highway patrolman, setting flares out on the road. Hot time in the old town tonight, Jamie thought. They didn't get too many calls like this one would turn out to be, of that Jamie was sure. Shots fired and two people down, lesbians assaulted by angry husband. It didn't get anymore tabloid than that. Jamie could just image the chatter on the radio and the number of locals glued to their scanners, listening for every detail. Jamie looked around. People from the marina began to huddle together, trying to see what was happening. Jamie looked up at Sandy and smiled.

"What are you smiling about?" Sandy asked.

Jamie grinned and said, "Well, baby. Welcome to your coming out party."

Chapter Eleven

Red and blue emergency lights circled and white strobe lights flashed against every surface in Jamie's yard. A small crowd of onlookers from the marina gathered in the yard, held back by the police tape strung around the property. The lights reflected off of their pajamas and housecoats, giving them the appearance of wallflowers at a disco, standing around a dance floor.

An ambulance sped away, carrying Jamie to the hospital. Another ambulance had already left with Doug. The sheriff deemed it necessary that the two injured parties not ride in the same ambulance, since Doug had tried to kill Jamie. Doug had been placed under arrest before they took him away. One deputy was assigned to ride in the back of the ambulance with Doug, in case he got violent again, and another deputy followed in a sheriff's department vehicle.

Doug was charged with vandalism for the brick incident, assault and battery, assault with a deadly weapon, and attempted murder, two counts. He was facing quite a lot of prison time, if he ran into the right kind of judge. Jamie hoped the "hanging judge," Judge Bailey, a legend in Currituck, was still on the bench. He would be all over Doug's ass. Judge Bailey did not tolerate domestic violence, because his own daughter nearly lost her life to an ex-husband. Doug could plead temporary insanity, maybe, but he was definitely going away for quite awhile, after the case went to trial.

There was a buzz among the emergency responders about the message on the brick and Doug's reasons for trying to kill both Jamie and Sandy. It was scandalous in the eyes of these locals, who did not deal with lesbian drama very often. Oh, sure there were other lesbians in Currituck County, but they kept to themselves and policed their own behavior, praying that the rednecks wouldn't find out who they were. Some redneck men, not all, but enough, felt it was their duty to change a lesbian back to being a heterosexual, by berating them in public and promising to fuck the lesbian right out of them, if given the chance.

There had been a case last year, in Currituck County, involving a semi-famous local writer and a professor at the university in town. Molly Kincaid, Jamie's friend, another very expensive, hot shot, lesbian lawyer from Durham, had represented the women and one of their fathers, when they were charged with conspiracy and murder. The father had killed the man, who was in the process of raping his daughter. The case uncovered misconduct on the part of several DA's and law enforcement officials and won the women a big settlement, in the subsequent civil suit.

The news of Doug's attack, on Jamie and his wife, and reasons for it would spread like a wildfire through the county and beyond. The little paper, printed in town, would definitely have at least one headline, because lesbian drama sold papers. The fact that a wealthy attorney, just moved back from Durham, and a public school teacher were involved would keep the story on the front page for awhile. The stories about the incident, circulating among the people in the county, would take on a life of their own. They would be embellished upon, until the facts became so distorted and sensationalized, that none of the rumors flying around would come close to resembling the truth.

The Girl Back Home

In crisis situations many people tend to mill around, all interested and actively involved in seeking information about what has happened. People begin to speculate and those speculations become part of the confusion of facts. In one small town, when a rape slaying occurred, a study found that there were no less than seventeen different versions of the attack reported. By the time the true nature of a crime comes out to the public, the damage has already been done. There would be people who would never believe the official story, even when confronted with the facts, due to their own prejudices.

Now that Jamie had been taken away in the ambulance, Sandy could no longer fight off the magnitude of the situation. She began to shake violently enough, that Beth went into the house and brought her a blanket. Beth sat Sandy down at the table on the patio, concerned that she might be going into shock. After all, Doug had tried to kill her. Sandy was lucky that he was too drunk to aim straight. Fortunately, his stray bullet had not injured anyone and ended up in the wall of the marina restaurant next door, startling a few of the staff, who happened to still be there. Sandy's hands and clothes were still covered in blood, where she had cradled Jamie's bleeding head in her lap.

All around the premises deputies were looking for evidence with their flashlights. A small woman in a Sheriff's uniform walked over to Beth and Sandy. Sheriff Cindy Mason had lived in Currituck County all her life, except for the time it took for her to get a degree in Criminology and attend police training school. She was a petite woman, with her graying dark hair in a bun, tucked under her Sheriff's hat. She wore the official tan and brown uniform, the brass on her left chest indicating she was someone to be reckoned with. The uniform looked good on her and the big gun on her side, made her look dangerous. She was married to the high school athletic director and baseball coach and had become the Sheriff in the last election. Sheriff Mason smiled at

Beth and Jamie. She knew all the parties involved and although she hadn't seen Jamie in years, she had remembered her well.

When she reached the patio, Sheriff Manson asked, "Sandy, are you okay?"

"I'm okay, Cindy. I'm worried about Jamie and I'm pissed as hell at Doug, but I'm okay. I just need to get to the hospital."

The Sheriff continued, "I know how worried you both must be. The EMT thought Jamie might have a concussion and she needed some stitches, but he said she was in good shape. Doug's leg is brok…"

Sandy cut her off, "I don't care what happens to him. He got what he deserved and he's lucky he's still alive."

Sheriff Mason nodded that she understood. It was easy enough. Sandy made no bones about how she felt about each of the parties involved.

The sheriff reached into her jacket pocket, producing a small pad and a pen, before continuing, "I talked to Jamie, before she left. She didn't know much about what happened. She was unconscious through most of the incident. I need to get your version of events and then Robby's. It won't take long, I promise. It looks pretty cut and dry as it is. Now, Beth, did you see what happened?"

"No. I got here after Doug was already down."

"What made you come here, Beth?"

"Jamie called Robby and told him Doug had just thrown a brick through her bedroom window. Jamie asked him to find Doug and make sure he stayed at home. When Robby found Doug's truck down the road, he called me. I called Jamie and got Sandy on the phone, instead. I told her where Doug's truck was and that Robby was on his way, and then, I assume, she dropped the phone. I knew something bad was about to happen, so I drove over here."

The Sheriff turned to Sandy, "Why didn't you call us when the brick came through the window?"

Sandy pulled the blanket around her tighter. "We thought Robby could handle it. Doug had to be drunk and I didn't want him arrested. I didn't want to ruin him, I guess." She lied. It even sounded like a lie to her. The sheriff was no dummy, she knew what was going on, and let Sandy know so with a turn of expression, but Sandy just couldn't bring herself to say it aloud, not yet.

"Sandy, tell me what happened, after Beth called," the sheriff said, taking notes on the little pad.

"When Beth said, Doug's truck was down the road and he wasn't in it, I knew he was outside with Jamie. I dropped the phone. Then I saw the gun on the counter and realized Jamie had forgotten to take it with her. I picked it up and ran out on the patio. It was really dark, but Jamie had a flashlight."

Sheriff Mason interrupted, "So, you could see Jamie."

"Yes, she was aiming the flashlight down at the ground, but I could tell it was her. Before I could say anything, I saw Doug step out of the shadows. He swung that board so hard. I don't know how he didn't cave her skull in. I thought he had killed her, but then she moved a little. Doug pulled out his gun and threatened to shoot Jamie. I tried to talk Doug into putting his gun down, but then he turned the gun on me and tried to kill me."

Sheriff Mason asked, "Did you see Robby tackle Doug?"

"Hell no, I hit the deck when he shot at me. I pulled my trigger, at the same time he did, but I forgot to take the safety off, so I just fell to the ground."

"Sandy, I have to ask you about your face. That isn't from tonight, is it? How did it happen?"

166

Sandy looked away, not wanting to talk about the fight with Doug and what had caused it. Sandy said quietly, "I had an argument with Doug last night. He was drunk."

The sheriff was persistent, "What did you argue about?"

Sandy reacted with, "Do you really have to know all this?"

"Considering Doug tried to kill you and Jamie tonight, I think it's relevant," Sheriff Mason explained.

Sandy gave in, but tried to cover up the substance of the argument, "I asked him for a divorce."

"Why do you think Doug tried to shoot you and Jamie? What does she have to do with your divorce?"

Sandy was indignant, "She has nothing to do with why I want a divorce. Doug's crazy. He came here to kill me and Jamie got in the way."

The sheriff took off her hat and sat it on the patio table. She ran a hand over her head and then sat down, so that she was eye to eye with Sandy. She said softly, "Sandy, I saw the writing on the brick. I know what's going on here. You don't need to hide things from me. I am here to help. The nature of your relationship with Jamie does not matter to me personally, but it is relevant to this case."

Sandy took a deep breath, and then told the truth, "When I asked Doug for a divorce, I explained to him that I had not been happy for a long time. He accused me of sleeping with Jamie, which I had not. He couldn't face the fact that our marriage had just failed. I made the mistake of telling him I was in love with Jamie. That's when he hit me."

The sheriff wrote in her notebook, saying, "I see."

Sandy continued, "Doug threatened Jamie this morning. He must have followed us here from Beth's house, when Jamie came and got me this afternoon. And yes, now I am romantically involved with Jamie."

Sheriff Mason did not respond at all to Sandy's declaration of love for Jamie. She wrote in her notebook and then looked up, with an understanding expression and little smile on her face.

She put her hand out and lifted Sandy's arm, examining the bruising on her wrists. "Do you want to file charges for the first assault?"

Sandy contemplated the ramifications of all that had happened in the last twenty-four hours. Everyone was going to know about her relationship with Jamie, now. She had not wanted to file charges against Doug, for the first attack or the brick throwing incident, because she wasn't ready to face the world as a lesbian.

It was all happening so fast. The cat was out of the bag and Sandy would have no secrets anymore. The whole world would know she was a lesbian by tomorrow morning. She would have to explain it all to her mother and Dawn, before someone else got to them. She prayed Doug hadn't called them already.

Sandy said, "Yes, I want to file charges."

Sheriff Mason stood up and tucked the small notepad back in her pocket. She gave Sandy a light pat on the back, before saying, "Get some pictures of those bruises, preferably with a camera that records dates and times. A good solid domestic violence case will probably make that divorce go a lot smoother. Call me, if you want me to give a statement to your lawyer."

Beth, who had listened to the entire interrogation, spoke up, "What about Doug? What happens when he gets out?"

The sheriff straightened, taking on a more professional air. "We have him in custody, and as soon as he is released from the hospital, he will be taken to Pasquotank County for holding. He will be arraigned and his bail will be set. If he makes bail, he will be free to walk the streets. I suggest Sandy and Jamie have protection orders put in place right away and get that motion detection light up as soon as possible. Jamie said it was in the office."

"I'll get Robby to put it up tomorrow," Beth assured her.

Sandy was growing anxious. She asked, "Okay, now can we go to the hospital?"

"Yes," the sheriff answered, "I will need to talk to you both again to get your written statements, but that can wait until tomorrow."

The sheriff went to talk to Robby. Sandy went in the house, Beth following close behind her. Beth put away Jamie's clothes, in the bedroom, the day they helped Jamie unpack, so she picked out some clean clothes for Jamie. It was dark in the yard, but Beth was sure Jamie's clothes were covered in blood, after seeing Sandy's clothes in the light. She also grabbed pajamas and toiletries, in case Jamie had to stay overnight.

Sandy took out another tee shirt and a fresh pair of sweat pants. She found the towels and washcloths, in the hall closet, and took a shower. The blood had soaked through the tee shirt and dried on her abdomen. It ran off her hands and down her thighs, turning the water pink. Sandy watched as the blood flowed down the tub and circled the drain, reminding her of the shower scene in Psycho, only there wasn't as much, thank God.

Sandy showered and then Beth took pictures, with her I-phone, of the bruises Doug had left imprinted on Sandy's skin. Then Sandy dressed quickly and they were out the door, in fifteen minutes. All of the emergency vehicles were now gone, except for one lone county sheriff's car, but there were no more flashing lights. The driver of that car was talking to Robby when Beth and Sandy walked past them to their respective vehicles.

"Beth, where are you going?" Robby asked.

"To the hospital. I'll be back in a couple of hours, okay?"

"Sure, honey. Be careful." Robby was a good man and the perfect match for Beth. He put his foot down, only when absolutely necessary, other than that, he let Beth be Beth.

The Girl Back Home

They drove separate cars, because Sandy was not leaving the hospital without Jamie. At this point, she didn't know if that would be this morning, it was now after midnight, or later in the day. Sandy didn't think Jamie's injuries were serious enough for the hospital to keep her over night. Sandy had seen Jamie take a line drive to the head, but she got up that time, wiped the blood off and kept playing. Jamie played three more games that day, and only discovered later she had a concussion, but that was twenty-five years ago. Sandy hoped Jamie would bounce back quickly this time, too.

Jamie requested she be taken to Chesapeake Regional, across the Virginia line, less than forty miles away. It was twice as far as the hospital in Elizabeth City, but Jamie didn't like that hospital. When she was in high school, a basketball player on her team took a really bad spill and was dropped off at the hospital, after a game. Her parents met her there. They were told she sprained her ankle. A week later, when there had been no improvement, her parents took her to Chesapeake, where they were told, not only was her ankle broken in two places, so was her knee. After that, Jamie never went to the other hospital. She always asked to go to Chesapeake.

It usually took thirty minutes, in the summertime, to get from Coinjock to Moyock, the last little village before the road passes over the state line, into Great Bridge, Virginia. Currituck County was formed like a long finger, pointing southward from Virginia. The county was surrounded by water on both sides, with waterways and canals cutting through it, like the rough scars on a farmer's finger. More than fifty miles in length, it could take well over an hour to drive from the state line to the southern tip of the county, where a long bridge awaits the tourist crossing over the sound and onto the Dare County beaches. Coinjock sat almost in the middle of the county, forty-five minutes away from Chesapeake hospital.

Sandy pushed her Ford Escape to a speed she thought she could get away with, but there were slow speed zones all along her route and tourist traffic clogging the roadway. Highway 168 had been widened to four lanes, to accommodate the summer traffic, but there were five highway patrolman assigned to scour the long road through the county, looking for drunks and speeders.

Sandy was anxious and pushed her speed beyond the legal limit and then some. Her heart sank when she saw the blue lights in her mirror. She slowed the car, but didn't pull over, because the blue lights passed her and the state patrol car pulled in front of her. Sandy's cell phone rang through the hands free device. She touched the button on the mirror and said, "Hello."

Beth's hoarse laughter echoed through Sandy's vehicle. "How's that for an escort?" she said.

"What?" Sandy didn't understand.

"That's Joe Early, in front of you. I called him and he was on duty. He said, he would be delighted to escort us to the state line," Beth said, continuing to laugh. "Get on up there behind him and let's go."

Chapter Twelve

Jamie was sitting up on the bed, inside a curtained off area of the emergency room. Because she was a still somewhat dazed when she arrived, Jamie had already been scanned and x-rayed, before she fully got her senses back. She wasn't enjoying the sense of pain. The throbbing on the back of her head didn't help. The doctor saw no serious head injury, just a slight concussion and a nasty gash, cut in the shape of a ninety degree angle, where the corner of the two-by-four had cut into her scalp. She was lucky. Either Doug had been too drunk to wield the lumber perilously, or Jamie's skull was extra thick where he hit her.

Jamie had a terrible headache. She felt of the white bandages wrapped around her head, covering the bloody wound that had now been closed. Her hair had been shaved around the area and then fifteen staples were used to seal the cut. Jamie could see her unfocused reflection, in the stainless steel cabinet door, next to her bed. The distortion in the mirror image, with the bandage on her head and white hospital gown draped around her, made her look like a mummy. It made her laugh, which made her head throb more. She was waiting for the extra strength Acetaminophen the nurse had given her, to kick in. Nothing stronger, the doctor had said, narcotics would cloud her neurologic recovery. Jamie didn't care about being cloudy. She just wanted the throbbing to stop.

Her neck was stiff from the blow, so she tried rolling her head around. That was a mistake. She felt like her brain was painfully bruised, and any movement sent shockwaves of throbbing through the inside of her skull. The nurse had gone in search of a top to a set of scrubs, because Jamie's shirt was too bloody, to put back on. The doctor said she could go home, if she promised to take it easy. She had a follow up in ten days to have the staples removed. All she needed now was her discharge papers and a ride home.

Just as Jamie was getting anxious about Sandy not having arrived, she heard Beth, chattering loudly, coming toward her. Jamie couldn't see past the curtain partition, but there was no mistaking that voice. Beth was giving someone the third degree on Jamie's condition. Jamie didn't hear Sandy, but who could get a word in, with Beth in the room. She was relieved to see the nurse pull the curtain back and Sandy appear, followed by Beth, who was still talking.

Jamie and Sandy made quite the pair. Jamie was sitting there with her head all bandaged up and Sandy's face and wrists were multiple shades of purple and black. Sandy went straight to Jamie and hugged her.

Sandy let go of the embrace and studied Jamie's face. "Are you okay?"

"Yes, evidently I have a hard head," Jamie said, smiling now that Sandy was with her. "I have a monster headache and some staples in my head, but nothing serious. The doctor says I'll need to take it easy, for at least ten days."

Sandy's relief rang clear in her voice, as she teased Jamie, "Looks like you're going to need someone to take care of you. As luck would have it, I'm available."

Jamie grinned and forgot about her headache, for the moment, "Are you offering to be my nurse. I always had a thing for nurses. Something about those scrubs is hot."

Beth broke up the flirting, "Oh, Jesus Christ, take her home will you, before you two get busy right here in the emergency room."

Sandy helped Jamie take off the hospital gown and pull the tee shirt Beth packed, gingerly over her head. Jamie received her discharge and aftercare paperwork a few minutes later. The three women stopped just outside of the emergency room doors to talk.

Beth asked Sandy, "I am assuming you are not going to Albemarle to check on Doug's condition."

Sandy looked at Beth, as if she had lost her mind. "Hell, no!"

Beth's husky laugh vibrated out of her chest. "I was just checking," she said.

Beth stayed with Jamie, until Sandy could bring the car around. Then they took Beth to her car and the little caravan started back home. Once they were alone in the car, Jamie leaned over, from the passenger seat, and kissed Sandy on the cheek, which caused a blare from Beth's horn behind them. Jamie stuck her middle finger up, in the glare from Beth's headlights, and kissed Sandy again.

Chapter Thirteen

Jamie spent her first night with Sandy on injured reserve, not what she had planned. Sandy read, from the internet, that Jamie had to refrain from "overexertion or overstimulation" saying they were not helpful for recovery from a concussion. She also mentioned, too much activity, noise, alcohol and caffeine were not recommended. This limited Jamie's activities to not much more than sitting on the couch or lying in the bed. Fortunately, sleep was all she wanted when her head finally hit the pillow.

Jamie's head hurt like hell, when she awoke Monday, around noon. She touched the bandages at the back of her head and it all came rushing back to her. Doug and the two-by-four had done a number on her scalp. Sandy was not in the bed, although she had been. After returning from the hospital, sometime just before sunrise, Jamie went to sleep spooning with Sandy. Sandy woke her every couple of hours, as instructed by the doctor, but for the most part Jamie slept peacefully for the first time in months. As soon as her arm went around Sandy's waist and she pulled her close, Jamie felt her body relax into Sandy's, as if it were a down pillow custom made for her.

Jamie sat up slowly, trying not to shake her bruised brain. It didn't help. The throbbing came in heavy waves, at first, and then subsided into a dull pain behind her eyes, after a few minutes. The next step was standing up, which added its own set of throbbing waves and then settled back down. She took a few cautious steps and felt a little dizzy. She held onto the wall for a second until the woozy feeling passed. Then, discovering that walking didn't add too much pain, she went into the kitchen.

Jamie still did not see Sandy. She went to the restroom, brushed her teeth, which had its on challenges, such as, not moving her head when she brushed, and washed her face. She went back in the bedroom, found a pair of pull on, gray cotton shorts, and went in search of the new love of her life. It was a small house. She shouldn't be too hard to find.

She found Sandy sitting on the sun porch. Jamie could see her through the windows, in the dining room, that opened onto the porch. Sandy was drinking tea and concentrating hard on what she was writing on a note pad, in her lap. Jamie stood still and watched her for a moment. She couldn't get over how beautiful Sandy was, even with her hair messed up from sleeping and wearing Jamie's clothes, which were a bit too big for her.

Jamie knew she had been incredibly lucky to have been given a second chance to fall in love with Sandy. They had both been too young before, especially Jamie, but this time they both knew what they wanted and it appeared to be each other. Jamie smiled, and even though her head was killing her, she felt it was a small price to pay to have the girl of her dreams sitting on her porch. "Thank you, God," she whispered.

Sandy turned and saw Jamie standing in the dining room. She stood up, as Jamie met her out on the porch, giving Jamie a big hug and a kiss, before sitting back down. Jamie took the seat beside her.

"How are you feeling?" Sandy asked.

"My head hurts, but other than that, I don't feel bad at all."

"It's time for some more Tylenol, but I wanted to feed you something first," Sandy said, setting aside the note pad.

Jamie picked up the pad, asking, "What are you working on?"

"A list of things I need to get from my house. I wanted to go over there today, while Doug is still in jail."

Jamie grinned at Sandy, before saying, "I guess I should officially ask you to move in here with me. I know it's not what you're used to, but it will do for now."

"For now, what does that mean? Is this a temporary arrangement?" Sandy asked this with that eyebrow cocked, the look that made Jamie grin every time she did it.

"If my head didn't hurt so bad, I would get down on one knee and ask you to marry me, so trust me, there is nothing temporary about you, as far as I'm concerned. I always planned to build a dream house down here. This house is just a temporary place to live."

Sandy leaned over and kissed Jamie on the cheek. "Yes, I will move in with you. Thank you for asking."

Jamie might have had a head injury, but her lawyer mind was still at work. "Sandy, you need to call a lawyer today. Start the paperwork on your divorce. And, you should know if Doug fights you, your living with me, will come up in court."

"Jamie, it doesn't matter. What's he going to fight me on? I don't want anything I didn't come into that relationship with. He can have the rest. I don't need any money from him, I have my own."

Jamie laughed, "No, honey, you don't ever have to worry about money again."

"Why, what's so funny?"

"Honey, Beth was right, I'm rich," Jamie said, smiling at Sandy.

Intrigued Sandy asked, "How rich?"

"Millionaire, many times over, rich," Jamie answered.

"I knew you had money, but wow. Okay, I don't have to worry about money, so let's just fly to Reno and get a no contest divorce and have it done with."

Jamie's stomach growled loudly. "Can we eat first?"

#

Sandy made Jamie sit at the table, while she made sandwiches for lunch. Jamie felt much better after taking the Tylenol and getting some food on her stomach. They wrapped a trash bag around her head, so the bandage wouldn't get wet and Jamie took a shower. She tried to get Sandy to take one with her, but Sandy said that wasn't a good idea. She was right. If Jamie had gotten Sandy naked, there would have been "overstimulation."

Jamie got dressed, while Sandy was in the shower. Jamie had just slid her feet into some flip flops when Beth's voice sounded from the kitchen, "Is everybody decent in here?"

Jamie answered, "Well, I am. I don't know about you." Jamie walked out of the bedroom to find Beth standing in the kitchen.

"You don't look too bad. At least your eyes didn't turn black. How do you feel?"

"Better than I thought I would. Sandy's in the shower. Do you want some tea?" Jamie offered.

Beth moved over to the kitchen table and set her purse down. She sat down and Jamie joined her, after grabbing a bottle of water from the fridge.

Beth explained why she was there. "Robby's coming with Jake, later. He's going to put up that motion detector light for you. He wanted to know if you needed anything else."

"After last night, I think I want to add another light over on that side," Jamie pointed toward the corner of the house, "where it could shine on the path and this side of the office.

"I'll call him. He can pick one up before he comes this afternoon," Beth said, digging around in her purse, for her phone. She stopped suddenly and looked at Jamie, across the table, her expression one of concern. "Jamie, we haven't had a chance to talk about you and Sandy. Is this what you want? It all happened so fast."

"Yes, this is what I want. I guess Sandy is the person I've always wanted. It just took coming home again, to find her."

At that moment, the bathroom door opened and Sandy stepped out. Her hair was wet and she was toweling it off. She was wearing another one of Jamie's oversized tee shirts and nothing else. Jamie broke into a wide smile at the sight of her. She said, "We have company."

Sandy snatched the towel down and peered over it, suddenly aware she was almost naked. Relieved at the sight of Beth, she said, "I thought you had let me walk out here half naked in front of somebody."

"I am somebody," Beth protested.

"Somebody that hasn't already seen me half naked," Sandy said, dismissing Beth.

Jamie entered the fray, playfully saying, "You've seen her half naked? Do you two need to tell me something?"

"No," the other women replied in unison.

Jamie laughed at their reaction. "Just checking," she said.

"Jamie, I hate to ask you this," Sandy said, "but may I borrow a pair of underwear. I really have to go get some clothes."

Jamie said sweetly, "Sure, they're in the top right hand drawer."

Sandy went to get dressed. Beth shook her head at Jamie, causing Jamie to ask, "What?"

"You two are just too in heat, it radiates off of you. I'm surprised it took as long as it did for you to get her into bed."

From the bedroom, Sandy added, "She didn't try very hard. It might have been sooner."

"Lucky for us, you were able to show restraint, both of you actually," Beth said, loud enough to be sure Sandy heard her.

Sandy came back into the room in the same shirt, but had added the sweats she'd been wearing and her sandals. She had brushed her hair and pulled it back with a clip. She looked refreshed, circling the table to sit beside Jamie. Jamie followed her every move. She was so fascinated with all things Sandy. At this point she couldn't take her eyes away from her. Jamie pecked Sandy on the lips, after she sat down.

Beth said, "See, you are both glowing. It's sickening."

"Don't look, then," Sandy said, pecking the smiling Jamie on the cheek. Then Sandy changed the subject. "I'm glad you're here. I need you to stay with Jamie, while I go get some stuff from the house."

"I don't need a babysitter," Jamie objected.

"Somebody needs to stay with you for at least twenty-four hours. Doctor's orders," Sandy reminded her.

Jamie was concerned. "You shouldn't go to the house alone. You don't know where Doug is."

Beth chuckled, "Well wherever he is, I don't think he's moving real fast. She could out run him." The image of Doug hopping after Sandy became very amusing to Beth, and she started to giggle.

Jamie was not amused, "I'm serious. He doesn't need to walk to shoot a gun."

Beth tried to stifle the giggles, "I know. I'm sorry. It's just funny that's all." She took a breath and gathered her composure. "Okay, we'll wait for Robby and then Sandy and I will go to get her things, while he is here."

That was satisfactory with all parties involved. Beth called Robby and he went to get two more lights for Jamie's back yard. The lights were there already, but they were not motion detection activated and the bulbs must have been blown out, because they didn't come on when Jamie hit the switch. Jamie was thankful that Robby was available to help today. She'd feel a lot better being able to see what moved in her yard.

Jamie had to remember, that now she wasn't behind gated walls with private security guards patrolling the streets. She was out here on her own and needed to become more security conscious. She had been good about locking up, but she had not anticipated getting whacked in the head by a crazed, soon to be ex-husband.

Beth called the Sheriff to make sure Doug was still in custody and was told that he was and would be for at least the night, which she repeated for the benefit of the other two women. He had an arraignment in the morning and then the judge would set bail. Beth thanked Sheriff Mason for the information and hung up.

While they waited for Robby, the three women moved into the living room. Sandy got a pillow and blanket from the bedroom and made Jamie lay down on the couch. She sat so she could hold Jamie's head in her lap and applied an ice bag to the back of Jamie's head. The ice immediately made the pain better and Jamie was able to relax. As they talked, Sandy absentmindedly stroked the pieces of hair sticking out from under the Jamie's bandage. Jamie was content and soon drifted off to sleep, listening to Beth and Sandy talk.

#

Sandy looked down at Jamie, who had fallen peacefully to sleep with a smile on her face. She gently wiped the stray bangs that had fallen out of the bandage, from Jamie's brow. Sandy had so many things happening at once it was overwhelming, but the one thing she was sure of, she did love this woman in her lap. She realized she had been looking down at Jamie, for some time, when Beth cleared her throat. She looked up to see Beth smiling at both of them.

"You do make a beautiful couple," Beth said, in hushed tones, trying not to wake Jamie. "You look like you belong together."

"It feels like that, anyway," Sandy said. "It's like I always knew, she was the one. I know that sounds corny and hard to believe, but when I walked in this house that day and saw her standing there, it just brought back so much."

"Sandy, what are you going to do about your job?" Beth asked. "You know people are going to talk."

"Beth, I have to deal with this one step at a time or I feel overwhelmed and unable to function. That's what was happening to me over the last month. There was too much to take in, you know. I finally got my act together and then this happened with Doug."

"Well, you dealt with asking for the divorce. I brought the lawyer information with me, in case you need it, but then again, Jamie's a lawyer. Bet she'd take it out in trade." Beth had to cover her mouth, to quiet a laugh. She was finding herself exceedingly humorous this afternoon.

"She can't. Conflict of interest. Besides, if he fights me, she'll be brought into it and she has way more to lose than I do," Sandy said.

Beth stopped giggling. "What do you mean?"

"If he finds out how much money she has, he'll try to sue her for 'alienation of affection,' which is ludicrous, but stranger things have happened," Sandy replied.

"You know, I have no idea how much money she has. I know it's a lot, but she's still the same person, she's always been. Except for the luxurious home she used to live in, the expensive clothes and the fancy car, Jamie didn't change at all."

"I just hope she doesn't get pulled into this divorce. She doesn't deserve it. I was leaving Doug, before she came back, it just sped things up."

Beth was thinking hard. Then she said, "I'm glad he hit you. I mean, I'm not glad he hit you, but I'm glad he gave you something to hold over him. The domestic abuse charges should make the divorce a matter of shuffling papers."

Sandy rubbed her hand along Jamie's shoulder, unable to stop touching her. She spoke to Beth, without looking up at her, "I hope some good, will come out of this. I didn't want to hurt Doug. I worried about how this would affect him, but now that he's done this, I don't care what happens to him."

Beth was checking off a mental list, and next was, "Now, how are you going to tell your mother."

Sandy raised her eyes to Beth. "I've been thinking about that and I think I better do it in person, with the whole family present. That way she can't manipulate the story and she certainly can't kill me in front of witnesses."

"Melinda Brown is not going to be happy," Beth warned.

"Believe me, I know. But Beth, I'm almost forty-six years old and I am not going to let her turn this into something perverted."

"Are you ready for how people are going to react? You have thought this through haven't you?"

Sandy thought about her answer. Yes, she had thought this through and she knew without a doubt, that nothing anyone said or did, would change the way she felt about Jamie. As long as they were together, the rest of it was just noise. She said to Beth, "Yes, I have thought it through and I am prepared to deal with it. I'm going to call Dawn tonight and go over to Mother's on Sunday. It's my nephew's birthday and the whole family will be there."

Beth sat back against the winged back chair. "It sounds like you've spent some time planning your coming out party. I hope it all goes well."

183

"I doubt Dawn will have a problem with it. She's so accepting of everyone and her best friend is a lesbian," Sandy added.

Beth perked up, listening. She said, "I think Robby is here. I'll go see." Beth left the room and called back into the living room, "Yep, it's Robby. I'll wait for you outside."

Sandy gently lifted Jamie's head, so she could stand up. Jamie's eyes opened slightly. Sandy said softly, "Go back to sleep, baby. I'll be back in a little bit."

Jamie closed her eyes again and sank back into the pillow. Sandy kissed her on the cheek and whispered into Jamie's ear, "I love you." A little smile crossed Jamie's face and then she drifted off again.

#

Jamie slept for two hours on the couch. When she woke up, there were people talking in the kitchen. She was a little disoriented, having trouble waking up entirely. Jamie sat up and put her feet on the floor. The room didn't spin out of control. So far so good, she thought. Her head did not pound with every heartbeat, as before. Dull thuds had replaced the throbbing. The cut, on the back of her head, was the source of most of the pain. She needed another ice bag. The one she had was warm and wet from condensation.

Jamie stood up, steadied herself and went toward the voices. Her first steps were a little shaky and she didn't feel quite right, her sense of balance askew. She let momentum take her to the door frame, separating the two rooms. She found Beth, Robby, Jake and Sandy, all seated at the kitchen table. As soon as Jamie appeared, Sandy stood up and came toward her.

"How are you feeling?" Sandy asked.

"Better," Jamie replied, but she couldn't let go of the door frame. She was weaker now than this morning. That knock on the head had really taken its toll.

It must have been evident to Sandy, as well, that Jamie wasn't really better. Sandy guided Jamie to a chair and made her sit down. Once seated, the fogginess cleared slightly and the uneasiness, temporarily subsided. Jamie was thinking that if she ever saw Doug again, she might just return the favor.

Robby interrupted the plotting of Jamie's revenge, when he said, "You have motion lights on the front of the office and both back corners of the house. If something moves out there, you'll know it."

"Thank you, Robby, and you too, Jake," Jamie said, her voice a bit fragile.

Robby answered back, in his slow drawl and nonchalant attitude, "Not a problem, your welcome."

Jamie turned to Sandy, who was bustling around the kitchen, pulling salad stuff out of the refrigerator. There was no real inflection in Jamie's question, as if she were so tired she could barely speak, "Did you get everything you needed from your house?"

"I did. I put most of it in the guest bedroom."

Jamie couldn't imagine where in the guest bedroom. Another bedroom set, with dressers and drawers, had not been on Jamie's list of high priorities. She had assumed she would be living alone, for a while at least, and was not expecting guests, but then, she had not anticipated Sandy either. There was nothing in there, except an empty closet.

Jamie wished she felt better, so she could help Sandy feel at home. She said, "You didn't just throw your stuff on the floor in there, did you?"

Beth joined in, "We didn't throw it. We stacked it."

"Sandy, just move my things around, I'm really not that particular about where things go, and anyway Beth put my clothes away. She knows where more of my stuff is than I do."

Sandy explained, "I wanted you to be awake, so you can help me find places to put my things."

185

The Girl Back Home

"Okay," Jamie said, weakly. She just didn't feel well, and there were too many people, and the lights were too bright. "Yes," she told herself, "you have a concussion." There was a beautiful woman moving into Jamie's home and all she wanted to do was lay her head down on the table and go to sleep.

She put her elbows on the table, clasping her hands together to form a pyramid, and then rested her chin on her entwined fingers. Jamie focused on the wood pattern in the small oak kitchen table. It curved and turned, creating the yellow hues and red tones that made the graining so distinctive.

Sandy was suddenly hovering over Jamie. She put her hand on Jamie's shoulder and bent down to look at Jamie's eyes. "Jamie, are you okay?" she asked.

"No, not really. Ouch." Jamie raised her head up too quickly and it made her neck hurt. She reached back and massaged her neck.

Now, all the other places she hurt were doing roll call, about her body. Her head must have been aching so badly, earlier, that she hadn't noticed the rest of it, until now. She wanted to take a long hot soaking bath and for god sake, could she please wash her hair? Jamie had held up well through the whole Doug event and aftermath, but she could feel herself starting to fall apart.

Sandy, whose concern continued to grow, said, "Hey, let's get you back in bed. I'll bring your food to you."

Jamie ignored the fact that other people were in the room. She was almost childlike when she said, "Can I please take a bath?"

Jamie stood up, collected her balance and took the few steps needed to reach the bathroom. She didn't say goodbye or good night, she just left, followed by Sandy.

Jamie heard Beth say, "I'll call you later," and she wasn't sure to whom she was talking. Jamie was just out of it. Fatigue had set in. Jamie lacked the energy to raise the tee shirt past the bandage, without a lot of difficulty.

A soft gentle voice spoke to her, "Jamie, let me help you." The tone of that voice said, "Let me take care of you." Sandy was quiet and calm with her movements. She tenderly undressed Jamie. Jamie didn't resist. She watched silently, as Sandy turned on the water in the tub, checking the temperature before turning back to Jamie.

"You look so tired, honey," Sandy said, still in her gentle voice.

Jamie blinked a couple of times, saying, "I am. I don't know, it just hit me all of a sudden, how absolutely beat up I feel."

Sandy reached into the cabinet under the sink, producing a bottle of bath salts, Jamie did not recognize. Sandy poured some of the salts in the roiling water under the faucet. She grinned at Jamie. "I only brought the important stuff," she said.

Jamie was so caught up in how bad she felt, she had not stopped to think about what Sandy must be going through. Sandy and Beth had packed up Sandy's life, as she knew it, in two hours, and moved it all to Jamie's, while she lay passed out on the couch. Jamie was naked now, sitting on the toilet, waiting for the water to fill the bathtub more. When Sandy crossed back by Jamie, to put the bath salts away, Jamie reached out and grabbed her, pulling Sandy down on her lap.

Sandy was caught off guard. Jamie had been so wounded just a moment ago and now she was grabbing her. She almost lost her balance and plopped down on Jamie's lap. "Stop," she said, "you're going to hurt yourself."

Jamie said, "Ssh, come here." Jamie studied Sandy's face. "How are you? This has been quite a forty-eight hour period for you. Are you okay?"

Sandy smiled into Jamie's eyes. "I'm better than okay." Sandy leaned her lips to Jamie's and they kissed sweetly, softly. Then Sandy stood up, saying, "Come on, Romeo, and get in the tub."

Jamie was touching the bandage on her head, when she said, "Can we take this off now? Didn't they say I could wash my hair?"

"Yes, with baby shampoo or just warm water. I think you're going to have to go with the warm water." Sandy moved to stand over Jamie, who was trying to find the end of the bandage. She said, "Sit still, I'll do it."

Jamie allowed Sandy to remove the bandage and then stood to see her reflection, in the medicine cabinet, while Sandy held a mirror behind her. Jamie moved her head around, examining the shaved area, which wasn't so bad, her other hair would cover most of it. The nurse had been nice enough to leave as much hair as she could. The nasty gash, with its shiny staples, was surrounded by matted bloody hair.

"Yuck," Jamie said.

"It's not that bad, really," Sandy commented, trying to make Jamie feel better.

"No, the blood. Yuck. You got to get this off of me." Jamie was more concerned about the blood clotted in her hair than the actual wound. It just looked gross.

Sandy found Jamie amusing. "In the tub, you," she said, grinning at Jamie, the big baby.

Jamie obeyed and stepped into the tub. The heat immediately began to soothe her, as she lowered her sore body, into the lavender scented water. "Just lay there and relax. Here's a towel for the back of your neck." Sandy handed a rolled up towel to Jamie. "I'm going to make a chef salad for dinner. Is that okay?"

Already settling back, Jamie said, "Sounds great," and let the water envelope her.

"I'll come back and wash your hair, and then we'll have supper. After that, you are going back to bed."

"Sandy?"

Sandy, who was on her way out, turned back to her patient. "Yes?"

Jamie looked up from her towel pillow. "Hey, I'm sorry our first days together have been so... crazy. I'll make it up to you, if you'll go with me to Durham, next week."

Sandy cocked her head to one side, asking, "Why are you going to Durham?"

"I'm closing a case, on Tuesday. I have to leave here Sunday. You come with me. I have a reservation for a suite at the Washington Duke Inn." Jamie paused and grinned. "Let me wine and dine you."

"That sounds wonderful, but I have that family thing on Sunday, where I intended to tell them about you." Sandy wanted to go to Durham. Jamie could see it in her face, but she was committed to telling her family, right away. Sandy said, "I need to do that. It's important."

Sandy squatted down, so she and Jamie were more eye to eye. She put her hand in the water, pushing gently waves of warmth over Jamie's chest. Jamie wanted to take her new girl out on the town and make her feel special. Jamie also knew she should be with Sandy, after she made such a huge announcement to her family, but Jamie could not postpone this meeting.

She pleaded, "Come after, you're done. I'll rent you a car, so you can drive up and ride back with me. You can fly. Whatever you want to do. We can stay as long as you want."

"Why can't we wait until, after I tell my family, Sunday afternoon? Then we could go together."

The Girl Back Home

Jamie tried to sound casual, when she said, "I have to meet Mary Ann's lawyer, to finalize the dissolving of our legal bonds, so to speak. This dinner was set up a long time ago."

"Will Mary Ann be there?"

"I honestly don't know," Jamie said, sliding, as far as she dared, down into the warm water.

Sandy watched her fingers in the water for a moment, and then stood up. "We'll see," she said and went to make the salad.

Jamie knew from her experience with Mary Ann and Tara that "we'll see" meant, "I need to think about this, and then I'll tell you what we are going to do. That was fine with Jamie. She closed her eyes, relaxed into the water, and concentrated on not feeling anything.

#

Sandy faced her fear, by leaving the bathroom. Since the beginning, since Jamie came back into her life, she had lived with the trepidation that Mary Ann would come to take Jamie away. It had actually happened and Jamie was still here with her, not back in Durham. Still, Sandy kept the smallest doubt tucked away. The doubt that she could withstand an all out attempt, by the stunningly beautiful Mary Ann, to reclaim Jamie's heart. Look how easy it had been for Mary Ann to get Jamie into bed.

Sandy lived with that fear, because this was so new, it was happening so fast, as if she and Jamie just stopped living those other lives and began to live this one. For all Sandy knew, Jamie could be living out a high school crush and then wake up a week or a month from now, to realize what she'd done. What Jamie had given up could not compare to Sandy's little country world. Jamie going to Durham, possibly to meet Mary Ann, did nothing to ease Sandy's fears.

Sandy was facing her own marriage ending, but somehow hers was so cut and dry compared to Jamie and Mary Ann's split. There had been doubt on both Mary Ann and Jamie's part, when their relationship reached the breaking point. There was no doubt in Sandy's mind that she was done with Doug, completely. Sandy could only hope Jamie had reached the same conclusion about Mary Ann.

All the while she was thinking, Sandy chopped vegetables for the salad and mixed in sliced boiled eggs, turkey and ham, with bright red cherry tomatoes on top. She set the table in the kitchen for two, complete with a candle she found in the hall closet. Sandy reminded herself that Jamie had taken this giant leap of faith, with her, into this unknown future. By the time she was ready to go back to Jamie, in the tub, she had made up her mind that Jamie should go to Durham on her own. Maybe Sandy could join Jamie later, but Sunday they would both be dealing with huge events, with irreversible consequences, on their own.

Sandy wanted Jamie to finish with Mary Ann, once and for all, because she could hear the pain in Jamie's voice, when she spoke to Mary Ann on the phone. Sandy heard Jamie's hesitation to tell Mary Ann that Sandy was with her, now. It was sweet and endearing of Jamie not to want to hurt Mary Ann, but Sandy needed Jamie to wrap it up. Sandy had not been a lesbian long, but she was aware of the tendency to let the ex hang around, until the breakup gradually became a reality. Sandy would prefer to keep Mary Ann at a distance.

Sandy turned the lights down, in the kitchen, so the brightness would not hurt Jamie's head. She looked around. It wasn't the romantic first dinner she'd wanted, but it would have to do. Her mind made up, she headed back to Jamie.

#

The Girl Back Home

Jamie heard Sandy return to the bathroom. She opened one eye, looking up at Sandy, who was smiling down at her. The few minutes Jamie had spent in the rapture of the hot bath, had done wonders for her body and her spirit. The tension no longer coursed through her body, as her muscles released their strangle hold on nerves in her neck and lower back. Peace fell over her, when she saw Sandy standing there. She smiled and slid up out of the water to a sitting position.

"Hey there," Jamie said, to Sandy. "That was amazing. Thank you."

"Are you ready for me to wash your hair?"

Jamie said, "Yes, please," eagerly.

"Do you want to sit in the tub or stand in the shower?" Sandy asked.

Jamie, who was already pulling herself into a standing position, pulled the stopper on the tub and winked at Sandy. She was feeling much better. She asked Sandy, "How are you going to wash my hair, if I'm in the shower?"

Sandy smiled and cocked her head just enough to let Jamie know, she wasn't going to fight her on this. Sandy said, "Well, I guess I'm going to have to get naked and get in there with you."

Jamie reached out and pulled Sandy's shirt off, over her head and watched as Sandy did the rest. Jamie wasn't miraculously healed enough for a full on sexual episode there in the shower, but she was well enough to hold Sandy's naked body against hers and dance in and out of the warm water, from the raining shower head. Jamie kissed Sandy, thinking she could never get enough of this woman. Sandy moved against her, in a way that said, I can't get enough of you either. They melded together, kissing slow and long, fitted like a glove.

Jamie's head went in and out of the warm water. Neither of them noticed, because their eyes were closed, that the blood from her scalp was running out of her hair and down their bodies to the drain. Jamie opened her eyes to see the crimson streaks running down her arms and onto Sandy.

She pushed Sandy back. "I'm getting blood all over you."

Sandy was intent on continuing the kissing; she grabbed Jamie and pulled her to her. Sandy said, through her quickening breaths "I've already had your blood all over me. Kiss me."

Jamie kissed her. Then Jamie made love to her, there against the shower wall. Sandy's hands clutched at Jamie's back, as she came quickly, shuddering in Jamie's arms, whimpering against her neck. Jamie held her until the shudders stopped. Jamie shuddered along with Sandy, as shockwaves shook her body.

Dinner was late, Sandy was satisfied and Jamie began to feel much better.

Chapter Fourteen

Jamie spent the remainder of the week recuperating and loving Sandy. Jamie couldn't remember being this happy, not ever. It was almost frightening, because she knew they couldn't sustain this level of bliss forever. Jamie knew that in the beginning of a love affair chemicals flew about the body making each partner more attractive to the other, until the affair grew longer and their bodies stopped making those chemicals. Then the overdriven passions would wane and the partners would settle into a more normal existence.

Somehow, Jamie didn't see them settling down for a good long while. They had so much lost time to make up. Jamie was fascinated by all things Sandy. She made Sandy fill her in on the years she had missed, things she never knew about Sandy, like, how she got that scar on her knee, what it was like having a baby, why she wanted to be a librarian, anything was fascinating to Jamie. She could gaze at Sandy talking for hours and never grow tired of what she saw and heard. Jamie was simply captivated by this woman.

Jamie would never have left the bedroom all week, if Sandy had not made her go to the courthouse with her, on Tuesday, to file protective orders against Doug. Sandy also made Jamie get up and run, after Wednesday, because she said, if the sex didn't kill Jamie then running wouldn't either. So, Jamie got out of bed and did a little work in her office and followed Sandy all over the county, shopping for things they needed.

However, being out of the bedroom did not stop Jamie from undressing Sandy, every chance she got and to her delight and joy, Sandy sometimes had to stop what she was doing and undress Jamie, too. They christened the office several times and every other room in the house. There was a mutual lust between them that frankly had been missing, in her relationship with Mary Ann. Jamie was right to crave it. Sandy made that all very clear to Jamie every time she touched her. Sandy was what Jamie had wanted all along.

On Wednesday night, Jamie called Mary Ann to get the details of the meeting on Sunday.

Mary Ann had been quiet and unchallenging, at first. "I won't be there," she said.

"Okay," Jamie said, "I guess that's it then."

"Yes, I guess so," Mary Ann replied, weakly. Then she asked, "Jamie, are you sure? We don't have to do this, yet. It can wait. Let's just separate for awhile and then see how it goes."

Jamie couldn't help the condescending tone in her voice, when she replied, "Mary Ann, this isn't a separation. We are not getting back together."

"You could change your mind... I did," Mary Ann said, the tenor of her voice changing, in mid sentence, as she caught a quick breath.

Jamie could tell Mary Ann was trying not to cry. It still hurt Jamie to hear that in Mary Ann's voice. Jamie asked, "Are you alright?"

"No, I can't believe this is happening. I know I'm the one who started dissolving our relationship, but I never thought it would go this far."

Jamie spoke softly to Mary Ann, "I'm so sorry that it happened this way, but we both know it was going to happen, eventually."

"No, I don't know that Jamie. I don't know what happened. I thought we were strong enough to make it through anything. I planned on loving you my entire life. I thought we were going to grow old together. Now, what do I do?"

"Mary Ann, you are a beautiful woman, smart, and sexy. You will have no trouble finding someone who will love you..."

Mary Ann had heard enough, her pride wouldn't let her listen to more. "Oh, please, I don't need your dating advice and don't give me that, 'I just want you to be happy,' shit, either."

The tone of the conversation had taken a turn. The very one Jamie had not wanted to take, again. She took a breath and let it blow out slowly, into the receiver. Jamie wanted Mary Ann to hear it, to understand that she was growing tired of these repeated attempts to engage her in an emotional struggle for her heart. Mary Ann was counting on the guilt Jamie still felt to overpower her obsession with Sandy. Mary Ann didn't have any details about Sandy and Jamie, unless Beth was talking to her. Jamie didn't believe Beth would get involved in this little triangle. She would have Jamie's back above all others, of that Jamie was sure.

Jamie finally came up with a plan. "Mary Ann, after I meet with your lawyer, would you have dinner with me at the hotel. We could talk then."

Mary Ann brightened. "Okay, what time?"

"How about eight?"

"Great, I'll see you then," Mary Ann said, cheerfully. Then adding, "I love you, Jamie," she hung up the phone.

Jamie decided the best way to tell Mary Ann about Sandy was face to face, in a public place. Mary Ann would have to behave in the Washington Duke Inn, among its English antiques and fine paintings. Jamie had already reserved a table in the Fairview Dining room, for the meeting with Joseph White, Mary Ann's attorney. It was a cocktail meeting, where they would exchange amenities, have a drink, and swap signatures. They would smile at each other and then, their business done, part ways. Jamie would just need to extend the reservation through dinner and beyond. The beyond being, ever how long it took to make Mary Ann understand, Jamie wasn't coming back.

Jamie didn't tell Sandy about the dinner date. Why make her worry? Sandy would have worried, if her reaction to Jamie just going to Durham was any indication. If she had asked, Jamie would have told her, but she didn't. In fact, neither of them brought Mary Ann's name up at all. Now it was Saturday night and Jamie was leaving tomorrow around noon. Sandy was busy in the bathroom and Jamie had already gotten into bed. All the doors and windows were locked and there had been no further intrusions by Doug, after her got out on bail. All the lights were off in the house except for the night light, in the hallway, in front of the bathroom door, and a dim bedside light on Sandy's side of the bed.

Jamie saw the bathroom light against the hallway wall, as the door was opened, and then the light clicked off. Only the glow of the nightlight cast shadows, as Sandy moved through the light, coming toward Jamie. Jamie was leaning up against the pillows, behind her. The sheets that were just barely covering her naked chest, slipped down when she saw Sandy and sat up in the bed.

Sandy had spent the time in the bathroom making herself more desirable, as if that were possible or necessary. Her hair was perfectly wispy enough to look like the wind blew it there. She had on only a touch of makeup to accentuate her natural beauty. Jamie didn't even notice the bruises anymore. It looked like Sandy was moving in slow motion toward Jamie, reminiscent of some fantasy Jamie had long ago, about how Sandy would come to her one day, and there she was.

The Girl Back Home

The white satin slip she wore was appliquéd with lace, matching the pattern on the kimono wrap, draped over her shoulders. Sandy moved, as if she knew Jamie was watching and for good reason. Jamie had not taken her eyes off Sandy for seven days. She felt the smile creeping up from the corners of her mouth, until Jamie was in a full blown grin. The grin was accompanied by a dip of her head and raising of her eyebrows, in the best come hither expression she could muster. Sandy smiled, showing her dimples, stopping in the door frame to pose and tease Jamie.

Sandy said, "From that expression on your face, I gather you like what you see."

"Do I really need to answer that," Jamie said.

"No, I can see that you do. Now, while you're gone, I want you to remember, this is what's waiting at home," Sandy said, playing the perfect tease.

Jamie had tried all week to get Sandy to come with her. It was no use asking again. Instead she said, "I know exactly what's waiting at home, you don't have to worry. I'll be back as soon as I can, believe me. I don't want to leave you here."

Sandy couldn't play tease anymore. She closed the distance in a flash. Jamie met her in the center of the bed on her knees and they came together in an embrace. Sandy kissed Jamie so deeply it made Jamie's head spin. Jamie pulled the kimono off Sandy's shoulders, sliding it down her arms, dropping it behind Sandy, onto the bed. She laid Sandy down on the bed and pulled her close, leaning on her elbow, so she could see into Sandy's eyes.

"You have no idea what you do to me," Jamie said, in a whisper.

"I think I have a pretty good idea."

Jamie kissed Sandy gently, but long and sweet. She couldn't stop kissing Sandy. She wasn't sure how she was going to make it three days without her.

The way she craved this woman was all consuming. The pure physical want and need was overpowering. Getting in that car and driving away from Sandy, was going to be easier said than done. Sandy was making it harder every second she lay in Jamie's arms.

"Everything I can think of to say, sounds so corny in my head," Jamie said.

Sandy reached up and pushed the hair back behind Jamie's ear, so she could see Jamie's face. She smiled and said, "Like what? Tell me."

Jamie bit her lip and bared her soul, "Sandy, I've dreamed about you all my life, well, at least since the first time I ever saw you. Through the years those dreams changed, but it was always you. Nothing I ever dreamed could compare with what's happened between us."

Sandy was playful, grinning, showing her dimples, she said, "Oh yeah, nothing. You have no fantasies left for me to fulfill?"

Jamie chuckled. "We're not talking fantasies. We'll get to those later."

"Why not now?" Sandy asked this, while sliding her hand up to Jamie's chest, circling one of Jamie's nipples with her finger.

Jamie's breath caught in her throat, as she tried to say, "Because, I'm trying to tell you something."

Sandy was tired of talking. "Show me," she whispered.

Jamie bent her lips to Sandy's. Sandy pulled Jamie down on top of her and they melted into each other. Jamie felt her head spinning and her heart leaving her body, to beat side by side with Sandy's. It was not her own to control, anymore. Sandy had her heart, to do with, as was her want, because Jamie realized this was all beyond her power. She surrendered to the higher authority. This one, this one woman, was the one she had been created to love. Their souls had been made especially for one another and they had found each other not once, but twice.

199

The Girl Back Home

In Jamie's mind, the gospel choir sang and the preacher said, "This was meant to be." Fate had taken the power out of Jamie's hands, and landed her right where she needed to be, at just the right time. How often does that happen, in a lifetime? The choir reached a crescendo, when Sandy slid down Jamie's body, kissing her skin as she went. The preacher said, "Thank you, God."

Jamie added, breathlessly, "Amen."

Chapter Fifteen

Jamie drove out of the driveway with a lump in her throat. She really didn't want to leave Sandy alone to deal with her family announcement, but she had to go to Durham, she had no choice. Judges didn't wait for private lives and busy lawyers only met other busy lawyers on Sundays, because there was no other time to meet. Jamie had to keep this appointment tonight or wait another month to finalize her life with Mary Ann.

Then, of course, there was the dinner with Mary Ann she had to face. Maybe she should have been worried, but she wasn't. How big a fuss could Mary Ann make in a public place? She would quietly tell Mary Ann to move on with her life, because Jamie certainly had. This morning, Sandy had made them breakfast in bed and then made love to Jamie one more time, before she packed her bags. On yeah, Jamie had definitely moved on.

Jamie pushed the car up to speed, out on the highway. Top down, radio blasting, and the Carolina sun beating down on her shoulders, she turned west away from the coast. She smiled at the memory of this morning, as she held Sandy close to her and told her she loved her.

Sandy had smiled back and said, "I've always loved you. I know that now. There's never been anyone else."

#

The Girl Back Home

Sandy watched Jamie drive away and let out a big sigh. Alone, she now had to face her family, who were, at this moment, gathering at her mother's house. Dawn was even driving down at Sandy's urging. Sandy only wanted to say this once and be done with it. She went inside to dress for the party and her crucifixion, which she was sure, would shortly follow her announcement.

Sandy wanted so badly to be in that car with Jamie, speeding away from here. It would have been so easy to put off telling her family, but she had to do this now, before word spread of her new living arrangements. She owed them that much, at least. Sandy had just stepped into the shower when her cell phone rang.

She answered, after looking at the caller ID, "Honey, you just left."

"I wanted to make sure I had the right cell phone number," Jamie's voice said, over the wind noise, in the phone. "You know, I'm still close enough to come back and get you."

Sandy closed her eyes and fought off the urge to say, yes, please come get me, instead she said, "Baby, please don't tempt me. I have to do this. It's the only way I can catch everyone together, in one place. It will be easier this way."

"I miss you, already," Jamie said, over the wind.

"I miss you, too. Now, concentrate on driving. I have to get dressed."

"You mean, you're naked," Jamie said, laughing. "I might have to come back anyway."

"No, you keep driving. Call me tonight, after your meeting. I love you. Now, hang up."

"It will be after nine, probably. I love you, too. Bye."

They already had that conversation, in the driveway, before she left, but Sandy smiled at Jamie's inability to be gone ten minutes, without talking to her. Sandy had no doubt that Jamie was infatuated with her. Sandy also knew that Jamie would see Mary Ann in Durham. Jamie had not mentioned she would, but Sandy knew the woman she had seen in Jamie's bedroom doorway, wearing nothing but a sheet, was not walking away, without one more go at Jamie Basnight. Sandy was wise enough not to underestimate Dr. Best. Sandy could only hope that Jamie would come home to her, in the end.

Currently, Sandy had bigger fish to fry. Sandy's grandmother had been the grand dame of this branch of the wide and vast Formbee family tree. At her passing, Sandy's mother had taken up the cause. With that cause, came a certain decorum she expected her family to uphold, as well. She had been mortified when Sandy got pregnant, in high school, but being a lesbian was going to send her over the moon.

Sandy's two older brother's were of no concern to Sandy. They had their own crosses to bear. Her middle brother, John, went through women and gallons of liquor, at about the same pace. How he held down a job, Sandy would never know. Even with his drinking, he was on that tractor plowing fields, every day, half-lit, she was sure. Her oldest brother, Robert, the lawyer, couldn't keep it in his pants and had caused quite a few scandals and at least one illegitimate child. Sandy felt safe that she wouldn't be judged by them.

On the contrary, her brothers would be ecstatic that Sandy finally did something wrong, again. She had been the good one a long time now. It would be refreshing, to them, to know she wasn't mother's perfect child, with just a slight blemish. The blemish could never be removed. Now, Sandy was going to change the blemish to a big black spot. An image of big black spots covering her face, in all the family photos, made Sandy laugh, as she applied her makeup.

Sandy finished dressing and checked herself in the mirror. The bruises on her face had faded and the makeup covered most of it, but it could still be seen. That would make leaving Doug self explanatory. She wore a simple sundress and white sandals. It was just a kid's birthday party, not an occasion. She looked radiant, if she had to say it herself, despite the bruising. Her complexion glowed and she looked relaxed and happy. Satisfied with her choice of dress, Sandy grabbed her purse and headed out the door, for the short trip down the road to Mother's house.

On the way, Sandy tried out different ways to say it. "I'm gay." "I'm a lesbian." She didn't think she'd go with either of those. Her mother wouldn't get, "I'm gay," and she'd have to explain. "I'm a lesbian," didn't roll off her tongue, as well as, "I'm in love with a woman." That's what she'd say, "I'm in love with a woman." That was all they need to know, but they would want the details. Sandy would divulge as little as possible to the group, but she would tell Dawn everything. Maybe, she should tell Dawn before everyone else.

Sandy would never get the chance to tell Dawn first. When she pulled into her mother's driveway and followed it around to the back of the house, she saw that most everyone had already arrived. The family had gathered underneath the tall oak trees, by the picnic tables. All eyes turned to her, as she pulled the car to a stop. The crowd parted, and there, at the table, sat Doug with a very startled looking Dawn sitting beside him.

The anger hit Sandy like a bolt of lightning. She was out of the car and moving toward the picnic table, before she knew what was happening. Gone were all the plans to make a calm announcement to the family. Sandy was beyond angry, when she stopped in front of Doug, still seated beside Dawn.

"How dare you?" Sandy shook her finger in Doug's face. "How dare you come here? Get out and stay away from my family."

Sandy's mother interjected, "Wait a minute Sandy. Doug was just explaining what happened."

"What happened is, he hit me and then he damn near killed me, that's what happened. There is a protective order against him and he's out on bail for attempted murder. Did he tell you that?"

Dawn looked at her mother. Sandy could see Dawn's eyes tracing their way around the bruising on her face and around her wrists. She stood up and went to Sandy. Sandy had begun to cry. Dawn put her arms around her mother and Sandy pulled her daughter close.

Sandy said, "I'm sorry you had to find out this way. I was going to tell you today"

Dawn said nothing. She let go of Sandy and turned around to speak to Doug. She said, "Doug, if you thought for one second, that coming here to tell my mother's family that she left you for a woman was going to make us forget that you abused my mother..."

Sandy saw where this was going and chimed in, "and shot at her."

Dawn looked back at her mother. "He shot at you?"

Sandy nodded yes.

Dawn went back to berating Doug. "You shot at my mother. You asshole. I'm glad she left you for a woman and if she's happy, then more power to her." Dawn looked around at the rest of the family. "And you all knew about this, didn't you? You let him come here. I am so glad I live in Richmond."

Sandy's mother started to say something, but Dawn cut her off, "Grandma, Mom has been making you happy for years. I think it's about time she made herself happy for a change." Dawn turned back to Sandy, "Mom, I'm proud of you and I can't wait to meet her."

Sandy, who had never been prouder of her daughter in her life, smiled and said, "You already know her. She used to be your baby sitter."

#

The Girl Back Home

Jamie drove straight to the Washington Duke Inn, when she arrived in Durham. She gave the valet her car and paid to have her bags sent up to her suite. She checked in and then spoke with the concierge to make sure her reservations were being taken care of. She also asked the concierge to have a bottle of champagne, Taittinger 1998, sent to the table at eight p.m., because it was Mary Ann's favorite and Jamie felt like splurging a bit, on their last dinner together. She tipped well and headed up to her room. She still had time for a workout and a swim before the evening's events. The recreation facilities here were incredible and the view of the golf course made Jamie miss the greens. She had not thought to put her clubs in the car. Jamie had been so busy playing kissy face with Sandy that she hoped she had remembered to pack underwear.

The floor plan of Jamie's suite was called the Terrace. It had a seating area, dining table and huge king sized bed. It was the same style suite she and Mary Ann had stayed in once, while the house was being worked on. Jamie liked the big dining room table to spread out her work and she was a creature of habit, so when she made the reservation, almost six weeks ago, she chose the same suite.

Her bags had been unpacked and her clothing hung up or stored in drawers. Her toiletries remained in their bag, but it had been placed on the bathroom counter, in the master bedroom. There was something to be said about luxury. Jamie appreciated the finer side of life a little more, now that she had been away from it for awhile. There was a clean elegance to everything around her. The décor was inspired by traditional English country inns, and had a warm homelike feel to it.

Jamie changed into workout clothes. Before leaving the room, she tried Sandy on her cell phone. She got voicemail, but didn't leave a message. She went down to the fitness center to work off the stiffness from the drive up and the cravings for Sandy, her body was putting her through. No matter what she was doing, Sandy was never far from her mind. Her capacity to concentrate was in serious peril. ADHD or not, Sandy was detrimental to Jamie's ability to think past her naked body. She was so lost in thought; she walked by the entrance to the fitness center, and had to go back.

#

Sandy sat on the end of the dock, dangling her feet in the water. Dawn sat beside her, doing the same thing. This was where they came to share big news, good or bad. Sandy brought Dawn down here to tell her, she and her father were divorcing, although she was too young to remember that. They had come here together when Dawn's father moved to Texas, without saying goodbye, when Dawn's heart was broken for the first time, when Sandy told Dawn she was marrying Doug and many of life's other challenging moments in between. It made sense that they would come here now, to talk about what just happened at Sandy's mother's house.

Sandy patted her daughter on the knee. "Thanks for sticking up for me back there."

"No problem, mom. He deserved it. They all did," Dawn said and hugged Sandy again. "So, tell me what's going on with you."

"It's a long story," Sandy sighed.

"I've got time. I didn't bring the girls, because I had a feeling, from your phone call, that this was going to be a dock day."

Sandy smiled at her daughter, the grown woman beside her, looking so much like Sandy did at her age. She was proud of Dawn. She was a beautiful, educated young woman, with a happy family and a great job, with James River. Dawn was wise beyond her years, because she and Sandy had grown up together, each in their own way.

The Girl Back Home

Sandy kicked at the water, sending spray out in front of the dock. It scattered a small school of minnows across the surface. Sandy watched their reflections, on the water, ripple with the waves. Without looking up, she began, "I have never regretted one day of being your mother. When I say, I've made some mistakes in my life. Please don't ever think that you were one of them."

"I know that, mom."

"Okay then, well, this story starts way back when your father and I were getting a divorce. A girl from the high school started playing on my softball team occasionally and I asked her to babysit for you, while I attended class two nights a week."

Dawn started to say something, but Sandy stopped her.

"Let me get this all out at once, before you ask me any questions," Sandy said. "Jamie Basnight was her name. We became good friends. She was seventeen and brilliant and I was only twenty-one and lonely. Nothing happened between us, but it could have. I took you and moved away, before anything did."

"I don't remember her," Dawn said.

"You were just barely five. Anyway, I pushed those feelings way back somewhere and lived the life I thought I was supposed to live. I just assumed everyone felt like I did. Like what they had should be enough. That feeling incomplete was just how I was supposed to feel."

"Mom, that's so sad."

"I know that now, but back then I didn't know any different. One day, about four weeks ago, Jamie Basnight walked back into my life, after twenty-five years. Actually, I walked into her kitchen and in that instant those twenty-five years vanished. I was standing there looking at her and it all came rushing back."

"Have you always been a lesbian?"

"No, I really didn't think about it. Like I said, I put that away and threw away the key, I thought."

Dawn laughed at her mother. "You can't really do that, you know. Lock away part of who you are."

"Okay, smarty pants," Sandy said, flicking water on Dawn with her fingers.

Shielding herself from the water, Dawn giggled and said, "Finish the story."

"I was already trying to figure out what to do about my marriage to Doug. I was beginning to be resigned to living out the rest of my days with him, even though I knew I wasn't happy. Then Jamie came home and I had to get out of my marriage. Nothing happened, really, between Jamie and me, before I asked Doug for a divorce, but I was already in love with her. I told him so and he hit me."

"That rat bastard."

"The next evening, he tried to kill both Jamie and me."

"That's when he shot at you?" Dawn asked.

"Yes. He hit Jamie in the head with a two-by-four. She still has the staples in her head."

"He's being charged, isn't he?"

"Yes," Sandy reassured her, "he's going to have to go to court and possibly spend some time behind bars. I don't care, as long as he stays away from me."

"Tell me about Jamie, Mom. What's she like? Where's she been for twenty-five years?"

Sandy felt her face blushing when she started describing Jamie, "She's forty-two and gorgeous. A little taller than me, with blonde hair and baby blue eyes. Jamie is an attorney, a very successful one, and she's moved back to Currituck, from Durham, to be a country lawyer."

"Mom, you're glowing. She really makes you happy, doesn't she?"

"Yes, she really does."

Dawn asked, "Where is she? Is she waiting for you at her house?"

"No, she had to go to Durham for a few days. She wanted me to come with her, but I had to tell the family." Sandy paused, kicking at the water again, "She said, she wanted to wine and dine me."

Dawn began to stand up, saying, "What's stopping you from going now?"

"Well, nothing, I guess."

"Then go. Let your new girlfriend wine and dine you. You deserve to have some fun."

Sandy stood and hugged her daughter. "Do you know how much I love you?" she said.

"Yes, I do. Now, go. Surprise her," Dawn said, shoving her mother up the dock toward her car. "I'll walk back up to the house. I could use the solitude."

Sandy took a few steps then turned back, "Are you sure?"

"Go, and don't forget to pack something sexy."

Dawn was much more enlightened than Sandy had anticipated. She smiled at her daughter and said, "Jamie is going to love you."

#

Jamie ran five miles on the treadmill and then swam for awhile. While running with her IPod set on random, she listened to everything from Nora Jones, Sugarland, Etta's James and Jones, Eminem, Reba, The Eagles, Willie Nelson, and BB King. Jamie's eclectic taste in music was a marvel, even to herself. With her favorites in her ears and the flat screen, in front of her, on the golf channel, her body ran, while her mind reviewed the last few weeks of her life.

It was mind opening to realize that a different perspective can make a life shattering event an actual opportunity, to find that thing she had been looking for. Jamie thought she had ruined her life when she cheated on Mary Ann. What she had actually done was set in motion a series of events that led her back to Sandy. Her life had not been shattered by her cheating. She cheated, because her life was shattered, in the first place. Sandy helped her put it all back together.

Jamie thought Mary Ann was the love of her life, but then she found Sandy again, and something clicked. It wasn't something she thought she could put in words. Etta James sang, "At Last," in her ears. Jamie smiled and laughed to herself, thinking, "Sing it, girl." Jamie had been bitten by the love bug. So much so, that she did not notice the hot chick on the treadmill beside her, until she was leaving.

During her laps in the pool, Jamie tried to imagine how the upcoming conversation with Mary Ann was going to go. The outcome Jamie was looking for was Mary Ann to move on. Jamie didn't want to hear from her for a long time. She wouldn't mind a Christmas card, but Jamie was ready to cut all ties with Mary Ann. It was only fair to Sandy, that Jamie not be distracted by drama created by an ongoing relationship with Mary Ann.

This was the beginning of Jamie's life with Sandy and she didn't want it marred with anymore crisis moments, like last weekend. Right now should be a happy time for both of them and Jamie was going to do what it took to clean up her end of the calamity that occurred in that forty-eight hour period. She would wrap things up with Mary Ann and then help Sandy close things up with Doug. It all sounded so cut and dry and easy. A girl could dream, couldn't she?

In a two day period, Jamie had witnessed, or been a party to, her ex showing up out of the blue. Her new love interest being there when it happened, with her husband. Jamie's ex figuring out something was going on, fighting with her, fucking her and then telling her she no longer was in love with her. Sandy confessing her love for Jamie, in front of the ex, who's been told there was nothing going on between Sandy and Jamie. Sandy's husband hitting her when she confessed that she was in love with Jamie. Finally being with Sandy and then almost being killed by Sandy's husband. It was too much to believe, but it had happened and Jamie had seen it all.

To think that this evening was going to be anything, but a bad memory in the making, was wishful thinking, at best. Her mind wandered back to Sandy, as she swam the last of her cool down laps. Jamie had wanted Sandy to be here with her, but then she had not told Sandy about the dinner with Mary Ann. In hindsight, she wished she had. She didn't want to start off not being totally honest. She had not told her to spare her the worry, but it felt like a lie of omission to Jamie now.

Jamie decided to call Sandy when she got back up to the room. She got out of the pool, dried off and put on one of the fluffy house robes, offered by the attendant. Jamie went up to her suite, found her cell phone and dialed Sandy's number. She got voicemail again. This time she left a message.

"Call me, when you get this. Hope everything went well. I love you."

Jamie hung up and got into the shower. She didn't hear the phone ringing when Sandy called back.

#

Sandy missed Jamie's call, because she was packing her car. When she got back to the house she quickly packed everything she thought she would need and then some. Luckily she had taken a few dinner dresses with her, when she and Beth had removed some things from her former home. She wasn't sure what Jamie would want to do in Durham, so she packed for almost anything, remembering the sexy lingerie Dawn had suggested.

When she saw the missed call on her cell, she immediately called Jamie back. She got voicemail and left a message.

"I have a surprise for you when you finish your meeting. Call me back."

Sandy chose to wear something comfortable on the drive and then change into different clothes before she went in to Jamie's hotel. She made another check through the bathroom and the bedroom, grabbed a book she had started reading, for when Jamie was working, and decided it was now or never. She was going to drive all the way to Durham to surprise the woman she was in love with and have a romantic few days in a fancy hotel, as a bonus.

Sandy locked up the house with the key Jamie had given her and left Currituck County in her rearview mirror. She stopped to get gas and missed Jamie's return call, while she was in the store getting a snack for the trip. She didn't look at her phone for hours and by then she knew Jamie was in her meeting and couldn't answer the phone. She drove on happily listening to the OnStar directions and NPR radio to pass the time.

During the three and a half hour drive, the sun began setting over the horizon, as Sandy drove straight into it. Sandy had not been to this part of the state in several years and much of the view had changed. Sandy drove away from the shores into rolling green hills covered in evergreen forest and farmland. It was a beautiful early evening, with the sky full of yellows, blues, and pinks and mixtures of those colors.

Sandy thought about how much her life had been altered in the last week. It was frightening how fast things changed, but as she drove closer to Durham and further away from home, her fears and anxieties receded. All she could think about was finding Jamie and beginning the rest of their lives together. Jamie was going to be so surprised.

#

The Girl Back Home

Jamie returned Sandy's call, as soon as she got out of the shower and missed her again. They were playing phone tag. It was amazing that in this technology mad world, neither was able to talk to the other and "Hey, I'm having dinner with my ex," wasn't something Jamie needed to share in a text message.

Jamie blew her hair dry, being careful not to heat up the staples, still in her head. She wore it in a style, parted to one side, pulling the bangs loosely across her forehead and tucked some of it behind her ears. It was a flattering cut and the look said, business does not necessarily mean a woman has to look less feminine or less attractive. The style also covered her stapled scalp fairly well. She put on makeup, for the first time in months, and did a pretty good job, she thought. It might have been the radiance of her tan that made the blue pop in her eyes, but the sparkle was there because of Sandy.

She sat at the table reviewing the paperwork that dispensed of her relationship with Mary Ann. All that they had owned together was divided up there on the papers in front of her. Sixteen years of Jamie's life represented by black words on white paper. Luckily Mary Ann didn't sue her for more money. It seemed Mary Ann had been ready to dispense with Jamie, at the time she had her lawyer draw up this agreement. After she checked the legal document for the third time, she put it in her briefcase and decided it was time to get dressed.

She brought her Bill Blass white pants and matching long, white duster jacket to wear. The pants were broad legged and cut like men's pants with buttons for suspenders. She put on a white shirt with big cuffs and collar to match. The shirt had a thin vertical, black stripe pattern that worked extremely well with the suit. It made her look taller and sophisticated.

The white Jimmy Choo pumps and black suspenders, with the gold hardware, were icing on the cake, She added jewelry for accessories, but left the diamond ring, Mary Ann had given her, in the zippered case. She dabbed on Karl Lagerfeld Kapsule parfum, because that's what was in her bag. She checked herself one more time in the mirror. Briefcase in hand, Jamie looked the part of the expensive, hot lawyer when she left the room.

Chapter Sixteen

The meeting with Joseph White went as Jamie predicted. They said hello, ordered a drink, caught up on old times for a few minutes and then signed some papers. The drinks finished, they shook hands and parted ways. Jamie ordered another drink and because the restaurant did not allow cell phones, she stepped into the lobby to try Sandy again. This time she got an answer.

"Hello, Jamie?" Sandy's voice said in the handset.

"Hey, I've been playing phone tag with you," Jamie said.

"Ja ie, I ca bar ly ear y u. I' n a ba ace." Sandy's voice broke up and then she was gone. Wherever she was, the cell reception was nonexistent. Surely she would call back when she was able. Jamie went back to the table and sipped on the scotch the waiter had delivered.

As she walked back into the restaurant, heads of both women and men turned. Jamie never paid much attention to her looks, but she was aware that at times she made everyone pay attention. It was useful in certain situations and she had shamelessly used her looks to get what she wanted on a few occasions. Jamie carried herself with confidence. It showed in her walk, even in the way she sat and sipped the scotch, alone. She was sure someone in the room was wondering who she could be waiting for.

The answer came in the form of Mary Ann, in a black Vera Wang dress and matching high heels. The only thing missing was the vamping music, "ba ba ba ba, ba ba," when she was escorted to the table, where Jamie sat waiting. Jamie saw her come in. She saw every head in the room turn. Mary Ann was stunningly beautiful. She could have been a model or a movie star, as far as the people in the restaurant were concerned. Jaws dropped and full forks stopped in motion to open mouths. Jamie stood, gave and accepted a peck on the cheek and then sat down, just as the champagne was brought to the table.

People were still staring and beginning to talk among their respective tables about the two gorgeous women, seated near the terrace doors. Jamie had always enjoyed that about her relationship with Mary Ann. It always made her so proud to be the one with the woman who turned heads. Jamie knew they looked good together, too. She had seen the pictures. Jamie smiled across the table at Mary Ann.

"You look breathtaking, as usual," she said.

Mary Ann smiled back. She looked relaxed and at ease. These were good signs to Jamie.

Mary Ann said, "Thank you and so do you. I like it when you wear your hair like that and your tan really adds to that suit. I'm glad I talked you into buying it."

The wine steward showed the bottle label to Jamie and then Mary Ann. Jamie nodded in agreement that this was the bottle she ordered. Mary Ann smiled across the table at Jamie when she realized Jamie had selected her favorite, for the evening. The steward popped the top and poured a little of the golden liquid in a champagne flute. He offered it to Jamie, who indicated with her hand that he should give it to Mary Ann. Mary Ann tasted the champagne.

"Yes, that's perfect," she said to the steward, who poured them both a glass, sat the bottle in the bucket, on a stand beside the table, and left them alone.

"Thank you for the champagne. That was very thoughtful, but what are we celebrating?" Mary Ann asked, holding her glass up, waiting for a toast.

Jamie lifted her glass to Mary Ann's, tapping it gently, she said, "To new beginnings."

They drank to each other and then Jamie sat her glass down on the table. Mary Ann hung on to hers, sipping as she talked. "I assume the papers all were signed and we are officially unattached."

Jamie answered, "Yes, that all went quite well. Joseph sends his best, by the way."

"I'm sure I'll be hearing from him soon," Mary Ann acknowledged, sipping more of her champagne.

Jamie could see the wheels turning behind those gorgeous eyes. Mary Ann was studying Jamie, sizing her up. Jamie decided the best way to deal with the elephant in the room was to just start talking.

"Mary Ann, I asked you to dinner so I could tell you something. Something I thought you needed to hear from me, face to face."

Mary Ann smiled. "Jamie, might we order first. I'm starving."

"Sure, it can wait," Jamie said, signaling the waiter.

The waiter came to the table and offered the women menus. He stood by the table to answer questions and make suggestions. Jamie settled on the seared scallops and Mary Ann chose the slow roasted Scottish salmon. The waiter suggested a Cabernet Sauvignon Cono Sur, a red wine, not the usual with seafood, but it would go nicely with both dishes and was a favorite among guests. They took his suggestion and he left to bring their Carolina Caprese salads, but not before refilling Mary Ann's champagne flute.

Mary Ann started talking about some friends of theirs who were having a baby. It was obvious to Jamie that Mary Ann was putting off the conversation, they had come there to have. She babbled on about the baby shower she attended and how big their friend had gotten. The cute little baby dresses were of particular interest. Jamie played along, listening intently and speaking appropriately when prompted by a question or comment.

Jamie was grateful when the salads came. It gave her something to do, while Mary Ann talked about the flowers in their yard and a seminar she had just given. Jamie watched as Mary Ann finished another glass of champagne, imagining she was using it as liquid courage for what was to come. When the wine arrived, Mary Ann did not let the waiter take her champagne flute. She told him it was her favorite and she intended to drink every last drop. Jamie finished her glass of champagne and let the waiter pour another for her, just to keep Mary Ann from drinking it. She was already sure she'd be sending Mary Ann home in a taxi, as it was.

Once the entrées arrived and Jamie was sure Mary Ann had eaten something, she steered the conversation back to the real purpose of their meeting. "I've enjoyed catching up, but there have been a few events in the past week, I need to talk to you about."

Mary Ann was polite, but a bit energized by the alcohol buzz, when she replied, "Oh, do tell. What happened in Peyton Place since I was last there?"

"For one, Doug hit me over the head with a two-by-four. I still have the staples in my head." Jamie turned her head and pulled the hair back so Mary Ann could see, then realized that probably wasn't a good idea. "God, I'm sorry. I forgot we were eating."

When she looked up at Mary Ann, the other woman was staring in disbelief back at her. Mary Ann's head was cocked in a questioning pose, as she said, "Good Lord, Jamie. Did he do that because of his wife?" She took a drink of the wine the waiter had given her earlier.

"Yes, I believe that's why he said he did it. He was going to shoot me, but Sandy held my gun on him. He shot at Sandy instead, but he missed. Sandy forgot to take the safety off the gun, but Robby came out of nowhere and tackled Doug, breaking his leg. I missed it all, because I was knocked out cold. Everybody survived and Doug is going to jail."

Mary Ann put her fork down. She picked up the wine glass and sat back against the chair, holding the wine in front of her with the fingers of both hands. She focused in on Jamie's face.

"Jamie, what have you done? Did you take his wife away from him?"

"No, she left on her own. You heard her say that."

"What happened, after I left? Have you begun your fling with the charming Sandy? Do the lesbians of the world owe you a toaster?"

"Hey, now we were doing fine. Don't turn this conversation into another argument. This isn't about Sandy. It's about you and me."

"Then why are you telling me about her husband whacking you in the head? Did he knock some sense into you?"

"Mary Ann, you make it very hard to be nice sometimes," Jamie said, hearing her defense mechanisms beginning to affect the tone of her voice.

"I'm not planning on making this easy for you. I'm not going to say, go have a nice life, without me," Mary Ann said, pouring more wine into her glass.

All Jamie's hopes for a simple goodbye were dashed. Mary Ann was going to make this as difficult as possible.

#

When OnStar warned her she was close to her destination, Sandy pulled off at a gas station, on Durham Chapel Hill Road. She grabbed the small bag she packed for this moment. Hanging in the back was the simple black dress she was going to wear. Her black heels were on the back seat and her pearls were in her bag. She picked up the shoes, laying the dress over one arm, and went inside the station to become dazzling for her surprise entrance.

Sandy smiled to herself, as she looked in the mirror of the tiny bathroom. This wasn't the most ideal place to get dressed. At least it was clean. She slipped out of her jeans and tee shirt and slipped into the little black dress. It fit her like a glove. Sandy knew from the looks she got when she had worn it before, that this dress looked good on her. She wanted to see the look on Jamie's face when she showed up, dressed to kill, looking like sex and candy.

#

Jamie sat up a little straighter in her chair. She took a sip of wine and then set the glass back on the table. She was no longer hungry and pushed the half eaten plate toward the center of the table. Mary Ann was not going to be a big girl about this at all. She wasn't finished torturing her prey. Jamie knew Mary Ann liked to leave a fight feeling as if she had gotten in the last punch, especially, if it was evident she was going to lose.

Mary Ann grew tired of waiting for Jamie's response, "Go on, big girl. Spit it out. Say it. It shouldn't be hard for you."

"You already know what I'm going to say. I've said it before. I'm not coming back. We're done, Mary Ann." Jamie tried not to sound arrogant or trite, just matter-of-fact.

"So, she's the love of your life, is she?"

Jamie couldn't stop the grin, before it snuck out and she quickly tucked it away. "Yes, Mary Ann, she is."

Mary Ann took a drink. She stared angrily across the table, at Jamie, for a few seconds and then downed the contents of her glass. She went for the bottle. Jamie reached out to stop her, but Mary Ann snatched it away, glaring at Jamie, daring her to say anything. Jamie sat back, put her hands in her lap and watched, as Mary Ann slowly filled the wine glass almost to the top. She sat the bottle down beside the glass and then refocused on Jamie.

"What makes you think she's the one? You've actually known her, what, a month?"

"Do you really want to know, or are you trying to passive aggressively, suggest I'm being foolish?" Jamie could play this game, as well.

Mary Ann still had not touched the full wine glass in front of her. Her hands rested on the table on both sides of the glass, but she made no move toward it. Instead her eyes bore down on Jamie, so intensely that Jamie looked away, picking up her own glass and taking a much needed drink. She wished she still had the scotch from earlier.

"I can't believe after all those years of listening to you tell stories about that childhood crush and now, it comes back to haunt me. I guess I should have listened more closely, when you would wake up and tell me you dreamed about her."

"Mary Ann, this just happened. I didn't plan to run into Sandy, when I moved home. Hell, I didn't even know where she was."

"Well, from what I gather, you've come here tonight to tell me, it is completely over between us, because the fates have intervened and brought you the girl of your dreams." Mary Ann paused and then her eyes softened, as did her voice, when she continued, "Jamie, you do realize that there will be no turning back. There will never be a second chance for us, if you walk away from me tonight."

Jamie's first thought was, "She actually thinks that is some kind of threat, that she still has some kind of power over me." Her next thought wasn't really a thought, it was Melissa Etheridge singing, "Oh, this one's gonna hurt like hell," and she wasn't thinking about herself.

Jamie said, the very next thought she had, out loud, "Mary Ann, I walked away from you a long time ago."

Mary Ann did not hesitate. It was as if she had been waiting for just the right moment. She stood up, which of course drew attention from every eye in the room. Mary Ann reached down to pick up the full wine glass and ceremoniously dumped the contents down the front of Jamie's shirt and into her lap. She held the empty glass over Jamie for affect, letting the last drops trickle out and onto her victim. Then Mary Ann placed the glass on the table and stared down at Jamie in disgust.

Jamie stayed in her seat. She looked down the front of her thousand dollar white suit, which was now stained a light ruddy-pink. She picked up her napkin, from the table, and wiped the wine from her hands where it had splashed. Jamie then threw the napkin on the table, stood up and walked past Mary Ann and out of the restaurant. When she saw the waiter, she simply said, "Put the check on my room and add a two hundred dollar tip for you."

Jamie went into the lobby, got on the closest elevator and took it up to her suite. When she got to the room, she called the desk and asked for a bellman to bring her a large bottle of vinegar. She took off the jacket, filled the sink with cold water, found a small towel and threw it in the sink. She unbuttoned the blouse and used a towel to dry the still wet wine from her skin beneath. She took the towel out of the water, squeezed the water out of it and then began methodically dabbing the towel on the red wine, removing it from the fabric one dab at a time.

Jamie didn't really care about the suit, but she let her anger focus her on removing the wine stains. She kicked off her heels and bent over the bathroom counter, dabbing and rinsing, dabbing and rinsing. When the knock at the door came, she stopped what she was doing and went to get the vinegar from the bellman. No such luck. It was Mary Ann, who must have thought she had not done enough damage and was coming back for more.

Jamie left the door open when she saw it was Mary Ann and went back to the bathroom to continue her cleaning project, without saying a word. Mary Ann followed her through the suite and stood outside the bathroom door, hand on one hip, really wanting to fight, but not getting one. Jamie ignored her, while she dabbed the wine out of the jacket.

"Jamie, look at me," Mary Ann demanded.

Jamie stopped what she was doing and looked at Mary Ann. Jamie felt her face form the expression her mother used to call the "I don't care what you say," face, and still she said nothing. This infuriated Mary Ann. When in most cases the person dumping wine, usually uses that as a parting gesture, Mary Ann had used it for her opening volley.

"You are not going to throw away sixteen years on a crush that's going to wear off in a month or two," Mary Ann shouted. "I don't think you're being very rational. I'm not going to let you do this."

Jamie said, very calmly, to her own amazement, "No, you're the one not being rational."

Mary Ann closed the distance between them. She stopped just short of actually running into Jamie. They were eye to eye, staring at each other, frozen. Mary Ann unclenched her jaw and said, "There is no way you could make love to me like you did last Saturday and then turn around and say she is the love of your life."

Jamie felt anger she could not control, as much as she had not wanted to hurt Mary Ann, she now wanted to hurt her and she did. "I fucked you last Saturday, Mary Ann. And if you want to know the truth, that's when I decided I did not want you anymore."

"I don't believe that," Mary Ann said and then she tried to kiss Jamie, but Jamie backed up. She put her hands out in front of her, in the international, "no way this is happening" signal.

"Mary Ann, call a taxi, go home. You've done enough damage for one night."

Then Jamie went back to dabbing. She let the water out of the sink, closed the valve and began to refill the sink. Mary Ann slowly turned around and left the bathroom, without another word.

#

Mary Ann walked to the desk and picked up the phone. She dialed the front desk.

"Front desk, how can I help you Ms. Basnight?"

"Could you call a taxi for me?"

"Yes ma'am and it's funny that you called just now. There is a Sandy Brown here to see you. Should I send her up?"

"Yes, please do."

Mary Ann hung up the phone. She sat her purse down on the desk and kicked her shoes off. There was a white terry cloth robe lying on the bed. She put it on over her dress and went to wait by the door.

#

Sandy got plenty of looks and one cat whistle, before leaving the gas station. She was anxious, now that she was so close to the end of her mission. Sandy felt nervous and she wasn't sure why. Jamie would, of course, be happy to see her. There was nothing to be nervous about. Still, a little sense of dread nagged at her. What if Jamie had seen Mary Ann and changed her mind about Sandy? It was the old fear of losing Jamie, now that she'd found her again, that haunted her.

The Girl Back Home

Sandy found the hotel with no problem and gave the valet her keys, leaving her bags in the car, for the time being. She made her way to the front desk and asked the man behind the desk, if he would call up to Jamie's room and let her know she was there. She wouldn't have made it past the elevators, if she hadn't. She didn't get to do the knock on the door and see the shocked look on Jamie's face, but she was here and that had to be a surprise to Jamie.

The phone rang, just as the man behind the desk was about to answer her. He called the person he was speaking with Ms. Basnight and then told her Sandy was at the front desk. He hung up and said, "Ms. Basnight said to send you right up."

#

Jamie thought she heard Mary Ann talking on the phone, to the front desk. Then she didn't hear her anymore. Jamie hoped Mary Ann had walked out the door and out of her life forever. Jamie had tried to be civilized and Mary Ann just wanted to fight, or fuck, neither activity interesting Jamie. Now she hoped Mary Ann had moved on to the last f and fled.

Jamie kept the water running for a while and when she turned it off, she thought she heard another knock at the door. She was still wearing her shirt, except it was unbuttoned and the robe was out on the bed. Jamie put her jacket on the counter and thought it was a lost cause anyway, but she went to get the vinegar, from the bellman she thought was at the door.

Jamie immediately noticed the robe wasn't on the bed where she had put it. She proceeded to the door, around the corner, and froze in the hallway. Mary Ann was standing, in the robe, with the door open. Mary Ann closed the door, turning to Jamie with a wicked smile on her face. Jamie had no idea to whom Mary Ann had been speaking, but it was clear she wanted the person on the other side of the door to think she was naked, under that robe.

"What did you just do?" Jamie demanded.

Mary Ann untied the robe, at the waist, and let it fall open. As she passed Jamie, Mary Ann slid the robe off and placed it back on the bed. She picked up her purse, slipped into her shoes and headed back for the door, still wearing a satisfied smirk. Jamie stepped in front of her.

"Mary Ann, I asked you a question. Who was that at the door?"

Mary Ann broke all the rules. She crossed the line that Jamie would never forgive her for and she appeared to know it, even relish in it. Mary Ann, true to form, had gotten the last word, "I just told your dear Sandy to come back, in an hour. We were still working out some issues."

Jamie was moving before all the words registered. At the sound of Sandy's name, Jamie saw the remainder of her life going up in smoke. Sandy was here, in the hotel. Mary Ann had done the worst possible thing she could think of, and it was a disaster for Jamie. In all the years Jamie and Mary Ann had been together, even in the worst of their arguments, Jamie had never felt the level of anger she felt, at that moment.

On her way out the door, she turned back, "Fuck you, Mary Ann. Be gone when I get back. I never want to see you again."

She ran out the door of her suite and down the hall, bouncing off walls and door jams, her shirttail flapping behind her. Jamie didn't notice, and wouldn't have cared if she did, that her shirt was unbuttoned, revealing her wine stained, white lace bra and tight ab muscles to the guests she passed, running barefoot down three flights of stairs and out through the busy lobby. She pushed her way through a crowd of people entering the hotel through the main entrance. They were exiting an airport shuttle, in mass, and clogging the sidewalk, when Jamie made it outside.

She ran up to a young, cherry cheeked valet, who was handing a ticket to a customer. Panting between her words, she asked, "Blonde... very pretty... Ford Escape... where?"

227

"Ms. Basnight, are you alright?"

"Where, Goddamnit!" Jamie shouted, at the young man.

He was frightened and lost the ability to speak, so he pointed toward the small lot on the side of the building, before regaining his speech. He called after the already running Jamie, as if he had done something wrong, "She wouldn't let me bring her the car. She said she would get it herself."

Jamie had, by this time, drawn quite the crowd of onlookers, as she tore across the asphalt drive and out in front of the oncoming headlights of the Ford Escape, as it pulled out of the small side parking lot. Jamie didn't think. She just reacted to the situation at hand. If she let Sandy get away, this would all become a lot worse. Jamie had to talk to her now, and she wasn't letting Sandy leave until she had. She threw herself into the path of Sandy's vehicle, just as Sandy began picking up speed toward the main exit.

Sandy screamed inside the car and slammed on the breaks, but the car continued to slide toward Jamie. It came to a stop, just as it hit Jamie, throwing her up on the hood of vehicle. Sandy jammed the car into park and threw open the driver's door.

"Oh my god. Are you okay?"

Jamie moaned and rolled over to face Sandy. Landing on the hood had knocked the breath out of her and she was trying to pull it together.

Sandy screamed, "Is that blood? Oh, my god! Help! We need help! Call 911!" Sandy's face was streaked with tears and her mascara was smeared under one eye.

Jamie regained her ability to breath, at just the right time, before Sandy had the entire hotel in an uproar. She sat up and grabbed Sandy's wrists, just to get control of her. She needed Sandy, who was having a fit, to focus. "Sandy! Sandy! It's not blood, it's just wine."

Sandy stopped freaking out and became completely still. She looked Jamie up and down, examining the open shirt and the wine stains. She pulled away from Jamie's grasp and took a step back toward the open car door. Jamie hopped off the car and stepped in Sandy's path.

Jamie put up her hand, saying, "Stop. Just stop. Listen to me."

Sandy began to cry, again. She opened her mouth to speak, but nothing came out. She was completely crushed, unable to form words.

Jamie was desperate for Sandy to hear her. "Sandy, Mary Ann did that on purpose. I was in the bathroom trying to get the wine out of my suit."

Sandy was barely audible, when she asked, "Why was she in your room?"

"I don't know. I guess pouring wine all over me, in the restaurant, wasn't a strong enough statement for her. She came to finish me off, I guess. I don't know. I was just trying to get rid of her."

"I thought you…," Sandy said, but couldn't finish. She looked down at the ground.

Jamie put her hands on Sandy's shoulders, forcing Sandy to look at her. "Sandy, the only thing I have done tonight is to tell Mary Ann that you are the love of my life."

Sandy fell against Jamie's chest and Jamie wrapped her arms around her. The small crowd, that had gathered to watch, cheered when Jamie lifted Sandy's chin up and then kissed her deeply, as the smaller woman melted into her arms.

Chapter Seventeen

They left the Escape where it was and Jamie threw the keys to the rosy cheeked valet, who was still standing by his stand with his mouth open.

Jamie said, when he caught the keys, "Please, have the bags sent up to my suite."

Jamie heard him say to the other valet, who had driven up just as Jamie ran into the parking lot, "Dude, tell me you shot that with your phone."

The waiting crowd at the door parted for them, as Jamie led Sandy, by the hand, back through the lobby of people, who had just witnessed Jamie's mad dash out the front doors. Jamie was oblivious to the stares and pointing. She had accomplished her goal. She had stopped Sandy from leaving and letting Mary Ann ruin everything. If Mary Ann was still in her room when she got there, Jamie might actually punch her out.

The bottoms of Jamie's feet hurt, where the asphalt had torn away skin. Landing on the car had not been as bad as it looked, but her feet were going to require attention. This time they took the elevator up the three flights, instead of the stairs. They were alone in the elevator, but neither said anything. They were both trying to recover from the excitement of the last few minutes.

The door to Jamie's suite was ajar when they arrived on the third floor. Jamie went in first, because she half expected to see Mary Ann still in the room, but she was gone. Jamie led Sandy into the suite and closed the door behind them. Finally, they were alone. Sandy remained quiet and followed Jamie into the bedroom of the suite. Jamie went to the dresser, removed a tee shirt and a pair of worn sweatpants and tossed them on the bed.

Jamie saw that Sandy was standing in the room, still shaken from her run in with Mary Ann. She went to Sandy and enveloped her in her arms. "I am so sorry that happened. I've been trying to call you all day. I wanted you to know she was here."

Sandy squeezed Jamie tightly and said, "I thought... I thought..."

"I know what you thought and I'm so sorry." Jamie took Sandy's face into her hands and staring into her eyes, she said, "I promise you, Sandy, you never have to think that again. You're the one I want and I'm going to love you forever. Do you hear me? Forever."

Sandy finally managed a weak smile. "You mean that, don't you?"

"Every word."

They kissed. Not the hungry, lust filled kiss of their previous encounters, but a passionate kiss of promises made, of a life to be filled with love and devotion to one another. When their lips parted the emotions of fear and anguish, which had followed them up from the parking lot, vanished. They both let out a huge sigh of relief.

"I can't believe you're here," Jamie said, still with her hands around Sandy's waist.

"Dawn sent me."

"Really, how'd that go?"

"Doug was there, but Dawn stepped up, told everybody she was glad I was happy and for the rest of the family to fall in line, or shut up. She was amazing," Sandy said, with pride.

231

"I was so worried. I didn't want to leave you there to face that alone," Jamie said, hugging Sandy again, as if she were afraid to let her go. "I'm glad it went okay."

"I wanted to surprise you."

Jamie laughed. "You did that."

Sandy started laughing, too. The two women laughed together, as the tension released, until a knock at the door startled them. Jamie pulled her shirt together, suddenly conscious of the way she was dressed. She went to the door to find a bellman there with Sandy's luggage. She came back in the bedroom, grabbed some cash off the dresser and tipped the bellman. Closing the door behind him, she bolted it and turned off the lights in the other rooms.

When Jamie came back into the bedroom Sandy was nowhere to be seen. She saw the bathroom door was closed and heard the water running in the sink. Jamie started peeling off her wine stained clothes and put on the tee shirt and sweats, before Sandy came out of the bathroom. She was sitting on the edge of the bed when Sandy reappeared.

Sandy had washed her face and brushed her hair and looked much more her normal beautiful self. She walked over to Jamie and stood in front of her.

Jamie looked up at Sandy and said, "God, you're beautiful."

Sandy smiled at Jamie and then turned around, saying, "Would you unzip me?"

"With pleasure," Jamie answered, reaching up to pull the long zipper down.

What happened next would be seared in Jamie's memory for her lifetime. Sandy turned back around to face Jamie. She lifted her hands to her shoulders and slid the black dress down her body and let it drop to the floor. Underneath the dress she wore a lacy black slip, which she agonizingly slowly pulled up over her head and dropped on the floor beside the dress. She stood in front of

Jamie wearing a black lace bra, black matching thong and garters holding up her black stockings. She was still wearing the heels and pearls.

Jamie swallowed hard. She was frozen in place with a look on her face that made Sandy smile. Sandy stepped between Jamie's legs and leaned down very close to Jamie's face. Jamie didn't take her hands off the bed, where she was gripping the comforter, holding herself up. She could feel Sandy's breath on her face and her smell was intoxicating.

Sandy whispered against Jamie's lips, "Surprise."

#

Just before she fell asleep, with Sandy sleeping soundly, her head on Jamie's shoulder, Jamie had a last conscious thought. She had spent her life looking for something that had been waiting at home all along. Jamie would never leave the girl back home, again.

Made in the USA
Lexington, KY
06 March 2011